# Pirate Magic

## Book 1:

## Jonah and the Pirate King

# Pirate Magic

## Book 1:

### Jonah and the Pirate King

BY

Tara L. Nielsen

If you purchased this book without a cover, you should be aware that this book is stolen property. It was reported as "unsold and destroyed" to the publisher, and neither the author nor the publisher has received any payment for this "stripped book."

This story, in its entirety, is the sole creation of the author's imagination. Any resemblance, real or imagined, is purely coincidental.

Copyright © 2021 Tara L Nielsen
All rights reserved.

No part of this publication may be reproduced, stored, distributed, or transmitted in any form or by any means, including photocopying, recording, electronic or mechanical methods, or otherwise, without the prior written permission of the author, except in the case of brief quotations and certain other noncommercial uses permitted by copyright law.

Printed in the United States of America by IngramSpark

ISBN: 978-0-9973881-5-2 (paperback), 978-0-9973881-6-9 (hardcover), 978-0-9973881-7-6 (ebook)

Cover Art © 2021 Beth Nielsen
Artwork © 2021 Beth Nielsen
All rights reserved.

No artwork from this publication may be reproduced, stored, distributed, or transmitted in any form or by any means, including photocopying, recording, electronic or mechanical methods, or otherwise, without the prior written permission of the artist, except in the case of certain noncommercial uses permitted by copyright law.

To My Children -

May you find your way through the journey of life, and may you never forget where you come from. You are meant for great things.

# One

The salty sea air tousled Jonah's hair, pulling it in all directions. Jonah didn't mind. He loved the smell of the sea that would linger long after he'd returned to his chores. He looked up from the small carving he was working on and looked out beyond the trees to the waves of the sea. The cove was his special place.

When his ma had first told him about it, she'd said he was to never go there. When he'd questioned why, she'd shook her head and repeated the warning. Jonah had often wondered why she'd bothered to tell him about it at all if he was never allowed to go near it. Sometimes, it seemed, grown-ups weren't all that smart.

Still, Jonah couldn't help himself. Even if he'd never known about the cove, he was certain he would have found his way here. There was something about it. Something that compelled him to come. It would have beckoned to him, pulling at him until he'd found it. And he would have stayed, just as he was now.

*Only I won't be staying*, he thought with a sigh. He knew he'd have to hurry home soon, or his mother would discover him missing. Jonah looked at the wood in his hand. It wasn't much yet, but in time, it would be a carving of a small ship for his ma. He'd been making her pieces from the images that came to his mind ever since he first started visiting the cove. He tucked the wood back into the little hole in the tree where he was perched in. The knife he slid back into its case on his belt.

Jonah looked out across the treetops toward the water. It called to him, stronger and stronger each time he came. But Jonah knew he would never be able to go to it. He wanted to. Everything inside him screamed to get closer. But to do so would mean his ma would know he'd disobeyed her, and that he'd be banned from ever returning. He couldn't bear the thought of never coming here. It was the only place he felt at peace.

For as long as Jonah could remember, he and his ma had lived in Delmar, a small village that ran along the sea. Fishermen dominated the town, while others, like Jonah and his mother, ran small farms further inland. Jonah wished he could be part of the fishing crowd. He was certain he'd love it; but it was man's work, and without a pa, Jonah had no chance of learning the trade. Not that his mother would have let him anyway.

The other boys teased Jonah relentlessly. He hadn't had his growth spurt yet, and the other boys were bigger and stronger from their work on the mighty seas. They spent their summers, and much of their springs and falls, saviling out to sea on the mighty fishing boats alongside their pas. These boys sneered at Jonah, taunting him not only for his size but for his lack of a pa – for not being like them.

Jonah shimmied down the tree and stuffed his hands in his pockets. He kicked his boot hard at the dirt in front of him. He didn't know anything about his pa because his ma wouldn't tell him. The boy didn't even know his own last name. The town's people only ever called his ma Ms. Emily, so even her name didn't give Jonah a clue to his identity. His ma had always said it was better that way. Better that he not know. No, better wasn't what she'd said. Safer. It was safer that he not know. But that just made Jonah wonder all the more.

It would seem that a woman with no last name was nothing short of trouble. Sometimes Jonah caught the whisperings of people as they wondered if Ms. Emily were really a witch. Jonah knew better. Everyone ought to know better. There were no such things as witches. At least, there was no way to prove it. Jonah knew his ma was just a simple woman who kept to herself and ran a small farm. A small farm, of course, that specialized in natural herbs.

With the rumors including him as a bastard son, a boy without a father, born of the devil, well, sometimes Jonah wished his ma really were a witch. Then she could put an end to all the gossip, could make them pay for their meanness. Sometimes Jonah caught himself daydreaming about the kinds of things his ma might do if she were a witch. But then he'd remind himself that she wasn't, and wishing wasn't going to fix anything.

Ms. Emily, for her part, had cautioned Jonah time and again not to get involved with others. Not to worry about their petty thoughts or their hurtful comments. To ignore them. That was  certainly easier to do when he was busy with the farm and had more time to spend at his cove. But when school days came around again…Jonah shuddered. He hated school. He hated having to face the other boys, but his ma wouldn't hear of him staying home. She always insisted it was better for him to get an education.

The breeze picked up, a soft wind that tugged at his body. *Come,* it seemed to whisper, *Come and see.* Jonah closed his eyes, feeling the light sea spray against his face. He licked his lips, the taste of fresh sea salt lingered on them. He liked it. He tipped his head back and put his arms out letting the sea wind run along his body.

*Just a few steps*, he thought. *I'll not leave the edge of the trees.* He inched along, the wind singing in excitement around him. He breathed deeply of the salty air and nearly lost his senses. He grabbed onto the nearest tree to steady himself. He wasn't sure he was strong enough to resist the temptation. Not this close. With two hands on the tree, he clung to the one thing he thought could keep him back.

The sound of shifting sand brought Jonah back to his senses. It wasn't much of a sound, but he recognized it, though he didn't know why. He looked around, trying to make out where it was coming from. His eyes scanned the cove, and stopped on a large ship sitting in the water. It was bigger than any of the fishing boats he'd seen in town, so he knew it wasn't a fisherman lost on his way to the main docks. He continued to scan the cove letting his eyes run along the shore. Then there, not more than twenty yards down the beach, Jonah saw a long boat being dragged through the sand toward the tree line.

The man pulling the boat was dressed in a long black sealcoat, black boots, with a large, black tri-cornered hat sitting on his head. "A pirate," Jonah exhaled, his eyes large in disbelief as he took in the sword and pistol hanging at the man's waist. Jonah could not take his eyes off the man. Suddenly the wind shifted, the playful tousling of Jonah's hair became a tangled pull, and the pirate stopped. He turned his head and looked in Jonah's direction.

Breathless, and heart thumping, Jonah pushed back against the trees hoping he had not been seen. The wooded area near the cove was not particularly thick, though the undergrowth was tall. Jonah was thankful for this because, he hoped, it hid him well. On the other hand, it would make it more difficult to escape without notice. The rustle of long leaves would surely give him away. Jonah decided his best chance was to climb the tree in case the pirate chose to come after him. It would be less likely that the man would look up in his search. Chores would have to wait.

From his perch in the tree, Jonah could just make out the movements of the pirate down on the beach. He had not come after Jonah. At least not yet. Instead, he had turned his attention back to the long boat, intent on getting it to the cover of the trees on the far side of the cove. Jonah knew dragging a long boat must have been hard work for one man, yet the pirate seemed to be handling it with ease. Jonah trembled a little at the thought of just how strong this man must be.

With his heart beating wildly in fear that he would shortly be surrounded by a whole gang of pirates, Jonah scanned the beach and as far out toward the ship as he could, trying to see if there were others. He wished he had a telescope so he could see better. He looked wildly around him, and then back out to the cove. Not seeing anyone else, Jonah's eyes darted back to the pirate on the shore. The long boat was nowhere to be seen, though a wide, deep line indicated where it had been drug through the sand. The pirate was walking back down toward the water's edge, carefully brushing away any evidence of the boat's path with a large palm leaf.

When the pirate reached the edge of the shore, he stepped into the sloshing water, wetting his boots up past his ankles. He tossed the branch out into the sea, which, Jonah could have sworn, came up like a giant fish and swallowed it. Then, before his eyes, Jonah saw the pirate tip his face toward the sky and lift his arms out wide, a gesture that seemed strange for such a large man. Once again, the sea seemed to respond, saltwater spraying over the pirate. And then the ship began to disappear.

Jonah rubbed at his eyes, sure he'd just gotten too much salt in them, but no, the ship was gone. He looked around, knowing a ship that big couldn't have gotten out of the cove so quickly. But it was nowhere to be seen. Gone. He searched the beach. No pirate. Nothing. It was just the quiet cove Jonah was used to.

With thoughts that it must have been one amazing daydream, and that he was likely in for some serious trouble for being so late with his chores, Jonah decided he'd better get home to the farm. He shifted his weight in the tree, preparing to climb down, when out of the corner of his eye, he caught sight of black. Lots of black. He turned back to get a better look. This time he saw the pirate. The pirate was still on the beach, but much closer to the tree line where Jonah was hiding, which, Jonah reasoned, must have been why he'd missed him before. The black-clad man was walking toward the same tree that Jonah was in. Jonah froze. He didn't dare return to his previous position for fear of attracting unwanted attention.

The pirate came up the beach with long, purposeful strides. He was at the tree line in no time and entered the area with the same purposeful gait. Jonah held his breath, waiting for the pirate to look up and find him. Waiting to die.

But the pirate never looked up. Never looked up and never looked back. Instead, he continued forward, and with each step something happened. At first, it was just the pirate's hat. It was missing, and Jonah wondered if it had fallen off. He couldn't imagine anyone leaving behind such a nice hat, but the pirate didn't slow or even bend over. A moment later, in place of the tri-cornered captain's hat he had been wearing, the pirate now wore a simple traveler's hat. The kind many of the farmers outside town wore.

Sea weathered boots dissolved into sturdy work boots, the black giving way to a well-worn brown. The long, well-oiled sealcoat shimmered in the fading light, and then it, too, had given way. This time the pirate was in nothing more than dungarees and red flannel.

Jonah blinked his eyes. What was this? Surely his eyes were playing tricks on him. Maybe his mind was making it all up. Whatever was happening, it couldn't possibly be real.

The pirate glanced over his shoulder, and Jonah pulled back against the tree he was in. A small breath escaped his lips as he noticed the beady black eyes become a soft grey-blue, and the long, scraggly beard fall away to a gentle five o'clock shadow. Jonah wasn't sure, but he thought the man knew he was there. He held his breath, and waited to be discovered, not knowing his fate.

After a moment's hesitation, the pirate-turned-farmer spun back around, continuing his deliberate stride through the trees, and disappeared from view. From his perch in the tree, Jonah watched the little stretch of country road at the other side of the trees, hoping to catch a glimpse of the strange man again. But he never did. The road remained quiet. No travelers, ordinary or otherwise.

Either his mind was playing tricks on him, or Jonah had just witnessed the pirate make a complete transformation. Whatever had happened, one thing Jonah knew, whoever that man was, he was anything but ordinary.

# Two

Millie mooed softly as Jonah finished the last of the milking. He patted her on the side as he stood up with the pail. "Thanks, girl," he said to her. "Sorry for being so late." He rubbed the jersey cow with his free hand as he talked to her.

Jonah had waited as long as he dared sitting up in his tree. He'd watched for the stranger to emerge, but when there had been no sign of the pirate after half an hour, Jonah decided he must have made it all up and raced home. He had been certain his ma would have been waiting for him, wondering why he hadn't brought the milk in yet, or why Millie was uncomfortably mooing. But much to Jonah's relief, his mother was nowhere to be seen when he'd returned to the farm. He'd felt himself more than a little fortunate that she had not been waiting for him, and he'd simply slipped into the barn and taken care of the milking.

He was glad the evening chores didn't take as long as the morning ones, but he knew if he wasn't quick about them no amount of explaining would prevent his mother from knowing he'd slipped away. Jonah didn't even want to think about what would happen if she mother knew he'd been at the cove.

Now that Jonah was done milking, thoughts of the cove and the pirate returned. Maybe it had been his conscience catching up with him after all this time. He managed to push that thought to the back of his mind with the promise that he wouldn't go back to the cove for a while.

He set the milk aside, put Millie back in her stall, and reached over for the pitchfork he kept leaning against the wall. There was something comforting in tending the animals. He'd just give the cow and horses some hay, and then he could take the milk to the house.

Grabbing the pail of milk, Jonah headed toward the house. He could see the soft light of the lantern already lit, and could smell supper cooking. They might not have much, but his mother could cook up a real delight for any boy's stomach, and Jonah's was mighty happy to know there was a good stew ready and waiting.

Three quarters of the way to the house, Jonah realized the front door was slightly ajar. His ma rarely ever left the door open, and certainly never at night. She was afraid of the snakes that liked to hide in the woodpile and, on occasion, make their way inside the house. Whatever she could do to prevent that from happening she would; so, the door was never left open unless she was sitting right by it. This time of night, with a stew over the fire, Jonah was certain the door should not be open.

He slowed his steps, not sure what to expect. A snake, maybe. More likely it'd be his ma sitting just inside the door to give him a good what for. He wasn't sure he wanted to encounter either with a pail full of milk. He crept forward, preparing himself for the worst. He stopped when he heard a man's voice. It wasn't one he recognized.

"Come on, Emily," the man pleaded in an angry tone, "just one night. Give me one night and we'll work this out."

"No," his ma's voice replied. "No. It's not a good idea."

Jonah almost felt sorry for the man, because even though ma

was soft spoken, she was firm. When she made up her mind about something, there was no negotiating. And it sounded like this man had been trying to negotiate for some time now.

"And what about the boy?" the man asked.

"Jonah?"

"Yeah, the boy. Jonah."

"He doesn't know anything. It's better this way." His ma's voice sounded strained.

Not for the first time did Jonah wonder what she was hiding. Part of him wanted to march right inside and demand that she tell him whatever it was. He wasn't a little kid anymore. He was nearly grown. Well, thirteen anyway. And after all, they were talking about him.

"It ain't right, Emily. The boy's got a right to know."

"He's my son. And I say he doesn't. He's gone through so much already."

"But it's different this time," the man pleaded again.

Jonah imagined his ma shaking her head in that resigned way of hers, knowing her words would remain true to her decision.

"You've said that before. No, Miguel, no. It just won't work. Please," this time she was pleading, "Please, Miguel. Please just go."

Jonah had never heard his ma's voice sound so desperate. His heart ached, and part of him wanted to barge through the door to her, but he resisted not wanting his ma to know he had overheard. He gripped the handle of the pail even tighter, his knuckles turning white from the strain of it, and willed himself to stay where he was.

"I won't stay here, Emily, but I'm not going away either. Not this time."

The sound of boots on the wooden floor told Jonah the

conversation was over. He didn't want to get caught eavesdropping, but he couldn't very well run with a pail of milk back to the barn before the man left the house. Looking around quickly, he decided it couldn't be helped. He was too close to the door, and too far from the barn. Hefting the pail up, Jonah started walking toward the house just as the man exited. In his haste, Jonah stumbled, sloshing milk over the side of the pail. Steadying himself, Jonah looked up and nearly dropped it altogether. Standing before him was a man dressed in red flannel and dungarees. Jonah took in the five o'clock shadow, brown farmer's hat, and well-worn boots. But it was the piercing grey-blue eyes that confirmed it. The man who had been in Jonah's house was none other than the pirate-turned-farmer. The man from the cove.

"Careful there, son," Miguel said as he reached out a hand to help steady Jonah.

Jonah flinched. "I ain't your son, mister," he said as he sidestepped around Miguel.

The pirate didn't move. He watched Jonah with a look that said he wanted to say something. Instead, the pirate shook his head and continued away from the house as Jonah went in with his pail of milk. His mind was racing; his stomach was in a knot.

Jonah took glanced quickly around the cabin as he came in. A stew boiled over the fire, but the dishes weren't set out yet. His ma sat at the table, her shoulders slumped forward, looking more exhausted than she ought to. Jonah carefully carried the pail to the kitchen and began straining it. He poured it into set pans, where it would rest overnight so his ma could make butter in the morning from the cream that rose to the top.

He heard his ma get up and gather bowls. She began dishing up stew directly from the pot still hung over the fireplace. Even if Jonah hadn't overheard part of the conversation earlier, he would have known something was bothering her. His mother always insisted on setting the table out full, which meant the stew would have been on the table in full reach of both of them.

He wanted to ask her who Miguel was. He wanted to, but he knew if he did she'd know he had been listening.

"Here, Jonah, have some supper," she said as she held the bowl out toward him.

Jonah finished setting up the milk, and took the bowl from her. She looked tired and worn, and Jonah found he couldn't stop the words from coming out of his mouth. "Who was he? What'd he want?"

Instead of answering, she took her own bowl and two spoons to the table. "Not now, Jonah. It's time to eat."

If history were any indicator, that was short for "we're not going to talk about it." Jonah didn't like it, but obediently made his way over to the table with his bowl of steaming stew. The smell was tantalizing, and his stomach rumbled at the thought of it. He'd known it was late, but hadn't realized he'd become so hungry. He'd just been worried about getting into trouble for not being back to do his chores on time. That, and for being at the cove.

At the thought of the cove, Jonah's cheeks flamed. He tipped his head closer to his stew to keep his ma from noticing. Surely the unexplained flush would have brought a question or two from her, and he figured that if she weren't asking any questions, he wouldn't give her any reason to start.

As his stomach filled up, Jonah couldn't help but wonder about the man once again. Miguel. The man's name was Miguel; and his mother knew him. *But how? Who was he anyway? Did Ma know he was really a pirate?*

Jonah glanced at his mother and decided she couldn't possibly know that. She would never associate with a pirate. Even with all her generosity toward others, she wouldn't. *Would she?* Jonah just couldn't see his ma as part of that life. No, his ma might not have everything the other ladies in town had; she might not dress as fancy, and she might have to work hard to keep them clothed and fed, but she was a respectable woman.

"You get enough to eat?" his mother asked.

"What?" Jonah could feel a slight heat creeping up from the nape of his neck at having been caught in his own thoughts.

"Did you get enough supper to fill you up?" She nodded at his empty bowl. He hadn't remembered finishing it, he'd been so deep in thought.

"Oh, um, could I have some more?" Jonah asked, a light crimson hue creeping up his neck once more.

Emily refilled his bowl and set it down in front of him. "Seems we both have things on our minds tonight," she said as she gathered up her own dishes and headed to the sink. "What's troubling you?"

"Uh," Jonah stumbled. "Nothing really."

"For a boy who's so hungry he doesn't pay attention to the stew in his own bowl, that seems to me you've got more than nothing on your mind." Emily poured hot water from the kettle into the sink, then peered back over her shoulder toward him.

The blush Jonah had hoped wouldn't tip her off came rushing to the top of his forehead. Emily's eyebrows rose up into her hairline, letting Jonah know she hadn't missed the tell-tale sign he wasn't telling her something.

Jonah swallowed hard. "Who was he?" he blurted out quickly, hoping to steer the conversation away from where he'd been most of the day. He did want to know who Miguel was, and that had been on his mind, but really he hoped it would keep his mother from prying too hard.

His ma turned back to the sink, and for a moment Jonah thought she wasn't going to answer him. After what seemed a very long time, she finally spoke. "He's not anyone you need to concern yourself with. Just someone I met once, a long time ago."

"What'd he come here for?" Jonah asked, figuring that if she'd answered his first question then maybe she'd answer more.

"That's none of your concern. Just you make sure if you ever see him you keep your distance."

Jonah had no intentions of being anywhere near the man. Still, he felt compelled to ask, "Why?"

His ma wiped her hands on the towel and came over to sit next to him again. She sighed with the exhaustion she felt from the encounter. "There are some things you just wouldn't understand. Not now. I need you to trust me, Jonah. I only want what's best for you. Okay?"

"Okay," he replied, though he wasn't really satisfied with her answer.

"Good. Just stay as far away from him as you can. Remember, you can't trust everyone."

# Three

Those last summer days went by much too quickly; and as the harvest season came into full swing, Jonah knew his days of freedom were numbered. He dreaded the thought of returning to school. It wasn't so much the school. It wasn't even the book work. Jonah was different that way - he actually liked to read. He liked to learn his numbers. There was something satisfying in figuring all those sums. It wasn't school. No, it was the other boys.

Thoughts of those dreaded days looming ahead of him crept to the front of Jonah's mind. He did his best to push them away, not wanting to ruin his last few days of summer with reminders of the cruelty of the other boys.

Jonah shifted his weight and hefted a bale of hay, throwing it on the stack he was building in the barn. He grabbed another one, and tossed it up as well. It was hard work, but Jonah was proud of the strength he had developed over the summer.

*Bet I could take 'em,* he thought, his mind shifting back to the dock boys as he sat down on one of the bales. He took a drink from the jar of lemonade his ma had sent out with him. *I could take 'em all, if Ma would let me.*

He wasn't certain he was stronger than all the other boys, but he couldn't imagine much more a boy could be doing to build up muscles than throwing bales of hay around. Unless, of course, it was working on the boats. That was something Jonah knew he'd never get the chance to do. Ma would never allow it, even if there was someone who would take him on.

He flexed his muscles, and frowned. There wasn't much to see for all the strength he'd built up. But he knew he was strong; and his arms were powerful even if they didn't look it. *Yeah,* he thought, *I could definitely take 'em.* His ma would never allow it, though, so Jonah knew he never would.

It wasn't that Jonah was a particularly obedient child. At least not the kind who always did everything he was told. After all, he often snuck away to the cove even after his mother had forbidden it. Maybe even because she had. But when it came to the town folk, Jonah sided with his ma, for better or worse. He wouldn't disgrace his mother by sinking to their level. *Though it'd sure be nice to put 'em in their place. Even just once.*

"No need to look so glum there, Jonah. We're just about done here," Ol' Man Wimple announced, pulling Jonah back from his thoughts. Jonah took another drink, leaving his mostly empty jar on the rail at the side of the barn as he returned to the work of stacking hay bales.

"What's gotcha brooding today?" Ol' Man Wimple asked.

Jonah frowned, his brow furrowing together. "Nothing," he muttered, not wanting to tell Ol' Man Wimple his troubles.

"Been a long time since I've seen a look like that on a young lad's face that didn't mean there was something going on inside his head."

Jonah didn't want to hurt the man's feelings, but he didn't want to admit he was having trouble. He knew Ol' Man Wimple would want to help. He'd probably go right to town to show those boys what was what. And that would be downright embarrassing.

It wasn't that Ol' Man Wimple was really all that old; that's just what everybody called him. He was really only in his forties. Maybe fifties. It was hard to know for sure. Farm work did one thing for a man, kept him strong and healthy so it was hard to know for sure how old Ol' Man Wimple really was, but he certainly wasn't *old*. Not like his name suggested. Still Jonah figured Ol' Man Wimple could take on any one of those boys. He could probably take them all on and they'd go home with their tails between their legs.

"It's nothing really. Just not looking forward to going back to school," Jonah said as he tossed up another bale of hay.

"Any particular reason?"

Jonah leaned down to grab another bale. "Nope. Not really."

"Well, I reckon a boy's entitled to his secrets. Even if they are of the brooding sort." Ol' Man Wimple gave Jonah a look that said otherwise.

Jonah squirmed inside. He knew Ol' Man Wimple was just trying to be nice. He was a good man. He'd helped with the farm ever since Jonah could remember. And he was good to Jonah and his ma. Still, he couldn't bring himself to admit he had troubles with the village boys.

"Pretty sure Ma's got more of that apple pie," Jonah said. "After we finish up here, you ought to stop in and we can have a piece. Bet Ma would like that."

At the mention of Jonah's mother, Ol' Man Wimple smiled one of those crinkly eyed smiles. The kind reserved for really old folk, but somehow fit well on Ol' Man Wimple's face. "That sounds mighty nice. It won't be no inconvenience for her, now would it?" he questioned, the crinkles around his eyes falling a little at the possible disappointment.

Jonah shook his head. "Nah. You know Ma loves it when you stop in. Bet she's already put the coffee on." *And probably already cooked up a storm for supper,* he told himself. Ma almost always invited Ol' Man Wimple to supper after days like today, when he was here helping them out.

After they'd finished putting up the hay, they started in on the normal evening chores. Ol' Man Wimple mucked out the stalls and put down fresh straw while Jonah set about to milk Millie. His thoughts drifted in and out, mostly about school and the dock boys, but sometimes about his cove. He missed going there; missed the salty sea air.

"You seem distracted, there, Jonah." Ol' Man Wimple said.

Jonah started from his thoughts.

"Looks to me like you missed the bucket as often as you hit it." The man's voice was tinged with surprise.

Looking around him, Jonah noticed the straw at his feet was wet, and the bucket had precious little in it. Ol' Man Wimple was right. He'd been distracted and probably lost at least half the milk.

"Why don't you head on back to the house? I'll finish up here and meet you inside."

Conceding the point, Jonah left the barn and was met with a brilliant red sky. He stopped to look at it, marveling at the brilliance of color, deep and rich, like painted blood. Then something sparked in his mind, like a flame hitting an oiled canvas. The night before he'd first seen Miguel, there had been a sky like this. He had come out into the barnyard to see his mother staring up at that sky, her face a little pale. She'd said it was known as a sailor's delight, but it was what she'd said before that - something he was sure she hadn't meant for him to hear - that he remembered now. She had been standing there, staring into that red sky, the kind of sky Jonah had never before seen in his life; and she'd whispered, like a breath of breeze in the air, "He's back." When Jonah had questioned her about it, she'd only told him about the sky, her words floating somewhere out of mind, until now. The following day the pirate had shown up.

Now, as he looked out at that blood red sky, Jonah wondered if his mother had been expecting Miguel. If that was, perhaps, what she had meant that night.

# Four

School had started a week ago for Jonah. Like the other farm boys, he was starting a couple months behind because of the harvest. Now he'd have to work harder to catch up. Jonah wasn't really worried about it though. The nights would be getting colder, the dark coming sooner, and he'd have little to do inside the farmhouse to keep himself busy. The school work would take care of his boredom and by the end of term, Jonah would be caught up and excelling alongside his classmates.

So far, things had gone smoothly. He had managed not to get into any fights, which was helped along by the fact that the normal heckling he would have endured had been scarce. It was strange, this new routine, and Jonah had little hope that such days would last forever. He'd walk into the village each morning expecting to come face to face with the gang of boys from the docks, blocking the schoolhouse entrance. Each day he'd come, each day he'd smell the salt air and the fresh fish catch, and each day the entrance remained clear. Jonah knew this meant they were up to something, he just didn't know what.

Then it happened, the day he had dreaded. He arrived at the school house just a little earlier than usual, apparently having grown comfortable in the new routine that did not include being threatened, only to find his path blocked.

"It's the witch's boy," Brigg called out. He was one of the prominent fisherman's sons. His father, Captain Amos Montagurell, was well known and respected by the local villagers. Captain Montagurell was consulted on matters of importance both for the village and for personal families. This gave Brigg an inflated sense of importance, and a position all the village children seemed to accept.

Jonah kept his head down, ignoring the boy's taunts as he made his way to the schoolhouse steps. Blood pounded in his ears as he tried to force the older boy's voice out of his mind. He hoped Brigg would get bored and move on. Although Brigg didn't try to stop him as he moved past, Jonah was aware that Brigg had lowered his voice, and was now talking with the other dock boys. Jonah couldn't make out what the older boy was saying. It was probably for the best.

Slipping into the one room school house, Jonah made his way to his seat. He shared a desk with a shy boy two years younger, but Jonah didn't mind. The younger boy never seemed to be warm enough, and though it wasn't winter yet, the air had a bite to it. The little pot belly stove wasn't stocked up this morning. The stove, barely big enough to warm the school house, wouldn't be put to use until the first flakes of snow began to fall. Toughens the kids up, or so they'd been told. Jonah figured it was a way to conserve wood. Of course, most of the kids came from fishing homes, where the families wore layers upon layers of treated wool. The wool kept the men warm on the waters, and the women and children warm at home. It might just be that these families really didn't know how cold it was for everyone else.

But Lucas, the boy he shared a seat with, was like Jonah and didn't come from one of the great fishing families. Jonah took off his own coat and wrapped it around the boy's thin shoulders. It would be chilly in the school room, but he knew his body could handle it better than Lucas' would.

"Thanks," Lucas whispered.

"How's your ma?" Jonah asked in return.

"Fine," Lucas said, though his eyes betrayed him. Lucas' ma had been sick with a mysterious illness for several years. The boy's father had tried many different things, selling off most of what the family once had to pay for doctors. Nothing they'd done had seemed to help, and Lucas' mom had progressively gotten worse.

"Ma could swing by. She might be able to help. 'Least make her feel a little better," Jonah offered.

Lucas quickly shook his head. "Father would never allow it." Even though Jonah expected this, it still stung. He knew the reason Lucas' father would never allow Jonah's ma to visit his wife was that, like many of the villagers, he feared the rumors were true.

"Maybe I could bring you some herbs. Then you could make your ma a tea."

The younger boy thought about this for a moment. Jonah sensed the boy's hesitation, and wondered if he had bought into the rumors as well. But Lucas wasn't like the other kids. He respected Jonah, and appreciated the friendship he'd been given. The hesitation was only due to not wanting to upset his father. Finally, he nodded. "Okay. Maybe."

It was something. And if the herbs worked, then maybe Lucas' life might be a little easier. Jonah smiled at the thought. Anything that could make the boy's life better was a good thing.

"Take your seats, children," Ms. Winters said.

Those who had not yet taken their seats quickly sat down. Ms. Winters was much like her name, cold and bitter. Jonah used to imagine she was magical and alluring, like a snowflake, but that had never been the case. He'd heard a rumor once that she'd been rejected in love and that was what had made her so bitter.

"Take out your slates and begin copying the letters on the board."

Jonah groaned inwardly. Ms. Winters called this the morning warm-up. Something about loosening up their fingers, but Jonah hated it. It was menial work, designed to help the youngest students master handwriting. He wished she'd at least give the rest of them something else to work on. But, once the letters were written, the assignments for the day would be given, with students meeting with her in groups, and the real learning would begin.

"Didn't see you at the docks this morning," Brigg whispered to Lyle. The two shared a seat directly behind Jonah.

"Slept late," Lyle told him.

Brigg snorted. "The Captain says if you ain't up with the sun, you ain't worth your weight." Brigg always referred to his pa as "The Captain," just like everyone else in town. Jonah didn't know if it was Brigg's way of making sure everyone knew his place, or if his pa made him.

"There's to be no talking," Ms. Winters warned.

Brigg dropped his voice even lower, "You could've made it. The ships left late."

"Why?" Lyle asked, the scratch of his pencil stopping.

Jonah tried to tune them out. He glanced up at Ms. Winters, who was looking their direction with narrowed eyes. He tried to focus on his own letters. As long as his pencil was moving, he should be okay.

"Eels on the ships," Brigg whispered.

"Eels? What are you talking about?" Lyle sounded as if he thought Brigg had lost his mind.

"Seriously. Every ship had 'em. Eels covered every deck. It was quite a sight! Had to push 'em off with the mop, 'twas so many."

Jonah stopped writing. A twinge of butterflies hit his stomach. Eels were fine on their own. They were even fine when the men were trying to catch them; and they made great soup. But to find them on the ship first thing in the morning - on every ship, and for the decks to be covered - that was not good. *How would something like that happen anyway? Who could possibly catch that many eels?* It must have been a prank. Still, dread clutched at his heart as he waited for the answer to the question he couldn't ask.

"That's enough!" Ms. Winter snapped. The whole class turned their attention to the schoolmarm. She had started a brisk walk toward Jonah's side of the room. "I told you there was to be no talking."

Jonah turned slightly to look at the boys behind him, then back around. Ms. Winters had stopped, standing just between the two desks, and now looked back and forth between them. He didn't know why she was doing that. He hadn't been talking. He'd been careful to keep working.

She looked over at Brigg. "And just what is so important it can't wait for recess?"

Jonah quietly let out his breath. At least this time she had chosen the correct culprit.

"I don't know, Ma'am," Brigg said innocently. "It must have been Jonah." This he said in his most confident voice. The one that reminded everyone of who his father was.

Ms. Winters immediately turned to Jonah. "Up!" she said as she grabbed him by the ear and pulled him to his feet. "I will not be mocked in my own school!" For a lady, she was surprisingly strong. Jonah was likely stronger, but there was something about having your ear pulled so hard it felt like it would fall off that made a person follow and not fight back.

She dragged him to the corner where she let go of his ear, and placed the ever-embarrassing dunce cap on his head. He'd been taught not to talk back, but at that moment all he wanted to do was argue with Ms. Winters. After all, he wasn't the one at fault. The words of his mother came to mind reminding him how important it was that they not cause problems; not cause a scene and draw attention to themselves. Out of respect for her, Jonah managed to bite back his remarks, but the anger still boiled inside of him.

"You'll stand here until dinner," she informed Jonah as she placed the dunce cap on his head.

The knot of emotion was tightening in his belly. He dared a glance back at Brigg who sat with a smug look on his face. Heat raced through Jonah's veins, and for a moment he thought about putting his fist through the wall. He'd like to put it into Brigg's face.

The lesson proceeded, and though Jonah wasn't allowed to participate, he had a quick mind and was able to keep up. He knew he'd have extra work to do at home that night, but he didn't figure it would take him too long.

When dinner came around, the students filed out of the schoolhouse. Jonah waited for Ms. Winters to dismiss him. If he took the liberty of removing himself, the punishment would only increase. He watched as Brigg and Lyle headed out. Brigg stopped at the door, turned and made eye contact with Jonah. "You don't fool me," he mouthed.

Dinner was nearly over when Ms. Winters finally let Jonah go. He grabbed his pail, and headed out to the side of the building. Most of the other kids were in the middle of a game of stick ball, so he thought he'd be able to eat in peace. He had only taken a couple bites of his bread and jam when he saw the boots on the ground in front of him. Slowly he looked up.

"We know who's responsible for those eels," Brigg said. "Only one person 'round these parts could have done somethin' like that."

Jonah knew Brigg was referring to his mother and to the rumors of her being a witch. He felt his blood begin to boil. Brigg was waiting for Jonah to respond. Instead, Jonah deliberately took another bite and chewed it very slowly.

Brigg got tired of waiting. As he turned he said, "It's just a matter of time. We all know she's a witch."

Jonah saw red. His fists clutched so tightly, he got jam all over his palms and fingers. Before he could stop himself, he swung his leg out and tripped Brigg. He'd pulled his leg back, gotten up and was putting the rest of his dinner in his pail when Brigg got back to his feet.

The bell rang, calling the children back inside. "You'll pay for that," Brigg threatened, then turned and headed around to the front of the building.

The rest of the day was uneventful, but Brigg's words lingered in Jonah's mind. He knew Brigg would plan his revenge, waiting until after Jonah had let his guard down once more. Brigg was calculating like that. Jonah only hoped he'd be able to see it coming.

# Five

That night Jonah ate his supper quietly. He wasn't in the mood to talk. His mother sat beside him, glancing at him from time to time as she ate. It was obvious she knew something had happened. Jonah only hoped that he would be able to finish his dinner and escape into his school work without any questions. It looked like it might work, until his mother started clearing the supper dishes.

"Mr. Wimple stopped by earlier," she started.

"Yeah? What'd he want?" Jonah braced himself. His mother turned to look at him. He refused to meet her eyes.

"He came through town just past dinner time." She paused, waiting for Jonah. "Well," she began again, "is there something you want to tell me?"

The boy slumped in his chair. He didn't know how much his mother knew, but he wasn't interested in telling her about the rumors, or that it wasn't his fault that he was put in the corner, or worse, that he'd deliberately tripped Brigg Montagurell. "It's nothing, Ma."

"Well, if it's nothing, then how'd Brigg end up in the dirt?" his mother said as she came back and rested her hands on the chair beside Jonah. "Haven't I told you to stay away from them boys? Not to go causing problems?"

"It wasn't like that," Jonah argued.

"Then what was it like?"

Jonah knew his mother wouldn't quit until she'd gotten something out of him. He decided to save them both the trouble and stick to the basics. "Brigg and Lyle were talking during morning warm-ups, and Brigg blamed me. So, Ms. Winters put me in the corner."

"Why would Ms. Winters punish you if you weren't the one talking? Did you try explaining things to her?"

"You don't get it. Brigg gets away with everything because he's The Captain's son. Ms. Winters is just like everyone else."

"I'm sure you could have resolved things if you'd just talked to her."

"I think she's afraid of Captain Montagurell."

"And why would she be afraid of The Captain?"

"I don't know," Jonah said.

Emily pulled out the chair and sat down beside him. "Look, Jonah, you can't go getting' into scrapes like you did last year. Your education is too important. I don't want you growing up with your only option to be out fishin' for your livelihood."

"What's wrong with being a fisherman?" Jonah asked before he could stop himself.

"I guess nothing, for most folks," Emily said. "It's just," she struggled to find the words she wanted to use; like she wanted to be sure she used the right ones. "It's just that there's so much more you could experience. Don't you think it might be nice to live in the city, and be one of those big city people? Maybe a doctor?"

Jonah scrunched up his nose and shook his head. He tried to picture himself dressed all fancy in one of those city suits, but couldn't. Unlike his ma, Jonah loved their little village. Okay, maybe he didn't love everything about it, but he couldn't imagine life anywhere else.

"I," she hesitated, then started again, "I just want you to have options."

It didn't really answer his question, but he wasn't sure that pushing would get him anything else. She'd said things in such a way that he couldn't really argue. He was certain he'd love being on the ocean, but he couldn't tell her how he knew that. Being a fisherman for the rest of his life didn't seem like a bad thing to him. He wasn't sure he needed options; but then again, he didn't know that he didn't. He frowned as he considered this.

"I heard there was quite a commotion at the docks this morning. Got a late start, so the catch came in late," his mother said, changing the subject.

At the mention of the boats' late set out, Jonah tensed. This line of talk was dangerously close to the mess that got Jonah into trouble earlier. He wasn't interested in the conversation taking a turn back in that direction, and thought it best to push the topic along. "Do you need me to smoke a fish tonight?" Jonah asked, thinking that maybe his ma had picked up more fish than she needed for supper.

"No. I already sent it along with Mr. Wimple. He'll bring it by in the morning."

When Emily didn't continue, Jonah tried to turn his attention back to his studies, but images of eels covering every ship at port kept flooding his mind. He still didn't understand how it had happened, but he knew his ma had nothing to do with it.

"Oh, Ma," Jonah said, suddenly remembering Lucas.

"Yes, Jonah?"

"Do you have some herbs that might help Mrs. Thompson?"

She gave him a questioning look. "Did Mr. Thompson suddenly decide it'd be alright if I took a look at her?"

"Well, not exactly," Jonah said. "I told Lucas I might be able to bring some to him, and maybe he'd be able to use them for his ma that way."

Emily nodded. "I see. Well, it might be difficult seeing as I don't know exactly what ails Mrs. Thompson, but maybe we can put together a few things that might at least ease her pain." She got up from the table and started to remove a few dry bundles from the rafters. "Maybe it would be a start," Emily said. She knew Jonah was hoping that if they helped Mrs. Thompson that maybe her husband would allow Emily to check her out completely. It was a long shot. Some people weren't so easily persuaded. "I'll see what I can put together."

"Thanks, Ma. You're the best."

"Yes, well…just you be careful. Don't go getting your hopes up."

# Six

Talk about the eels died down after about a week. Jonah was glad as it meant that Brigg would have less to harass him about. Just the same, Jonah made it a point to arrive at the schoolhouse right as the bell rang, and to dash out as soon as they were released. The less time he had to be confronted by Brigg and his pack, the better off things would be for all of them.

Dinner hour was the hardest. Often Brigg and his friends would head home for their meal, as they lived down the street near the port. Jonah lived too far away, and even if he didn't, he preferred to share his meal with Lucas, who often came with nothing. However, Brigg didn't spend much of his dinner hour at home. He'd race down the street, scarf his food, and race back. Playing stick ball was a favorite of his, but since the eels, Brigg had been hanging back and watching Jonah. It was as if Brigg was reminding Jonah that he hadn't forgotten his threat; and that he still planned to prove Ms. Emily was a witch.

If Jonah hadn't promised his ma he would stay out of trouble, there were times he was certain he would have pummeled Brigg to the ground. Or at least gone down trying. The kid's arrogance alone irritated Jonah, but what bugged him most was everything Brigg had done to belittle and humiliate Jonah, as well as all the insinuations that his ma was a witch.

"Don't give him a thought," Lucas said one day when he noticed Jonah watching Brigg. "He's just a big bully."

Jonah looked over at him. "You're awfully smart for a little kid."

"I'm not that little." Lucas was nibbling at a bone, trying to get the last of the chicken that clung to it. Jonah smiled at him. "Here," he said as he handed Lucas a bright red apple. "They're especially sweet this year."

The younger boy grinned up in response and took it. "You know," Lucas said, "I could help you."

"Help me? With what?"

Lucas nodded toward Brigg.

"Oh, yeah? And how would you do that?"

Lucas shrugged, but there was a twinkle in his eye as he bit into the apple.

Jonah raised an eyebrow, then glanced over at Brigg. There wasn't really anything to do; and he certainly didn't want Lucas getting caught in the middle of whatever might come. "Never mind all that," he said. Changing the subject, he added, "How's your ma? Did you give her the herbs?"

A cloud seemed to pass over Lucas' expression. "I… I haven't yet," he said letting his hand and the apple drop to his lap. "It was awfully nice of you," he added quickly, "just that…"

"Your pa," Jonah finished for him.

Lucas nodded.

"It's okay, Luke. At least you've got them, you know, in case," Jonah couldn't begrudge the youngster for his father's fallacy, even if it did turn Jonah's stomach into a knot. He took another bite of his own apple, but it had a metallic taste from the bile that rose up against it, and he spit it out.

"Yeah, sure. Thanks," Lucas said, his own apple seemingly forgotten in the awkwardness that followed.

Jonah stood up, tossed his apple core aside, and thrust his hands in his pockets. His right hand settled on a piece of metal deep inside. He'd forgotten about the nickel Ol' Man Wimple had given him last night. When he'd given it to Jonah, he told him to spend it on something fun. It wasn't often that Jonah had an opportunity like that, and he felt guilty at even the suggestion. But Ol' Man Wimple insisted that he was not to give it to his mother, or feel guilty about a little pleasure. An idea settled on him.

"We've got some time left," he said, turning back toward Lucas, "want to go to the mercantile?" Jonah flipped the coin high in the air, and caught it.

Lucas' eyes got big at the sight of the coin. "Really?" he asked, his eyes lit up with childhood excitement - excitement that was contagious. And just like that, the awkwardness of the previous conversation, and all that lay unsaid, was gone.

"Yeah. Let's go."

The two boys hurried down main street to the mercantile, past the handful of shops that had come into Delmar as it had grown. There were several specialty shops along the street now, but the mercantile, Joe's Mercantile to be exact, was the oldest standing building in town. Next to the fish market, the mercantile was the oldest business in town, too. Some people liked the specialty shops that were starting to pop up, but the mercantile was great for a general one stop experience. It was also the most likely place to have prices the outlying families could afford.

Joe, or rather Joseph Tanner, the owner of the shop, was outside sweeping dust from the walkway just in front of the store. As the boys neared the shop, Joe stopped his sweeping and rested against the handle of the long broom.

"Whoa, there boys," he said with a twinkle in his eye. "In a bit of hurry, aren't cha?"

"Just a few minutes a'fore the bell, sir," Jonah said, remembering his manners.

"Well, then, what can I do ya for?"

Lucas glanced at Jonah, anticipation and a little doubt rested in his eyes. Jonah grinned back at the boy. "Ol' Man Wimple gave me a nickel and told me to spend it on something fun."

"More 'n likely, something sweet, then?"

"Yes, sir. I'd like to treat my friend here to some of your right good candy," Jonah replied.

"Well, best come on in then. See what this fine fellow here might like." Unlike most of the people in town, Joseph Tanner wasn't as easily swayed by gossip. He'd always been kind to Jonah and his mother, and treated them like ordinary customers. Now he was showing the same kindness to Lucas, the boy whose family had nothing extra at all.

"Tell me, son, how's your ma doing these days?" he asked in a gentle voice while Lucas looked over the candy.

There were so many choices, lemon drops, candy sticks, licorice, peppermints, and candies Lucas didn't even know the names of. He looked away from the jars to answer the store keeper. "Not much progress, sir," he said trying to be brave as he said it. "Doctors don't have much hope."

At this last comment, Joseph Tanner looked over at Jonah and raised an eyebrow in question. Jonah just shook his head; and the store keeper dropped his gaze back to Lucas. The unspoken question, and the silent answer, had said it all. And although Jonah felt sick that his mother wasn't allowed to help Lucas' mother, the silent acknowledgement that his mother did a world of good for some, was enough to help lessen the knot that seemed to reside in his stomach.

"Well, then, what can we getcha?" Joe asked the boys, changing the subject back to the candy in front of them.

Lucas couldn't decide. The choices were just too many. Jonah quickly noticed this, and said, "How 'bout a sample sack. A nickel's worth."

Joe put in a nickel's worth and then some, knowing the two boys rarely had the opportunity for such treats. "You boys best hurry along, so's you're not late," he told them as he handed them each a small sack. "Tell Ms. Emily I said hi," Joe added.

"Will do."

"And, Lucas, you let your ma know we're praying for her."

"Thank you, sir," Lucas said. Tears pricked at his eyes, but he managed to blink them back. Jonah knew things were bad, but now he wondered just how bad.

Jonah and Lucas joined the crowds on main street as they worked their way back to the road that would take them out to the schoolhouse. The smell of the salty sea air was refreshing for Jonah, and he found he missed visiting his cove more than he realized. He'd done well, keeping away from it ever since the night of the pirate landing, and things had been pretty quiet. The pirate-turned-farmer hadn't re-emerged at the farmhouse, and as far as Jonah knew, the man wasn't even in town any more. He hadn't seen him, anyway, and most who weren't from their little town didn't stay long.

The dinner hour was just about over, which meant the bell would start ringing soon. Other kids pushed past Jonah and Lucas on their way back to school, but Jonah couldn't seem to bring himself to hurry. He was enjoying the salty sea air maybe a little too much, the lap of the waves as they hit against the docks was like music to his ears. He stopped and closed his eyes, allowing himself to take it all in. Soon he felt an urgent tugging on his arm.

Lucas' voice pulled Jonah back, reminding him of what his current responsibilities were. "Come on," Lucas said, "we're going to be late."

Jonah sighed and opened his eyes. "I know," he started, then stopped short as his eyes came back into focus. Just in front of him, on the nearest pier, was the pirate. The man appeared to be working, helping to unload and restock some of the boats.

Jonah couldn't take his eyes off the man. "Have you ever seen him before?"

Lucas followed Jonah's gaze to the pirate on the pier. "No. Don't think I have." He looked back at Jonah, whose attention was fixated on the stranger. "Come on," he tugged at Jonah's arm again, "it don't matter who he is right now. You can figure it out later. If we're late, we'll get a lickin'."

The bell began to toll in the distance. Lucas tugged once more on Jonah's arm, then took off at a sprint toward the school house. But Jonah didn't move. He was still watching the stranger as he lifted crate after crate. Miguel turned and looked directly at him, holding his gaze for a minute. It was uncanny how the man seemed to know Jonah was watching him.

Captain Montagurell came out of the tavern, probably having just finished his own dinner, and marched over to the pier where

Miguel was working. Jonah watched as The Captain puffed out his chest, said something to Miguel, then spat directly on Miguel's boot. Miguel looked at his boot, then back at The Captain. Nothing was said, but his eyes seemed different to Jonah. He couldn't be too sure, after all, he was across the street from the pier, but it certainly seemed like something in them had changed.

The bell continued to toll in the distance, but Jonah knew it would stop soon. The chances of him getting back before the ringing stopped were slim. He knew he ought to hightail it back to the schoolhouse, but he couldn't take his eyes off the pirate. He sensed something was going to happen. Something big.

The Captain turned his back to Miguel and his voice boomed out, "We'll be back in a few days. Back before the first flakes fall."

And as the captain shouted out what Jonah figured was an annual announcement, Jonah watched Miguel behind him. The man had lifted one final crate and was placing it in the boat. But what Jonah noticed was the water, that had been gently lapping against the side of the boat, began to still. Jonah moved forward, walking across the street to get a better look.

"When we return," the captain continued to bellow, "there'll be a celebration on the green to honor these fine men and their families for their sacrifices in bringing us the fish that sustain this town."

Captain Montagurell's words felt hollow. A celebration was in order, but not because of the fishermen, at least not in Jonah's mind. It was always hard work for all the families getting ready for winter, and a celebration was a wonderful way to reward all the hard work.

As he neared the pier, Jonah looked down at the water. The lapping had died away completely. Crystals were forming on its surface, and, as he continued to watch, they ran down and linked together, creating a thick bed of ice completely locking in the boat.

Jonah looked up. The sky was clear. He wasn't wearing his coat, and only felt the slightest tinge of coolness in the air. Not cold enough to freeze anything more than a light mist. Certainly not cold enough to freeze the sea.

He watched Miguel climb out of the boat, the last crate tucked securely away ready for the trip ahead. Then Miguel looked over at him, and winked.

Jonah didn't make it back to school that day; and the boats never did launch.

# Seven

Ice held the harbor waters captive, locking the ships in tight, though the air stayed mildly cool. Families had to resort to hunting for their meat, as there was no fish to be had. Even the butcher could not keep up with the demand for meat to replace the fish normally used for daily meals.

When the weather turned warm again, as it often did just before winter took over, the sea still did not budge. If anything, it seemed the crystals multiplied, as if doubling their efforts to keep the ice in place. Even Mother Nature could not make the sea obey her rules.

Peter Jensen, a long-time resident who grew up by a lake in the north, eventually came forward to teach the men how to ice fish. He figured it couldn't be any different than doing so on the lake. However, the ice was so thick he couldn't get a good cut. After breaking three saws, he finally gave up.

In addition to the hardships revolving around the lack of fish, there still had been no celebration, and the people were agitated, their moods darkening by the day. It seemed the townsfolk were falling into an increased frenzy of panic as the days wore on.

Jonah had taken to spending his dinner hour by the pier, which is where he was today. After the sea froze, he'd begun spending time at the cove again, too. There, the water continued to lap freely, racing its way up the beach, as though unaware of the winter ahead. There was nothing unnatural about that. But here, at the pier, something was definitely going on; and he thought he knew who was to blame.

"'T'aint natural," Captain Montagurell muttered to his first mate.

He watched The Captain as he leaned down and tested the ice. It didn't budge. The captain's face turned red with rage. This was one thing he couldn't control. One thing even he had to accept.

"Something's gotta be done," The Captain sputtered. "Call a town meeting."

"For when, sir?" his first mate asked.

"Tonight. Seven o'clock."

The two men left in opposite directions, and Jonah assumed that meant they were passing the information along. A town meeting wouldn't normally be a bad thing, but with the present circumstances, Jonah had a very uneasy feeling about it. He looked around, trying to locate the one person he was sure had something to do with the ice, though he couldn't figure out how. Problem was, Miguel han't shown himself since that day. At least not down at the pier.

***

Seven o'clock came. Jonah watched as what appeared to be the whole town tried to fit inside the church. It wasn't very big, and was only really full when the men were out at sea. Few families were devout, attending weekly in good times and bad. The vast majority only attended when the men were gone, and their families were concerned with their well-being, so the church rarely saw this kind

40

of attendance.

People were jostling each other trying to wedge their way closer to the front where Captain Montagurell stood to conduct the meeting. Jonah had come early, knowing the little church would not be big enough, and positioned himself near enough to hear well, but close enough to the side entrance that he'd be able to escape quickly should the need arise. He deliberately neglected to tell his mother about the meeting, not wanting to worry her. His heart was pounding hard in his chest as he waited to hear what The Captain would propose.

"Thank you all for coming tonight. As you know," Captain Montagurrell shouted over the noise, and others repeated quietly to the people behind them, "we've experienced an unnatural freeze in our harbor this season. It has caused great trouble and tribulation to the families of our town. Thanks to Peter Jensen, we have learned it is impossible even to cut through the ice." Here he turned his attention to Peter Jensen who was sitting nearer to the front. "I do hope your saws have since been repaired."

Peter gave a curt nod, which really didn't answer the inquiry. It may have been an affirmative, but it may have been acknowledging the concern and being too prideful to ask for assistance in getting them repaired. In any case, Jonah noted, The Captain did not actually offer assistance.

"Even as the weather has turned warmer, the ice continues to hold. There is nothing for us to do, and winter is fast approaching," The Captain continued.

"Then why are we here?" someone in the crowd yelled.

"Yeah, if there ain't nothing we can do, why'd ya call this here meetin'?" another added.

The Captain raised his hands to quiet the murmurs that quickly rippled through the crowd. "Because, as I've already said, this is truly an *unnatural* occurrence." He paused, letting the emphasis on the word unnatural set in.

Jonah's heart pounded even harder, racing like it wanted to burst out of his chest. His hands and neck were now sweating. He knew what was coming.

"Surely you don't think…" Joseph Tanner began.

"Mr. Tanner, what else is there to think?" The Captain spat back.

"We've been over and over this," Joseph Tanner said, trying to make his voice heard over the crowd; but the crowd was restless and the murmur of voices rose higher, making it difficult to hear.

The crowd pushed forward as more people tried to make their way toward the front. Jonah sensed someone watching him, but with the crowd's movement, it was difficult to be sure. He scanned the crowd trying to find the source. Brigg was across the room, leaning against the wall, looking right at him. When Jonah's eyes met his, Brigg's lips turned up in a sneer. The uncomfortable knot that had tied itself in Jonah's stomach lurched upward.

"There's only one answer to the ice," The Captain's voice boomed over the crowd. The murmuring quieted some. "Such unnatural occurrences come from the devil himself. Only someone who consorts with the devil would be able to make such a thing happen."

Panic filled Jonah. He knew where this line of thought was heading. He couldn't explain it, but he knew the stranger had something to do with the ice; and Jonah wasn't about to have the town blame this on his mother. Frantically, he pushed his way through the crowd. Jonah looked around wildly. He had to find the stranger.

Had Jonah not been carefully searching, he would never have seen Miguel. The pirate had tucked himself against the door frame, barely visible through the mass of people pressed into the little church. He caught Jonah's eye, and held his gaze for a moment, then nodded and headed outside. Jonah fought his way to the door, determined to catch up with the man.

"It's high time we put a stop to this nonsense," The Captain's voice rose above.

"What do you propose we do?"

"Yeah, what can we do?"

Jonah heard the voices, and knew the next step would be a riot against his mother. With a final push, he found himself standing in the open doorway.

"We'll make sure everyone knows that her kind will not be tolerated!"

*BOOM!*

The sound split the air with such force it caused the very earth beneath them to vibrate. An uneasy silence settled over the congregation. Apprehension filled the air as they whispered to one another, "What was that?"

*BOOM!*

Popping and cracking split the sound, causing the air to ripple and vibrate. The villagers grabbed hold of one another as the little church shook violently with each resounding boom.

"Make way!" The Captain bellowed, and the crowd immediately parted, creating a direct path to the door where Jonah was already standing.

Jonah, and the rest of the crowd, followed The Captain out of the small church. Ice fragments littered the ground. Large chunks of ice jutted upward like a badly mismatched puzzle.

With the next booming-crack, the ocean spewed out another round of frozen shards, scattering the crowd. Everyone watched apprehensively from the shelter of the buildings as the frozen mounds shifted violently.

Eventually the booming cracks lessened to a series of light pops, and Captain Montagurell made his way to the docks. Jonah, and few brave souls, followed behind. As The Captain stepped onto a dock, it swayed under his weight. He looked down, and Jonah followed his gaze. The ice had broken, and was melting rapidly, giving way to lapping water. The ships were no longer ice locked, though it was apparent that several had sustained damage from the pressure the ice had put on their boards.

Although surprised at the sudden flow of water, Captain Montagurrell quickly saw the need for repairs and called out, "Men! To your ships! Check the damage!"

The command revived the shocked crowd; and fishermen from all over the village sprang into action. Carpenters raced off to gather supplies, not knowing exactly what would be needed, but knowing they needed to act fast. The whole town relied on those fishing boats.

In the frenzy of the needed work, it seemed the witch hunt had been forgotten. At least for now. But Jonah knew it was only a matter of time. Especially if this kind of thing continued to happen.

"Best get on home." Jonah turned to see Joseph Tanner standing near him. "Things seemed to have blown over this time. There's nothing you can do here."

"Thank you," Jonah said.

Joseph smiled. "No need to thank me. Anyone with half a brain would know your ma had nothing to do with the ice."

Though Jonah appreciated the sentiment, he didn't share Joseph's optimism. He nodded to the man and turned away from the crowd, heading out of town. As he walked, he saw the pirate leaning against the mercantile, hidden by the shadow of the building. Once again, Miguel winked at him.

# Eight

It took a several weeks working night and day to fully repair all the fishing boats. During that time, the older boys of the fishing families were kept out of school to assist in the repairs. This gave Brigg and his cronies leverage to expand their already big heads, and Jonah noticed, upon Brigg's return, that Brigg was more puffed up than ever before.

Jonah kept to himself, and avoided going into town. He worried that it was only a matter of time before people took up their witch hunt again. But in a town that had been deprived of their fish for the last couple of months, it seemed the vast majority of people were just grateful to get the boats back on the water.

With the fishing boats active again, the original celebration was rescheduled and preparations begun. The theme of the celebration would be the renewal of the fishing community – the reviving of the town that had recently been looking at its demise. It was good to see everyone had something else to think about and occupy their time.

"Hey, Jonah," Lucas said one morning as they waited for the school bell to ring. "I made ma that tea."

It took Jonah a minute to figure out what Lucas was talking about. When he did, a huge smile covered his face. "That's great,

Luke. Did it help?"

Lucas nodded. "Yeah. I think so. 'Least she seemed to be in less pain. Even Pa seemed more relaxed."

"So, he let you give it to her then?"

Lucas shuffled his feet uncomfortably. "Well, not exactly. I… I made it when he was out. I didn't want him to stop me."

Jonah's smile slipped. "That's okay," he said, "at least she was able to use them."

"Can I get some more?" Lucas asked hopefully.

"Yeah. Sure. Of course." Jonah was happy his mother's herbs seemed to be helping Lucas' mother. It wasn't the best situation, but it was better than the woman not having any relief.

The bell rang and the boys made their way up the steps.

"Hey, Demon Boy!" Brigg hissed in Jonah's hear as he pushed passed him.

Jonah felt his body tense. Having Brigg back in class was going to be difficult. And it was obvious that Brigg hadn't forgotten the almost witch hunt. He took a deep breath and continued into the classroom, taking his seat beside Lucas.

"Don't think I've forgotten," Brigg said as he leaned forward across his desk toward Jonah.

Jonah felt his muscles tighten.

Lucas touched his arm. "Never mind him. He's not worth it," he whispered.

"It's just a matter of time," Brigg threatened. "We'll get her. And you." He sat back in his seat.

*Breathe. Just breathe…in…out…in…out,* Jonah told himself as he focused on his breathing. It wasn't worth getting in a fight during school. Or getting on Ms. Winter's bad side this early in the day. *In…out…in…out.*

"Your essay." Ms. Winters was standing right beside Jonah, waiting. He hadn't seen her come to his desk. Hadn't heard her tell the class to take out their essays. He rifled through his satchel and pulled out a couple wrinkled papers. Ms. Winters crinkled her nose as Jonah smoothed them out and handed them to her.

Brigg snickered.

"And yours, Mr. Montagurrell?" Ms. Winters turned her attention to Brigg.

Brigg lifted his smooth, unwrinkled papers up and handed them to Ms. Winters with a grin. "Right here, Ms. Winters."

"Thank you, Brigg."

As Ms. Winters continued down the row, Brigg leaned forward again. "You best watch your back. Yours and your mother's."

Jonah jumped to his feet, his body tense and fists clenched tight. He whirled around to face Brigg who continued to sneer at him.

Lucas grabbed Jonah's arm and pulled. "Sit down," he pleaded through his teeth trying not to draw more attention to the scene.

*In…out…in…out.* Jonah began to turn back around to sit down.

"Chicken," Brigg's voice hissed just as Ms. Winter's asked, "Is there a problem, boys?" in a voice that clearly said, *There better not be a problem.*

The rest of the morning passed without trouble. Ms. Winters kept the groups busy with rhetoric and arithmetic, which came as a welcome distraction to Jonah's mind. But as the dinner hour approached, Jonah was on edge once more. He had trouble concentrating, and found he was tapping his pencil. Anxiety mounted as he thought about Brigg and what might come. His heart began to race, his hands started sweating, and he felt the familiar nauseous knot form in the pit of his stomach.

As it turned out, he needn't have worried, since Brigg and his buddies ran off toward town. Jonah had no reason to go to town today, so he found a quiet spot at the side of the building where his body and mind could calm down.

The air was bitter, and a cold breeze was blowing. Looking up at the clouds, Jonah could tell a storm was brewing off the coast. That was typical for this time of year, but it wouldn't be appreciated with the lost fishing time, but it wasn't as if anyone could do anything about it.

Lucas sat down beside Jonah. "You know he says that stuff just to get you mad."

"Yeah, I know."

"So why do you let it get to you?"

"How'd you feel if they were saying that stuff about your ma?"

The younger boy was quiet a moment. "Guess I see your point." They ate in silence for a while, both boys pulling their sweaters tighter around them. "Do you think they'll cancel the celebration tonight?" Lucas was watching the sky.

"Don't know," Jonah replied.

"Looks like a big 'un coming in."

Jonah nodded, watching the sky. It had started red that morning, a flaming dark red, and was now a rolling black pushing inland.

"I hope they don't cancel it," the younger boy said.

Jonah smiled at Lucas. "Yeah, that'd be a bummer."

The crunch of boots on the frosted ground caused Jonah to turn his head sharply in that direction. However, the person he saw wasn't Brigg, but rather someone else who made Jonah's stomach knot up almost as tightly.

Miguel stopped and tipped his hat to the boys. He looked up at the sky and a wide grin spread across his face. "Looks like a good one," he said, to no one in particular, then looked back at the boys and winked.

"He gives me the creeps," Lucas whispered to Jonah when Miguel was out of earshot.

"Me, too," Jonah said hollowly. "Me, too." Yet, unlike Lucas, Jonah was both disgusted and fascinated by the man. He just didn't understand why.

# Nine

“Are you sure it's a good idea?” Jonah asked his mother. She was busy watching her reflection while she pinned up her hair. She pulled at some of the curls on the sides, loosening them and allowing them to hang in wispy strains beside her face.

“And why wouldn't it be?” she countered.

What could he tell her? There are people who hate you? They think you're a witch? No, he couldn't tell her those things, though he was certain she already knew them. He just couldn't bring himself to let her know that he knew. Nor could he risk hurting her feelings. Still, he didn't like that she was so insistent on going to the celebration tonight.

“We could stay here,” Jonah offered. “There's a big storm blowing in.”

Emily walked over to the window and looked out. It was dark, and the darkness was growing, but the storm hadn't actually hit yet. The town was determined to have the celebration. “Seems to be holding for now. Besides, Jonah, it's been a long time since we've been out. It would do us both some good. Who knows when we'll have such a celebration again.”

“Next year,” Jonah muttered.

“Oh, come on. It'll be fun.” His mother grabbed up her shawl, and pinned her hat on her hair. "Grab your jacket. You don't want to catch cold."

Jonah did as he'd been told, not only grabbing his jacket, but putting it on and buttoning it before stepping outside. It was strange how dark the sky was. The wind wasn't blowing, leaving an eerie feeling in the air. It didn't feel natural, and that made Jonah think of Miguel. He wondered what the man was doing right now. His mind raced back to dinner, when Miguel had spoken to him. He had seemed so excited about the incoming storm. There was definitely something unnatural about it all. And yet, Jonah found himself wondering if the pirate would be at the celebration; and hoping that he would.

***

The incoming storm didn't appear to have kept anyone from coming to the celebration. The green was full of lanterns strung from tree to tree, giving the area a bright glow. Several small warming fires were spaced out around the edge of the green, making the area reasonably comfortable despite the cool air of the impending storm. A pig had been roasting all day, and there were tables set up with pies and sweets of every kind imaginable. Jonah's mouth watered at the thought of them.

Off in the far corner, a group of fiddlers sat on barrels, with a space marked out in front of them for dancing. The music was fast and riveting, and Jonah couldn't help but tap his feet. He was certain he wouldn't make his way out to the dance floor, though. Only the bravest of boys found their way there. They were the ones no longer afraid to ask girls for a dance. Either that, or they were still young enough not to be nervous.

Emily quietly looked around the area. "Why don't you go along and find your friends," she told him. Jonah didn't have the heart to tell her he didn't really have any friends - unless you counted Lucas. He looked around to see if he could find the younger boy now. The kid had been so excited about coming, but Jonah wondered if Lucas' father would actually let him come, especially with the growing storm. He scanned the area, but did not immediately find his friend. So, he found his way to a table full of punch cups, and took one. There he stood, watching the crowd of people as he sipped at his drink, hoping to avoid any interaction.

His mother, on the other hand, drifted off to speak with the farmers' wives. Women she was more comfortable with, and who, generally, trusted her. Occasionally, Jonah would see one of their husbands come over, take his wife by the arm, and they would walk away. Each time this happened, Jonah wondered why his mother insisted they come at all.

"Hey there," Lucas said as he came up next to Jonah. "Sure is something, isn't?"

Despite his frustration at the treatment of his mother, Jonah couldn't help but grin at the excitement of the younger boy. He'd forgotten the wonder of such events, and found it was contagious as he watched Lucas' big eyes dart around the place. Delmar really went all out for this event.

"What do you want to do first?"

The skinny boy was tapping his toes along with the music, all the while eyeing the tables heaped with food. "Suppose we ought to eat a little something 'fore we do much, don't ya think?"

Jonah laughed. "Reckon you're right." He handed Lucas a cup

of punch, and the two of them headed for the food tables.

They helped themselves to a couple of plates, filling them up with cookies, pie, roasted pig, and the fixings. You'd have thought the boys never ate looking at their plates, which wasn't too far from the truth for Lucas. Jonah was glad that at least this one night, his friend would have a full belly.

As they sat on the grass enjoying their food, they watched the men play horseshoes. Captain Montagurrell was facing off with his best mate. Both men were strong – muscles built by the sea – and both had a deadly aim. The clang of steel on steel as they set their horseshoes against the stakes was punctuated by applause. Jonah enjoyed watching the spectators. Some wore hard expressions, concentrating on the match as if their lives depended on it. Jonah knew these were the men who had bet money on the game.

"Want to do the sack race?" Jonah asked Lucas.

Lucas looked across the green to where most of the children had gathered. Large burlap sacks had been laid out, and several of the children were stepping into them and pulling them up. "I don't know," he said.

"Awe, come on. You ain't too old for racin' yet!" Jonah encouraged. As for himself, he figured he'd crossed that line. Though if they put together a group his own age, he'd probably join in. More than likely, it would be a foot race, though.

With Jonah's encouragement, Lucas agreed, and they made their way across the green to the gunny sacks. The younger boy grinned as he climbed inside and hopped his way to the starting line. Jonah laughed at the boy's excitement.

Lucas did the sack race, falling at least three times before he crossed the finish line. His smile never left his face, though, as he'd jump back up and keep going. It didn't seem there was anything that could keep him from enjoying himself.

"Your turn," Lucas told Jonah when the sack races had ended and the foot races were starting.

Jonah didn't need any extra encouragement. He came to the line eager for a chance to prove himself. A light breeze caressed his cheek, and he glanced up at the sky. The storm appeared to be holding off. In fact, it looked as if it might clear up before it made it to shore.

"You ought to the leave the racin' to us men. Ain't meant for no scrawny boys," Brigg taunted as he positioned himself at the line next to Jonah.

Ignoring the comment, Jonah leaned low, waiting for the gunshot that would signal the beginning of the race. Brigg might be stronger, but Jonah was pretty sure he was faster than his nemesis. He refused to let the older boy get under his skin.

"Ain't none of that black magic gonna help you now," Brigg sneered just as the gun went off.

The remark shot like a dagger into Jonah's stomach, causing him to miss the first seconds of the race. Belatedly, he launched himself forward, and pushed against the ground with everything he had. Adrenaline raced through him, hot with the anger, pushing him forward. The wind swirled around him, pressing at his back. Without much effort, Jonah caught up to Brigg and passed him, crossing the finish line just seconds before the older boy.

Brigg glowered at Jonah as he was awarded his ribbon and a pie for winning the race. "Better watch your back," he growled. Brigg turned and stomped off across the green, his buddies following closely behind.

"You sure showed him!" Lucas grinned ear to ear.

"Yeah. I sure did," Jonah agreed, though he felt a sinking in his stomach. Showing Brigg up was sure to come at a cost. He shook the thought aside, and handed his pie to Lucas. "Here. I want you to have it."

The younger boy started to protest.

"Really, Lucas, take it. I bet your mama'd like a piece."

A frown creased Lucas' face, but just as quickly it was gone. "Alright. Thanks." He took the pie gingerly. "I probably ought to get back." The two boys nodded to each other, then Lucas ran off with the pie in his hands.

Jonah looked at the sky again. It was nearly full dark now, but he could still make out the angry clouds in the distance. They appeared to be gathering again, doubling their efforts. This storm was not going to clear after all. *Probably ought to get Ma home before it hits.*

He looked out across the green. Light from the lanterns and fires flickered across everything making the images dance before him. It was difficult to see clearly past the dancing couples, so he made his way back around.

It wasn't until he reached the first of the tables that Jonah spotted his mother. She was chatting with several ladies, one of which Jonah knew was Mr. Tanner's wife, and seemed to be enjoying herself. Jonah picked up a cookie, and began to eat it as he watched her.

A low rumble cut through the air, reminding Jonah that a storm was rolling in. He glanced up, and though the sky was black, he could see the shifting of shadows as clouds covered what few stars were left in the sky.

He was about to make his way over to his ma, and suggest

they head home for the night, when he saw Miguel. Jonah was transfixed watching his strong, confident step. The pirate clearly feared nothing. Several women turned to watch him, then turned back to whisper among themselves. That would have made Jonah uncomfortable, but Miguel didn't seem to notice.

Miguel stopped by the table where chunks of roasted pig had been laid out. He tore off a piece and began chewing on it as he leaned back against the edge of the table and looked around. His eyes landed on Jonah, and he tipped his hat to him. Jonah blinked and looked around him, wondering if anyone else had seen what the man did. When he looked back at Miguel, the man winked at him, then left the table and strode across the open space right up to Emily. He said something to her, and she appeared to become flustered. Jonah imagined he could see the faint pink of a blush creep into his mother's face. He watched as she set her cup on the table, reach out and accept Miguel's offered hand with a curtsey before drifting out onto the dance floor.

A funny feeling found its way into Jonah's stomach, and made itself at home. The gall of the man! To waltz in here and pick his ma out of everyone here! Jonah wasn't sure if he was going to be sick, or if he was angry. His heart was racing, and his mind felt like it was on fire. Then he realized it wasn't just Miguel he was unhappy with. His mother had accepted.

Unease crept through him as he watched them dance. With it only being a few days since the almost witch hunt, Jonah didn't like that his ma had been singled out by the troublesome stranger. But his mother seemed at ease with the man. Quite the contrast to the conversation he'd overheard that first night a few months back. Now he wondered if Miguel had stopped by the house more than once. And what business would the stranger have with Jonah's ma anyway? Maybe he should have told his ma what he had seen at the cove when the pirate came ashore.

Jonah shook his head and walked over to another table laden with treats and helped himself to a handful of cookies. He leaned against one of the poles nearby, and watched as his mother danced and laughed. He'd never seen her like this before. After watching for several minutes, Jonah decided he really didn't like Miguel. Maybe he even hated him.

He stood there, staring daggers at Miguel, crushing the cookies in his hand. Crumbs drifted to the ground as he let his arm hang limp at his side, no longer interested in eating. A rustle behind him drew his attention away from the dancing couple. Jonah didn't have to turn around to know who was there, but he turned anyway. Brigg and his buddies were just ducking off into the shadows with a heavy jug between them. Certain it was mead they'd managed somehow to smuggle away from the fishermen, Jonah secretly hoped they'd get caught.

The song was just coming to an end, and Jonah turned back around to find his mother again. He scanned the area, but didn't see her. He'd lost track of Emily... and Miguel. When he found them again, they were in the shadow of a tree away from everyone else. Jonah felt his hands tighten into fists. That dirty, rotten pirate was kissing Jonah's mother. *How dare he!* Jonah was so mad he was shaking.

Jonah's mind raced back to the night he'd overheard Miguel in the farmhouse with his mother. He hadn't understood everything they had said; and his mother hadn't wanted to talk about it. But now Jonah was certain there were things she'd been keeping from him. Important things.

With hands still clutched tight, Jonah took two steps toward his mother. Then, filled with anger and being too overwhelmed to confront her, he whirled away from her and the celebration. He figured he would wait for her at home; and in doing so, missed seeing Emily slap Miguel.

Jonah stuffed his hands in his pockets and headed away from the bright lantern lights down the road toward home. He was more hurt than angry, and as he walked, that ache built inside. Lost in his own thoughts, Jonah forgot about Brigg and his friends, so he wasn't ready when the group ambushed him at the edge of the road.

"Whatcha think you're doing?" Brigg said, his words slightly slurred, but still fierce.

Jonah wasn't in the mood to deal with Brigg. "Ain't doing nothing, Brigg. Let me pass."

"Let him pass," Brigg mocked, laughing back at his friends. Turning his attention back to Jonah he said, "I don't think so, ya nitwit! Ain't nobody goin' nowhere."

"Yeah, no telling what he saw?"

"Or who he'll tell."

Brigg moved in closer to Jonah, and his buddies followed, forming a semi-circle in front of him.

"Oh, shove off!" Jonah said. "I don't give a hoot what you're doing. And I ain't got no one to tell. Not like anyone'd believe me, anyhow, now would they?" Jonah wasn't interested in a fight, especially right now. He just wanted to be alone to clear his head. He needed a chance to figure some things out before he confronted his mother.

"It ain't who you'd tell we need to worry about. Is it, Nitwit?"

Brigg spat back.

Jonah decided to ignore the bait, and tried sidestepping around the group. He just hoped the boys were all words tonight, and that it wouldn't escalate into something worse. But Brigg was itching for a fight, and wasn't about to let Jonah slip past so easily. The group had widened, spreading out to make getting around them nearly impossible. "Don't need to tell anyone, do ya? Can take care of things yourself. Or is it just your mama got all the power?"

Jonah's heart thudded, as it always did when Brigg started accusing his mother of witchcraft. It would be so easy to take a swing at the boy. But there were at least ten of them, and only one of him. The odds didn't look so good, even if the others were a bit tipsy.

"Heard your witch of a mother's done gone crazy," Brigg continued to taunt, his cronies laughing and encouraging him.

Jonah knew his mother was acting strange, but he was not about to give these boys something to hold over him for the rest of the year. *One. Two. Three.* Jonah counted slowly in his head trying to keep control over his fast-rising emotions. But the anger he felt now had a different target, and it boiled right at the surface.

The wind picked up, and large, heavy drops began to fall from the sky. It seemed the raging storm had finally made its way inland. Jonah glanced up at the dark clouds swirling overhead. It looked angry. This would be a big one.

"What? Cat got yer tongue?" This time Brigg gave a dull laugh, like he knew something Jonah didn't.

Jonah knew he was being baited. *Just breathe,* he told himself, repeating the words Ol' Man Wimple had told him many times before. Somehow it was supposed to help, but Jonah could feel the anger rising faster. He knew Brigg well enough to know there was probably something Jonah didn't know that the older boy did. Something probably the whole village knew; and it probably wasn't good.

Jonah looked up. He had to see it for himself in Brigg's face. Needed to know if Brigg really knew anything, or if the boy was just trying to get Jonah to make the first move.

"Your ma's been out dancin' with the devil," Brigg's taunt turned to a sneer, a wicked gleam in his eye. The nasty curve of his lip told Jonah that Brigg was enjoying himself way too much.

Jonah could feel the heat of his emotions crawling toward his face. The image of his mother dancing with Miguel flashed through his mind. That was all it took. The anger, so close to the tipping point, boiled over. Jonah's hand balled up into a fist, came up and connected with Brigg's jaw so fast even Jonah wasn't sure he'd actually hit the kid. Only the throb in his knuckles convinced him of the truth of what he'd done.

Brigg reached up to his jaw, shock registering on his face. No kid had ever hit him before. In that moment, Brigg's eyes snapped from wicked amusement to full blown hatred. "Oh, you did not just do that," he said in a low growl as he cocked his fist ready to retaliate.

Jonah anticipated the move and was able to duck in time; probably due, in part, to the older boy being a bit tipsy from the mead. This only angered Brigg further.

"Hold him down," he yelled to his cronies. The boys who'd been gathered just behind Brigg snapped to life, all heading toward Jonah on the command of their leader.

The other boys quickly surrounded Jonah. Now he was determined he would not go down without a fight. Suddenly the heavens opened. Rain came down in thick sheets, drenching the boys and muddying the road. Jonah threw a couple of wild punches, hoping to hit one or more of Brigg's friends before they overtook him. He knew there wasn't much he could do against all of them, even if they were drunk. His only hope was the slickening ground, which he knew could rapidly turn against him as well.

With arms swinging in all directions, and a few well-placed punches, it took Jonah a few minutes to realize the other boys beginning to back off. They pulled out, forming a ring around him and Brigg. In the midst of this surprising new development, he heard a voice calling out above the mayhem, "Make it a fair fight, boys."

It wasn't a voice Jonah recognized, and for a second he lost his concentration and turned toward the crowd to see who it was. In that moment, Brigg knocked Jonah so hard his head snapped back. The trickle of blood that came from his aching nose quickly turned into a gushing waterfall. Jonah lay on his back, his hands to his face as the blood seeped through his fingers. Brigg kicked him in the ribs a couple times, then turned away, already claiming victory and reminding everyone of his status.

Jonah wasn't going to let him get away that easily. He groaned once as he steadied himself, letting the blood from his nose run down his chin. Then, just as someone was pointing out to Brigg that Jonah was actually trying to get up, Jonah kicked his own feet outward and swept them directly underneath Brigg, taking down the older boy. Quick as a cat, Jonah was on top of Brigg, his arm pulled back ready to beat the kid to a pulp. He got in two hard punches before he felt his arm catch in a firm grip.

"That's enough."

Jonah looked up into the eyes of Miguel. The pirate, his mind quickly reminded him. The man glanced down and nodded toward Brigg as he repeated himself, "That's enough, Jonah."

Irritation flooded Jonah. This was his chance to prove himself. Brigg deserved everything he got. Then the irritation gave way to anger as he realized this man knew his name. Not only knew his name, but was preventing him from getting revenge on the one person who'd spent his whole life trying to tear Jonah apart. He could feel the heat of anger as it raced through his blood, blinding him.

"There are other ways."

Jonah shook his arm loose from Miguel's grip, and looked down at Brigg. Already the kid's eyes were swelling closed, and his lips were fat. A feeling of remorse tried to edge its way into Jonah's conscience, but he pushed it away muttering, "He deserved it. He deserved every last bit of it, and more." Still, it was enough to temper his boiling blood and he dropped his arm.

Jonah got up, freeing Brigg as he did so. He moved backward out of the circle, keeping his eyes on the boy in case Brigg tried again. "Don't you ever speak about my ma like that again or next time I won't stop," he promised as he turned and headed down the dark road.

After a few minutes of walking, Jonah remembered Miguel. He turned, scanning the road behind him as he tried to find the man, or at least pinpoint his shadow, but it seemed the man had disappeared as quickly as he'd shown up. He wondered what would make the man interfere; and what business was keeping him in the area. The village was small, and strangers were few, never staying more than a couple of nights. This man was still here after four months and was probably still working for Brigg's father, which meant that whatever business he had with Jonah's ma was nothing they wanted any part of. Not to mention, Jonah already knew Miguel held a very dangerous secret. Another good reason he and his mother should steer clear of him.

# Ten

Jonah had planned to go straight home and wait for his mother within the small farmhouse, but he never made it. Instead, he found himself in the familiar wood that led to the cove. Though he'd been back here before, he'd never crossed out of the tree line, having promised himself that he wouldn't go near the water. It was his way of justifying being at the cove, while having promised his mother he'd never actually go there. But, tonight he no longer cared about the promise he'd made himself - or his mother.

As he walked through the trees, the water called out to Jonah, more insistent than before. It was as if it were alive and had been missing him. Though deep down he knew he should stay clear of the water – knew he should stay deep in the trees as he'd done in the past - Jonah just didn't care anymore. He was tired and hurt. The ocean beckoned, and Jonah listened. He moved past the trees onto the sand, slowly making his way to the water's edge. As he came near, the sound that had urged him so intensely softened, becoming a soothing, gentle caress to his mind, if not quite his heart. Jonah let go of his senses, and for once, he felt at peace. He felt calm.

The wind had died down, and with it, the rain had subsided. The sound of lapping waves matched the rhythm of his slowing heart. As he calmed, Jonah began to feel the aftermath of the fight he'd just been in. His nose hurt, though it had stopped bleeding a while ago. Dried blood pulled at his face and covered his hands. He knelt near the water's edge, running his hands through it. Cupping his hands, he filled them and splashed water over his face. He knew he was a mess. His was nose broken, his face bruised, and his eye would be black before daylight, if it wasn't already. Everything hurt. The water was cool and felt good on his sore face.

The struggles of his life seemed to fade from before him. The more he felt the water in his hands and lapping at his feet, the more he wanted to join it. He never wanted to go back. The ocean seemed to sense his desire, and waves grew large, causing the water to rush higher and higher as it pushed up along the shore. Jonah wanted to lay down and let the water wash over him again and again. Oblivion. That's what he wanted.

"Careful there, Jonah," the stranger's voice pierced through the serene experience.

Jonah turned and could just make out the pirate-turned-farmer holding his hand out toward the sea as he spoke. The sea receded and calmed once again to a gentle lapping.

"It only wants to please you."

Jonah stood up. "What?"

"The sea. Surely you have noticed it." The man walked slowly toward him.

The waters had returned to a gentle lapping, barely reaching Jonah's feet. "I...," he began as he looked out at the sea, suddenly feeling uncomfortable. "I...I don't know what you're talking about."

By now Miguel was directly beside Jonah, where he sat down. Jonah inched slightly away from the man. He realized that something about the man both intrigued and frightened him, but he didn't want the man to know.

"I'm sure by now you've heard it," Miguel said. "It calls to you."

"I don't know what you're talking about!" Jonah said, with more conviction. Inside he felt dread. He had never told anyone about the sea, about its voice, or the calling. Not even his own mother.

The man turned to look at Jonah, his piercing grey-blue eyes, illuminated by the full moon, staring directly into Jonah's own. Jonah wasn't sure what he'd expected to see, but he knew it wasn't this. There was compassion, gentleness. Pirates were not gentle.

"I may be the only person to understand what you're going through. Not even your mother knows. Not really." He said this last part with a touch of sadness.

"How do you know my mother?" Jonah asked as he sat down beside Miguel. The question had been burning in his mind ever since he'd seen the man at their home. And more so now that he'd watched the two of them dancing together. The image of them dancing, and how easily his mother was taken in, made him feel sick. The water rocked violently at his feet as if it were trapped against a cage trying to escape.

Miguel let out a heavy sigh, the kind that makes the shoulders sag low, and which made the man look dejected somehow. "Don't change the subject, Jonah. I'm not here to talk about your mother."

"Well, I don't want to talk about anything else," Jonah told him stubbornly crossing his arms over his chest. Two could play this game, he thought as anger crept to the surface.

"I may not get another chance, Jonah. I need you to listen to me. To understand what I have to tell you."

"Listen to you! I don't even know you! Why should I listen to you?"

"This isn't easy, Jonah. But I don't have much time left."

"What do I care?" Jonah asked. The sooner Miguel left, the better. He wanted to tell the man he knew it was him who'd caused all the trouble these past four months. Wanted to make Miguel realize his secret wasn't so secret. But Jonah just couldn't bring himself to do it. The same thing that intrigued Jonah about Miguel was the same thing that now put a sense of fear in his heart. What was he doing with this man? He was dangerous. And yet, Jonah sensed the man would not hurt him. At least not as long as he kept quiet.

"Jonah, do you know who I am?"

A healthy dose of fear shot through Jonah's heart. Miguel knew. He must know. But why, then, had he not done something about it before now? Images of that first night sprang to Jonah's mind. His heart thumped wildly. Jonah was almost certain Miguel must be able to hear it, it was beating so hard. Still, he shrugged in what he hoped was a carefree way, and crossed his arms over his chest in an act that he hoped showed indifference.

"No, sir."

Miguel raised an eyebrow at the sudden formality. He studied Jonah. "That night," Miguel began, and Jonah felt himself panic. "That night, outside your house - do you remember it?"

Jonah gave a hesitant nod. His heart still thumped wildly in his chest, but curiosity was now creeping to the surface.

"I'm guessing you must have been standing outside the door for a while by the look on your face when I came out." Miguel gave him a questioning look. Jonah didn't respond. "What did you hear, Jonah?"

The nervous fear that had crept toward Jonah's heart tightened its grip. He felt certain this was a trick. A trap of some sort, though he couldn't figure it out. He forced himself to swallow, though his mouth felt dry. "I," he began, "I, um. I don't know. Nothing really."

"Nothing?" Miguel questioned as he stood up and walked just barely into the water. He moved his hand in a gentle wave over it. The water seemed to respond, lapping in time to his hand movements. Its gentle caress found Jonah's feet and he immediately felt a sense of relief. A calm feeling pushed the fear away, allowing Jonah to relax.

Miguel turned to face the boy. "Jonah, I'm sure you heard something that night. I don't know how much, because I don't know how long you were standing there. But I know you heard something. And from your reaction, I'd have to say you didn't understand everything you heard." He moved back over and sat down again. This time Jonah didn't move.

"Do you know who I am?" Miguel asked again.

This time Jonah nodded, then shook his head. "I heard Mom call you Miguel."

"And does that name mean anything to you?"

"No."

A hurt expression clouded Miguel's face. Sadness, maybe a hint of anger. Jonah wasn't sure.

"Your mother never mentioned me? Not ever?"

Jonah thought back as far as his memory would allow. He shook his head.

A spark lit in Miguel's eye. Now Jonah was certain the man was angry, but with the water lapping at his feet, Jonah did not worry. Something in his mind told him he should be afraid of this man, but he wasn't.

"Who are you?"

Miguel looked up at him with sad eyes, hurt showing in the

creases of his face. "Flesh of my flesh, blood of my blood. And yet you know not who I am. How is it possible you do not know? Even now, as I have been among your people. Even now, as I sit beside you."

Jonah felt a twinge of guilt at Miguel's words. He shook it off. There was no reason for him to know who this man was. But those words *flesh of my flesh, blood of my blood,* what was that supposed to mean? Was Miguel referring to him? But if he was, that would mean…"My father," he breathed, the whisper hardly more than a breeze on the sea. "But that can't be," his voice grew stronger. "My father was lost at sea before I was even born."

Sad, dark eyes looked back at him. A quick flash behind those eyes was the only indication that anger was boiling under the surface. "I was never lost at sea," Miguel said. His voice was quiet, as though the sadness was too deep to fight, but an edge caught and the strength behind his next words made it clear that anger was clawing its way to the surface. "I never wanted to leave you, Jonah. I didn't know your mom was expecting until we were well along in our voyage. I came back as soon as I could. I couldn't stay then. That was the night you were born. But when I returned, she was gone. I've looked everywhere trying to find her. To find you."

Jonah's mind was whirling. With all he'd been through, with all the years of dreaming and wishing for his own father, this man… but he couldn't be. This had to be a bad dream. A really bad dream. He turned away from Miguel as he fought the thoughts tumbling around in his head. *It's late,* he reasoned. His mind wasn't clear.

"Jonah, I was never lost at sea. I'm your father," Miguel said, the tension evident in his voice. He reached out a hand and placed it on Jonah's shoulder. "And I want you to come with me – out to sea."

For a mere fraction of a second, Jonah felt his heart leap with excitement. His father. He had a father. Then, just as suddenly, anger swept through him with a force he did not recognize. Jonah jerked his shoulder out from under Miguel's hand and took a few steps away before whirling around to face him. "No," he heard himself say. "No! No! Get away from me!" he yelled, now turning and racing off toward the trees. This man, the same crazy man who caused so much trouble to this town, could *not* be his father.

As he entered the tree line, the ocean cried out with a deep anguished song. He turned back. Miguel had not followed him. Instead, the man was kneeling in the water so that it lapped at his waist, his head thrown back, and with every apparent groan, the water surged faster and higher around him. The storm it had become mirrored the agony of the man in the water.

# Eleven

The shock of discovering that Miguel was his father engulfed Jonah in a complex array of emotions. He neither knew what to say nor what to do. He sat there, in his tree, watching the ocean's heartache, his mind racing like a panicked horse. There was something so unbelievable about what Miguel had just claimed. And yet somewhere deep down Jonah wanted to believe him - wanted so badly to believe him. The man scared him, at least that's what his mind told him. Yet the idea that maybe, just maybe, he really did have a father - one who was here in the flesh, alive, and real - was something he'd wanted for so long he'd have agreed with nearly any fatherly claim. But he hadn't. He'd yelled no over and over again. Why?

It was several hours before Jonah was ready to leave the cover of the trees. By then, Miguel had left the ocean and walked down the beach, where, it seemed, he had disappeared. Jonah still didn't have any answers. Still didn't understand why he'd so readily, and vehemently, denied Miguel's claim. But his mind was quieter, and he knew his mother would be worried. He climbed down, pushed his way through the undergrowth, and headed for home.

As he approached the door, part of him hoped his mother was not waiting for him inside - that she had not yet arrived home, or at least that she was already sleeping soundly. The other part of him hoped that when he opened the door he'd find her sitting at the table, anxious and worried. *It would serve her right,* he thought as he pushed open the door.

He was not prepared for the dark that met his eyes. In his heart, he was certain she'd be waiting up, lamp lit, worry etched across her face. The stillness that accompanied the dark gave the sense that the house was empty. Jonah wasn't sure what time it was, but he thought it was late enough that the celebrations ought to have finished. Walking across the length of the house, Jonah carefully took down the oil lamp he knew was sitting on the shelf above the sink. The matches were to the left, and he grabbed one. He struck it to catch light, then put the flame to the wick and adjusted the glow. Jonah held the lamp up to verify that his mother had not fallen asleep at the table or in her rocker before he moved to her bedroom. Her door was slightly ajar. As he pushed it further open, a light draft raced into the warmer room. He held the lamp out a little as he reached into the room, allowing the light to fill it. She wasn't there either.

Though unlikely, Jonah checked the loft, his own sleeping quarters, before confirming that his mother was not at home. A sense of relief flooded through him. He would not have to answer her questions tonight. That was good, as he had too many of his own, and was emotionally exhausted. While he waited, he restarted the fire, then sat in the chair nearest it. He intended to wait up for his mother, questions burning in his brain. He needed answers.

***

Thunder shook the house, jolting Jonah awake. Lightning

flashed across the windowpane, lighting up the empty room. He looked at the clock on the mantel. The clock, one of the few possessions his mother owned from the grandparents he'd never met, read midnight. He glanced at the pegs beside the door, and when the next flash of lightning lit up the room, he noticed it was still bare. His mother's cloak was not hanging where it ought to be. *Surely the celebration had long since ended.* He wondered what could be keeping his mother; especially with the cold and the storm.

Nearly an hour later, with rain pounding the roof, and lightning continuing to light up the sky outside, Jonah grabbed his coat and hat. His anger had, at first, grown as he waited for his mother to return. But as time had ticked by, his anger had given way to concern. Where was she? Was she looking for him? It occurred to him that he hadn't told her he was leaving, and she might be wondering where he was. If so, it was his fault his mother was out in this mess. Was she okay?

Thunder boomed like a giant hitting the earth with a club, while lightning slashed a silver blade through the sky. Wind beat against every board trying to tear the house apart. He hesitated, but couldn't wait any longer. He needed to know she was safe. Jonah pushed open the door, head bent to fight against the wind. The door ripped from his hands and slammed against the side of the house. As he turned to grab hold of it, he noticed there was a light in the barn.

The shock of seeing the light had nearly caused Jonah to forget about the door. It slipped from his fingers, banging hard against the house once more. As the shock wore off, a plan began to form in his head. Jonah swung around, and with a strength even he was unaware he had, yanked the door from the grasp of the wind holding it captive. He pushed it, closing and securing it against the storm.

It was a good thing he didn't need the lantern since the wind had caused it to sputter out almost immediately upon opening the door. Still, Jonah could see quite well, as lightning continued to ignite the sky. He didn't have much trouble getting to the barn. The unknown strength that had surged through him a moment before, remained with him. In fact, it seemed he was becoming stronger the more he endured the storm.

Rain raced down his face as Jonah made his way to the barn. He wasn't sure what he'd find inside, but it seemed the right place to go. With his mind firmly set on the light in the barn, Jonah forgot about searching for his mother. He pulled open the door and stepped inside. A soft moo drifted over to him as he closed the door. Blinking in the steady light, Jonah moved forward and patted the cow. Droplets of water clung to his eyelashes, and dripped off his nose and hair. Millie tossed her head as the cold drops fell on her.

It was warm in the barn, and the sudden surge of power Jonah had so recently felt seemed to melt along with the chill of the storm. Standing here, inside the barn with Millie, seemed to have softened his heart some as well. The calm he felt brought a sense of peace, and suddenly Jonah found he was tired. The day had finally caught up with him.

"A bit late, idn't it?"

Jonah turned at the voice, remembering now that the light had already been on. Ol' Man Wimple was leaning on a pitch fork in the middle of the barn. "What brings ya out this time a night? And in this storm, no less?"

"I could ask you the same thing," Jonah replied, a slight edge to his voice. Ol' Man Wimple raised an eyebrow in question. Jonah slumped a little in reply. He looked back at Ol' Man Wimple, "Why are you here so late?" he asked again, this time without the edge.

"Figured with the storm comin' on, I'd stick around. Make sure the animals have enough hay and such. Didn't look like this one'd be blowin' over."

At the mention of the storm, Jonah became aware once more of the thunder and the beating wind. This brought his mind back to his ma. "You haven't seen Ma, have you?" he asked.

Ol' Man Wimple looked at him. "Well, no, can't say's I have. Didn't she come back with you?"

Jonah shook his head. "I, uh, didn't stay."

"And she didn't know you'd left. Didn't tell her, did ya?" Ol' Man Wimple's eyebrow was raised again.

Jonah looked sheepish. "I was heading out to look for her when I saw the light in the barn." The guilt he felt dripped off every word.

"Out in this storm?" Ol' Man Wimple gave Jonah an appraising look. "Don't think that's such a great idea, Jonah." As if to emphasize the point, thunder boomed shaking the barn walls. "Ms. Emily's a smart woman. Don't think she'd let herself be caught in this mess. Certainly wouldn't want you out in it." He moved closer to Jonah. "She'd have found herself a place to stay for the night."

"How do you know she's not out there? How can you be sure?"

"I've known your mama a long time, Jonah. *A long time.* I just know."

Though he wasn't completely reassured, Jonah was too tired not to accept the small comfort that came with those words. "Are you sure?"

"Sure as I know fish love water."

Despite his worry, Jonah smiled. "I guess you're pretty sure."

"When you've known someone as long as I've know your ma,

you just understand a person. She'll be all right."

The barn shook again, causing Jonah to look up at the roof. "How long have you known my ma?" he asked. He couldn't recall a time in his life when he hadn't known Ol' Man Wimple, but for some reason, he hadn't thought Ol' Man Wimple and his ma had known each other for too long. When had Ol' Man Wimple begun helping them out? Jonah couldn't remember.

"Since before you'd been born. Knew her as a young'un, I did."

"You knew Ma before she came here?"

Ol' Man Wimple now wore a guarded expression, but he nodded.

"You mean, you didn't always live here?"

"Nope. Been around a bit." Ol' Man Wimple had moved into the stall with Millie and was now clearing out old straw and getting ready to lay down new. His movements were sure and steady.

Thoughts whirled through the air. Jonah heard the words *I'm your father, I wasn't lost at sea,* and *I looked for you* replay in his mind. Fragments of his earlier conversation with Miguel drifted in and out; and now he struggled with understanding. He had always known his mother had lived somewhere else before Delmar, but he'd never thought much about it. This was his home. It had always been his home. Even when he was teased - even when everyone else had a father and he didn't - still, it was his home. The only home he'd ever known. Or was it? Maybe this was just the only home he'd ever remembered.

"You look like a man with a lot on his mind."

Jonah shrugged. "Yeah, maybe. I don't know. Just tired." His mind was spinning with all that had happened. He wasn't sure he was ready to share. Would Ol' Man Wimple even *understand?*

Certainly, Jonah didn't. His mind and heart raced, full of questions and emotions that were constantly colliding. The one desire he'd had to know his father turning sour, instead of sweet. And Jonah didn't understand why.

The more he heard, the less sure of anything he was. He needed answers, but wasn't sure which question to ask. "Did my ma… Did you ever know my…my father?" Jonah was surprised by the question he voiced. He hadn't planned on asking about his father. Anything else, and maybe he could have pieced the rest together, but there it was.

Ol' Man Wimple stopped spreading the straw. He turned toward Jonah, obviously weighing his reply. "What brings him up?"

"Nothing. Forget it."

"A question like that doesn't come out of the blue. What's up?" Ol' Man Wimple pressed.

The man had moved over to sit on a hay bale, and indicated that Jonah should join him. Jonah hesitated before moving closer and taking his seat beside Ol' Man Wimple. Even then, Jonah didn't immediately answer. His thoughts were warring within. If he wanted Ol' Man Wimple to answer his question, Jonah knew he'd have to share at least some of what had happened. But Jonah wasn't sure he was ready to tell even Ol' Man Wimple.

"Jonah," the older man said after the silence had gone on for several minutes. He was now close enough to see the black eye that had begun to form, the light of the barn having been too dim to see it properly until up close. "Did something happen today?"

Jonah shook his head. He didn't want to talk about his experience at the cove. Not really.

"Nothing, uh? Don't look like no nothing to me," Ol' Man

Wimple said. "Last I checked, eyes don't black themselves."

Jonah had forgotten about his black eye, and he immediately reached up to touch his face. His nose was still sore, though the bleeding had been stopped for some time, and he couldn't see the eye that was now blackened. But when he touched it, he could tell it was slightly swollen. "Got in a fight," he said as he withdrew his hand.

"Well, I can see that. Wanna tell me how it happened?"

"Brigg." Jonah said. He wasn't interested in dishing out the details, because they would include him leaving the celebration, and Ol' Man Wimple would want to know why. The memory of his mother and Miguel dancing was hard enough without having to relive it as he shared the details with the man.

"Captain Montagrell's boy?"

Jonah nodded.

"Didn't he have something better to do on a night like tonight? Thought he'd a been chasin' after them young ladies."

"Don't know about any young ladies, but he was sure keen on downing some mead. And he wasn't the only one. Bunch of his buddies were with him when they'd stolen that keg and taken it off into the bushes with them."

"So, you saw 'em?"

"Yeah."

"Did they know you'd seen 'em?"

"Probably. Least they thought I was going to rat 'em out."

"Would have served 'em right."

"Maybe."

"Why didn't ya?'

"Why didn't I what?" Jonah asked.

"Tell somebody. Surely, they had it comin'."

Ol' Man Wimple was right, Brigg and his friends did indeed have it coming to them, but Jonah hadn't been thinking about that when he'd met up with them. His mind had been on his mother and Miguel. "Well, I, uh, had other things on my mind."

Again, Ol' Man Wimple raised an eyebrow in question and waited for Jonah to continue. The exhaustion Jonah felt seemed to have finally drained him of any arguing power, but he still wasn't sure he wanted to let the whole story out. "I was…I guess I was upset."

"Something happen at the celebration ta turn ya sour?"

"Yeah. You could say that. Anyway," Jonah continued not wanting to give away more details than he needed to, "I'd decided to head home. It wasn't like I wanted to be there anyway; and with the storm blowing in and all…So I'd started toward home. That's when Brigg and his buddies ambushed me. They were just in front of me at first, the mead already making them sloppy. Brigg said some stupid things – accused me of going to rat 'em out. He was itchin' for a fight. Been itchin' for one for some time now, really. Then they circled up around me and started saying things about ma – so I let him have it."

"He lookin' as good as you?"

Jonah reached up and touched his face again. "I don't know. He's bigger than me, and he weren't fightin' fair. All of them against me. But then, well," Jonah hesitated. Did he really want to mention Miguel stepping in?

Ol' Man Wimple nodded encouragingly. It seemed he knew that quiet encouragement was all Jonah would need.

"That stranger caught up to us. He told 'em to make it a fair fight. After that, it was just me and Brigg. That's when he gave me this." Jonah pointed at his shiner. "Knocked me right flat to the ground. Thought he'd won, he did, but I wasn't done yet. I knocked his feet from under him and started beating the tar out of him."

"And did ya?"

"Did I what?"

"Beat the tar outta him?"

"Nah." Jonah shook his head. "That stranger stepped in and grabbed my arm. Kept me from knockin' Brigg right out. Told me there were other ways." Jonah lightly punching the palm of his other hand. "I don't know what Brigg looked like when I left. Probably worse 'en me. But I wish Miguel hadn't stopped me. Brigg deserved everything he got and more."

"Miguel?" Ol' Man Wimple asked. Alarm clearly showed on his face, evidence that he knew exactly who Miguel was.

Jonah realized he'd slipped up, and tried to cover, "Yeah. The stranger." He hadn't meant to say the man's name. He hadn't wanted anyone to know he'd overheard Miguel and his mother inside the farmhouse that first night. Thinking fast, he decided to lie. "I've heard people call him Miguel." After all, Miguel had been in the town for over four months, and Jonah was bound to have overheard someone using the guy's name.

Ol' Man Wimple was quiet for a while. "You didn't come straight home after the fight, did ya?" The question was less a question and more a statement.

Jonah squirmed uncomfortably inside. "No."

"Didn't think so. Wanna tell me what happened after that?"

Jonah didn't want to tell him, so instead he said, "Didn't think ma would be back right away, and I needed some time to cool off."

Ol' Man Wimple nodded. "So, you went to the cove." It wasn't a question.

Bewilderment covered Jonah's face. "How did you know?" He flushed as he realized he'd just given himself away.

"I didn't. It was just a guess."

Jonah knew his secret was out. He just didn't know how Ol' Man Wimple would have come to that conclusion. "But…"

"It's what your father would have done." Ol' Man Wimple held out his hand and shook his head forestalling Jonah's next question. "Your ma wouldn't be happy knowin' that."

"I know," was all Jonah could manage; although he wasn't sure if Ol' Man Wimple meant about going to the cove, or about Jonah being like his father. Probably both.

"You alone at the cove?"

Jonah nodded, then squirmed uncomfortably under Ol' Man Wimple's gaze and looked down at his hands. "At first," Jonah admitted. Even though he sensed Ol' Man Wimple looking at him, Jonah couldn't bring himself to the man's eyes. "But then Miguel showed up." A sudden surge of irritation swept through Jonah. "He had some nerve doing that. Showing up after stopping me from giving Brigg what he deserved."

"Jonah," Ol' Man Wimple's voice was gentle, but firm, "you asked me earlier if I knew your father. Is there something more you want to tell me? Like maybe why you asked me that question?"

Not wanting to make Ol' Man Wimple angry, and not willing to share what Miguel had said to him, Jonah opted to settle on a half-truth. "Mom never talks about my father."

Ol' Man Wimple appraised the boy in front of him. It wasn't what Jonah had said, but rather what he'd left unsaid that tipped the older man off. "I knew your father, Jonah. But I think you need to talk with your ma."

The feeling came on so suddenly that Jonah wasn't sure what it was at first. The frustration he'd held all these years at not having a dad, not knowing who his father was, or if the man was even alive, finally boiled over to a deep hot rage. How could the two people in his life – the two people that he trusted, that he loved - have kept him from the truth all these years? And what was the truth? He didn't know. But one thing was certain, one way or another, he was going to get answers.

# Twelve

As determined as Jonah was, Old Man Wimple would not crack and eventually Jonah made his way back to the farmhouse. By then dawn was fast approaching and the storm that had matched the anger in Jonah's heart was finally abating. A slow drizzle was all that was left of the torrents of water from earlier. The lazy sun was slowly rising from its sleep, the first vestiges of soft golden light resting at the spot where the sky met the earth. It was peaceful. As if it had no memory of the storm, or of the raging emotions in the young man's heart.

"I'll stay awhile yet," Ol' Man Wimple called out to Jonah as he leaned against the barn door. "It's been a long night. You go on in and get some rest. I'll see to the chores afore I head home."

Jonah knew he should say something, ought to at least thank Ol' Man Wimple for his generosity, but Jonah just couldn't do it. He was emotionally drained, and the battle of feelings was still too close to the surface to speak. Part of him wanted to yell at the man, but he'd already done that. Another part wanted never to see him again, but he was too tired to make the threat real. Instead, he waved a hand in acknowledgment, and trudged along to the house.

He entered the house fully expecting to find his mother had appeared sometime during the night. One look at the hooks where he hung his coat made it clear she had still not returned. A part of him felt a tug at his heart when he asked himself why he'd not continued his search for her during the night. Another part whispered comfort that she had, as Ol' Man Wimple insisted, found shelter in town to wait out the storm.

In any case, Jonah was still angry, and still wanted answers. He felt he deserved answers, especially after the night he'd had, so he sat himself in the rocker to wait for his ma. It didn't take long for exhaustion to overcome him, and he slipped off to sleep with his head lolling against his chest.

His dreams were punctuated with raging seas, the waves of which reached the top of a cliff face. A ship rocked back and forth, tossed like a toy amidst an angry battle. Yet it never crumbled. It seemed a dance between the sea and the ship. A dance that culminated in an angry rise of a curling wave that wrapped itself over and back under the ship. The ship staying steady as the wave closed in around it.

Jonah jolted awake. Light was streaming through the windows from the sun that had broken through what was left of the storms depleted clouds. Was that what had woken him? He shifted, his body aching from having slept in the rocker. He heard a steady rumbling in the distance. He went to the door and swung it open. Coming up the lane to the house was an old wagon. As the wagon approached, the rumbling grew louder. When it was closer, Jonah could make out his mother seated on the buckboard. Relief flooded over him, and he felt guilty for having been angry with her last night. That was until he saw who was with her.

Miguel was holding the reins, bringing the horse drawn wagon closer to the house. Jonah could feel anger boiling inside him as he stared daggers at the man. *How dare he come here? What was Ma doing with him anyway? Wasn't that what started this whole mess?* The man was not welcome here.

Before Miguel had even stopped the wagon, Jonah was rushing up to it. "What are you doing here?" he demanded of the man. Miguel didn't respond, just locked the wheel, climbed down, and offered a hand to Emily.

Emily watched the exchange with concern. She'd never seen Jonah go off like this before. She wasn't sure what to do. For a moment, she stood in the wagon, unaware of the proffered hand, as she watched Jonah. Shock and disappointment were clear upon her face.

"Emily," Miguel said to get her attention. The way he said her name caused Jonah's blood to boil. He had spoken her name as tenderly as one who had affection for another. As a husband to a wife. But he was not her husband. Not since he'd abandoned them for the sea.

"What are you doing here?" Jonah demanded more angrily. He felt like his chest was going to explode with the pressure building there.

"Jonah!" Emily, having been helped out of the wagon by Miguel, had turned her full attention on her son. "I'll not have you speaking so to our friend." When Jonah continued to glower at Miguel, she added, "Please, wait in the house."

Jonah began to speak, but a quelling look from his mother was enough to remind him of his place. He took a slow step back toward the house keeping Miguel in sight, then turned and stormed away.

"Best I get going," he heard Miguel say.

"I don't know what's got into him," Emily replied.

Jonah didn't hear what else they said, as their voices were cut off by the door swinging shut behind him. He glanced out the window, and saw Miguel tip his hat as he climbed back on the wagon. Emily said something else, then turned and came toward the house.

She had barely come in and hung her bonnet when Jonah rounded on her. "What was that all about? Why didn't you come home last night?"

It was apparent that Emily was a little shaken, but even that would not allow her to permit such behavior from her son. "Jonah, you know that I will not tolerate disrespect. Not toward me. Not toward anyone. I have raised you better than that, have I not?"

Jonah did not want to admit she was right. "Yes, Ma. Sorry," he mumbled, though he didn't really feel sorry.

Emily returned to the task of removing her cloak before going to the kitchen to start a kettle of water. "I couldn't find you when the celebration was over. You didn't tell me you were leaving."

Guilt cut through Jonah. He should have told her. Even at the time he knew he ought to.

"I didn't feel like staying."

"I gathered as much when I realized you'd left. That doesn't explain why you didn't tell me you were leaving."

Jonah sat stubbornly at the table not wanting to explain himself. All was quiet until the kettle began to whistle.

"Well, then," said Emily, "at least explain how you got so banged up. Your eye is a right mess and your nose is crooked. What happened to you?" At these words, she raised herself and poured water from the kettle into two mugs to make a tea from herbs she had hanging nearby.

"Like you care," spat Jonah, his anger clearly still at the surface.

"Don't you take that tone with me. I *am* your mother. I have a right to know what happened to you."

"Got in a fight. Why didn't you come home last night?"

She sipped her tea. "I stayed with the Tanners above the mercantile. There was no way for me to get home in that storm." She returned to the kitchen and selected several more herbs. Crumbling a few leaves into the mortar, she picked up the pestle and began grinding them up. "Mind telling me who you were fighting with?" She poured a little hot water over the herbs and blended them together creating a paste. She wrapped the paste in a cheesecloth and handed it to Jonah. "Here, put this on your eye. It'll help."

Jonah held the cloth up to his swollen right eye. The heat felt good, almost as good as the ice-cold water had the night before. Rather than answer her question, Jonah asked one of his own, "Why didn't you tell me about my father?"

Emily was not expecting this, and the shock was apparent on her face. "I… I did…he was lost at sea when you…" her voice got quieter, "…when you were born."

"Liar!" Jonah spat at her. He pulled the cloth away from his eye, and slammed his fist on the table, causing the tea in his mug to splash.

His ma jumped at the sound. "It's the truth."

"No, it isn't. He was never lost at sea." The bitterness Jonah felt at having been lied to all these years put an edge on his words. He didn't really know that Miguel had spoken the truth, but he felt it was true.

Emily glanced at the window. "Who told you that?"

"*He* did. After he stopped me from beating Brigg into the ground."

"Who…wait, what? You were in a fight with Brigg? Captain Montagurell's son?"

"Yeah, so what?

"Jonah, how could you?" her voice held more than disappointment when she said this. Was it fear he heard?

He suddenly had the impulse to defend himself. "Brigg ambushed me."

"What have I told you about fighting? And with The Captain's son? Oh, Jonah." Disappointment and worry were etched on Emily's face.

"He had it coming," Jonah said indignantly. "Would have given him all of it if *that man* hadn't stopped me."

"*That man?*"

"Yeah, *him,* the one who brought you home just now."

"Miguel?" Emily's voice had become quiet again, while the blood drained from her face.

"He stopped me from beating up Brigg, then followed me. That's when he told me. Told me he'd been looking for us. For me. Said he was my father."

The blood drained from her face. "Jonah, honey, you don't understand," she pleaded.

"What don't I understand? That you lied to me? That I've had a father all this time? That he was looking for me and you kept me from him? Or is it that you're still in love with him?" He hadn't realized he knew this until he'd said it. He had wanted to hurt her – to tell her something she didn't know. But that part about her being in love – he hadn't realized he knew that.

"Jonah, it's complicated. Your father, he's a good man. Sometimes." She'd said the last word softly, as if an afterthought.

"If he were such a good man, why did you leave?"

"There are things. Reasons. You wouldn't understand."

"Wouldn't understand what?"

"Just… Jonah, please. You have to trust me on this."

"Is it because he's a pirate?"

"How did you…?" Emily was pale and shaking. "There are things you cannot possibly understand. When he went to sea…" her voice trailed off. When she spoke again, her voice was stronger, more in control. "He was lost at sea. Maybe not in the way you thought, but the sea took him just the same. Yes, I love him. I've always loved him. But, we had to leave, Jonah. It was all I could do to protect you."

"From what? From him?"

"Yes, no…" It was clear his mother wasn't going to tell him everything she knew. As if there were secrets that even now she couldn't bring herself to share. "From him, yes. And maybe, from yourself."

# Thirteen

The next few days Jonah spent down at the cove. He didn't worry about staying in the trees, or avoiding the call of the sea. Having felt betrayed by his mother, and still feeling angry, Jonah had enjoyed the lapping of the water against his legs. As it had before, the water seemed to soothe him; and, since he did not want to think, it seemed the perfect balm.

His primer and slate lay in a heap at the base of one of the trees, just at the edge of the sand. He wasn't interested in going to school anymore. His desire to study was gone. Emily wouldn't be happy to see the lack of care taken with these items. *Serves her right*, Jonah thought when it had occurred to him. He no longer cared about taking care of the few things his mother found valuable. Things that, up until recently, he had also found valuable.

For his mom's part, she seemed reluctant to talk, and therefore, the subject of skipped school had fallen by the wayside. Jonah didn't mind this either. Anger sat all too close to the surface to make conversation pleasant. So, often, they went without any.

The current shifted, the gentle lapping changed direction as if pulled by some other force. There was an energy to it, like it had woken up. Jonah sat up and looked around. Shielding his eyes from the glare of the sun, he noticed a figure at the far end of the beach.

The only person to ever join him at the cove in all his years of living here had been Miguel; and the thought of seeing Miguel right now didn't make Jonah very happy.

Though Miguel had been some distance away, it seemed he covered ground unusually quickly as he all but materialized in front of Jonah just minutes later. The time it took Miguel to reach Jonah hadn't left time for Jonah to fully decide whether he wanted to stick around. Somehow, Jonah figured, that was part of the plan.

"Thought I'd find you here," Miguel said.

Jonah didn't reply. The ocean had moved into light rolling waves that raced up his legs, matching the anxiety Jonah felt.

"Hoped we could talk," Miguel tried again.

"We've nothing to talk about," Jonah snapped bitterly. The water at his feet increased, now splashing against his legs.

"I think we do." Without being invited, Miguel sat down next to Jonah, staying just out of reach of the water.

Jonah was not happy that Miguel had joined him. He thought he'd made it clear he wasn't interested in talking. But it seemed Miguel either couldn't take a hint, or was ignoring the obvious. Anger-laced adrenaline surged through Jonah's veins. He could feel it pulsating, as if it were a living thing inside him. The water rocked more violently.

"We need to talk about the other day."

If Miguel really thought they were going to talk, the man was seriously mistaken. Jonah deliberately refused to answer Miguel, or even look at him. Maybe Miguel would take the hint and leave him alone.

It seemed the pirate was as hardheaded as the boy. "You were pretty upset when you left here the other night. I didn't get to explain."

"I told you, there's nothing to talk about." Jonah would rather pretend that night had never happened. He couldn't stop hearing those words, replaying that conversation. Part of him hoped that if he never gave voice to any of it then maybe, just maybe, it would all go away. Like a bad dream.

"Whether you like it or not, Jonah, you are my son and we have things to talk about."

"My father died at sea."

"No, Jonah, I didn't." Miguel must have been frustrated, but if he was, he didn't show it.

"Then you couldn't be my father," Jonah snapped. He didn't know why, but he wanted to hurt this man.

"Saying it's not true doesn't make it so." The irritation he surely felt was masked by the sadness in this voice.

Anger sprang to life inside Jonah, finally boiling over. The ocean came alive, throwing large towering waves toward the shore where Jonah and Miguel sat.

"Careful!" Miguel yelled. He jumped up and out of the way. The wave crashed down upon him and Jonah, and sent Miguel sprawling back on the sand. "Out of the water! Now!" Miguel grabbed Jonah by the arm and pulled him further up the beach.

The next wave struck. This time they both went sprawling forward, but Miguel never let go of Jonah as they made their way further inland, and out of the water. Immediately the water calmed. The giant, crashing waves gave way to the soft calling of the sea with which Jonah was so familiar.

"What was that?" Jonah sputtered, ocean water dripping in his eyes.

"That's what I need to talk to you about," Miguel responded turning around and watching the sea.

Jonah did the same. He was drenched from head to foot and shivering now that he was no longer in the water. His heart thudded, and he willed it to return to normal. The anger he'd felt earlier seemed to have been washed away. He had no idea what caused the enormous waves that came on so suddenly, or why they returned to normal just as quickly. He glanced up at the sky just to be sure there wasn't a storm brewing. There wasn't a cloud in sight.

"Have you ever experienced anything like that before?" Miguel asked, interrupting his thoughts.

"No. Never."

"Has anything unusual ever happened before when you were in the water?"

Jonah shook his head embarrassed to admit the truth. "I've never really been in the water before," he said quietly. "Not really."

Miguel looked at him with disbelief. "Never? Surely your mother brought you here? Taught you to swim?"

Jonah shook his head again. "Ma doesn't know I come here."

The man took a deep breath. "I guess we'll have to start at the beginning. But first, let's get you warmed up."

Miguel helped Jonah to his feet, turning them both down the beach to where he'd first appeared. Jonah was shivering too hard to protest. The thought of getting his numb fingers warmed helped propel him along. After they had walked several yards, Miguel turned them toward the tree line. Though Jonah was numb with cold, his mind was clear enough to recognize they were heading toward the very place where Miguel had hidden the longboat months before.

A thousand thoughts tumbled through Jonah's head. The most

prominent of which was that this could be a trick. Yet those words, *I'm your father*, rang out like a screaming gong repeating themselves over and over. Jonah didn't know if he should trust the man, but he was too cold to do anything else. He needed to get warm.

They had walked about a yard into the tree line when Miguel started pulling away large branches of leaves. They had been positioned in such a way that, had Jonah not already known what was hidden there, he would have thought it a miserable tangle of overgrown plants. The pile of branches kept growing. The long boat took more time than Jonah would have thought necessary to show itself. Miguel uncovered just enough of the boat to reach into the hull and pull out two blankets. He wrapped one around Jonah's shoulders and pulled it tight across the boy's body. He then restacked the tangle of branches to cover the boat before wrapping the second blanket around himself.

Jonah was grateful for the blanket. It was of a fine quality wool, wonderfully warm, and had soon done its job. Though he was still wet, he was no longer shivering. The two made their way back toward the beach. The warmth that ran through Jonah freed his mind to explore the thoughts that had been racing there.

"Why is that boat hidden back there?" It wasn't the most important question he had, but it was the first question to make its way across Jonah's tongue.

Miguel stopped walking and looked back at Jonah, who had been following just a few steps behind. His eyes darted to the tree line, then back at Jonah. Without saying anything, he made his way over to a piece of driftwood, halfway between the water's edge and the trees, and sat down. Even then, he did not answer Jonah's question.

"I saw you," Jonah said. "I saw you that night. When you came here. I saw you." He didn't know why he was telling Miguel this, but couldn't seem to stop himself. "I saw the ship. Saw it disappear." Something clicked, and Jonah's eyes sprung up with sudden clarity. "I saw you make it disappear."

Miguel sat quietly watching Jonah, as if he didn't know what Jonah was talking about. Yet, Jonah had the distinct impression Miguel was calculating his response.

"I'm right, aren't I?" Jonah pressed eagerly.

"You saw me?" Miguel's voice was calm and soft. "That was you?"

Jonah nodded. "Yeah. That was me."

Miguel rubbed the back of his head. "Come sit down."

Jonah didn't move. He stood facing Miguel, staring at him. "Who are you?"

"I told you, Jonah. I'm your father." Miguel sounded deflated.

"Yeah. But *what* are you?" Fear and intrigue had collided once more, but this time, intrigue won out. Jonah found he was eager to learn more about this man. Excited even.

"Please. Sit down." Somehow the image of the fierce pirate didn't ring true with the sad voice of the man seated before Jonah. "There is so much to tell you. It'll be easier if you're sitting down."

Jonah didn't budge.

"Have it your way." A little heat had reentered Miguel's voice causing Jonah to flinch inwardly. He wondered what he'd started.

"I come from a long line of seamen. Strong, powerful men. Generations on the sea have taught us the secrets of survival. But there's a price for knowing these secrets. A curse, some say, for we can never be long from the sea."

"That doesn't sound so bad," Jonah said, thinking of how much he longed for the ocean.

Miguel smiled. "Ah, well, most of us love the sea and the wild life it brings with it." His smile faded as he added, "A curse, though, for those who try to outrun it - to live without it. Some call us pirates."

"You're no ordinary pirate."

"No. You're right. I'm not."

Jonah waited for further explanation, but nothing more was said, so he asked, "Why'd you come here?"

"For you. I came here to find you." Miguel hesitated as he weighed his next words. "You're my son. And contrary to what you might believe, I care about you. Please always remember that."

"Pirates don't have children. They don't have families," Jonah interjected.

"Not in the traditional sense. No. Not usually," Miguel admitted. "Much of what you've heard about pirates is true. They never stay in one place long, they prefer not to make any attachments. But that doesn't mean they don't have kids."

"Is that what happened? You decided you liked the sea better than my ma? Better than me?" There was a bite to Jonah's words.

Miguel looked stung. "You forget, I didn't know about you."

"And my ma? You just left her?"

"She left, remember."

"Not until after you'd gone to sea." Jonah didn't know why he was defending his ma. He'd been just as angry about her leaving when he'd found out.

"I had to go. It's part of the curse, Jonah. I didn't have a choice. But I was never going to stay away. I loved your ma." Sadness crept into the pirate's voice once more. "I still do," he said softly.

Jonah squirmed, uncomfortable with the direction the conversation had just taken. He didn't want to talk about his ma, or the fact that Miguel thought he still loved her. "What curse?" he asked, letting his curiosity pull the conversation back away from his ma.

Miguel hesitated. This was the reason he'd come here, to tell Jonah about the curse, but now he wasn't sure. "There is a curse that comes with being a pirate. Some choose the life, and so you could say they also choose the curse. Most actually. And for them, the curse isn't as bad. Not normally. But some never have a choice. Some are born pirates. And the curse owns them."

"Like you." Jonah didn't need to ask, it was apparent to him that this was the case with Miguel from the way Miguel had spoken. A part of him felt sorry for the man.

"Like me." Miguel nodded. "I never wanted to be a pirate. I was never even curious about them."

"It couldn't be all bad," Jonah said. Unlike Miguel, Jonah had thought often about the life of a pirate, though not enough to actually consider seeking them out. It was just a childhood fantasy. Something that probably stemmed from being kept away from the water. The idea that something so compelling would be forbidden. "You know. If people choose the life of a pirate, it can't be all bad."

A sad smile rested on Miguel's face. "I suppose there are perks."

"Like what?"

"Power. Fame," Miguel said. But from the way he'd said it, it didn't seem that Miguel believed they were perks.

An awkward silence permeated the air between them. For several long minutes, the only sound was the gentle lapping of the waves against the sand. Under normal circumstances, Jonah would have enjoyed listening to the ocean. However, there was still one question he needed answered.

"Then why'd she leave?"

Miguel blinked as he processed Jonah's words. "That's a question you'll have to ask her," he said.

"I did. She wouldn't tell me."

"I don't really know. I can only guess that she must have learned what I was. About the curse. And it must have scared her."

"Why would it scare her?" Wrapped in the wool blanket, Jonah realized that his curiosity had finally gotten the better of him.

"It's called a curse for a reason, Jonah. She'd probably heard some things. Things that would scare anyone, really. At the time, none of them were true."

"At the time? Does that mean they are now?" The look on Miguel's face was answer enough. "So, she was right to leave you," Jonah said, feeling both relieved and angry. Angry that there would be a reason to leave at all, and relieved that his mother had good reason to take him away.

"It's important that you understand. That's why I came here. That's why I've been looking for you ever since I learned about you."

"Understand what, exactly? That you'd abandoned us?" He couldn't help himself.

Miguel regarded Jonah carefully before responding. "Remember that wave?" Miguel asked, nodding his head forward toward the beach where they'd been sitting when they got hit. Jonah followed with his eyes, and nodded. "That didn't happen on its own."

"You did that? You made that happen?"

"No, Jonah. You did."

The very idea that Jonah could have done anything, much less cause a massive wave to strike, was ludicrous. Even Jonah knew that wasn't possible. It wasn't possible for anyone to control something like that.

Jonah thought back to the ice – frozen more solid than anyone had ever seen. Frozen before winter had hardly begun to set in. Magic wasn't supposed to exist, but in his heart, he knew it was Miguel who caused the freeze. He couldn't prove it, he wouldn't have even known how, but instinct told him he was right.

He knew he shouldn't trust Miguel, yet here he was sitting on the beach wrapped in a wool blanket at the mercy of the man. The reality of the situation should have caused Jonah unease, but he found, instead, that he was much too intrigued by this man and the direction the conversation had taken to be afraid. The idea that he, Jonah, could make something like that wave happen thrilled him to his core.

"How could I have done that?" he asked.

Miguel gave him an appraising look, deciding whether or not to answer. "It's in your blood, Jonah. The Sea, she recognizes you even though you've never been allowed near her. You've heard her singing, calling to you." Jonah started to protest. "No, Jonah, there's no need to lie to me. I've heard her myself. In fact," Miguel hesitated, "she is getting louder. She'll not wait much longer for me to answer her."

Jonah decided not to deny what Miguel had said. "What does it mean?"

"It means, Jonah, that I will have to go to her." Jonah must have looked puzzled, because Miguel continued. "Do you recall our first meeting on this beach?"

Jonah nodded.

"I told you then that I didn't have much time. I have used up nearly all my allotted time on land. The sea will demand I return, and soon."

"I don't understand."

"It's part of the curse, Jonah. It's why your mother has kept you near the sea, but refused to let you go in the water."

"But that doesn't even make sense. Being in the water is the best feeling in the world. It's like nothing else matters."

Miguel nodded. "It won't be long then. You need the sea. It's what keeps you alive. She'll call to you, and you'll have to answer. It's in your blood. The curse will demand you answer; and in return, you'll have more power than you could ever imagine. You're like me." There was a change in Miguel. Something that looked like greed flashed across his face - his eyes just a little too eager. "Come with me, Jonah."

Jonah lost his own excitement then. He didn't trust the man. There was something about him that set Jonah's stomach in a knot. All the stories he'd heard of pirates raced through his head. Jonah was no pirate. He shook his head.

"Don't you see?" Miguel asked. "We're the same – you and me."

"I'm nothing like you!" Jonah spat, fear and anger clawing their way to the surface.

There was a gleam in the pirate's eye. "You're more like me than you know, boy. Come with me. I'll show you the way."

"No!" Jonah jumped from the log. Fear replaced intrigue, and he dropped the blanket as he backed away from the man. "I'll never be like you."

The gleam in Miguel's eyes vanished, replaced by sadness,

but Jonah didn't notice. He was too busy running back into the trees.

# *Fourteen*

For the next week, Jonah avoided the cove. He still saw Miguel around Delmar from time to time, but he'd stopped going to Main Street so as to avoid seeing him as often. It wasn't because he'd made up with his mother. He was still angry with her, but he now had his own reasons for avoiding Miguel. So, he was finally heeding his mother's warning to stay clear of the man.

At night, Jonah slept fitfully. Dreams of a ship tossed roughly by the sea came more and more frequently, often ending in a thundering storm that would wake him. His heart would be pounding, and as sweat dripped off him, he found he couldn't remember anything else about them.

By the end of the week, Jonah had grown so weary of the nightmares he'd refused to go to sleep at all. When his mother had turned in for the nights, and Jonah was certain she was asleep, he would slip outside. Even from as far away as he was, he could hear the cry of the sea. He didn't remember ever hearing it this far inland before. Maybe it was because it was so much quieter at night that the sound carried farther. Whatever it was, Jonah found he couldn't resist the call. It was almost as eerie as the nightmares he'd been trying to escape.

On Saturday night, Jonah made his way to the copse of trees at the cove. Instead of turning down the well-known path he'd always taken before, he climbed along the ridge, up onto the cliffs. From there, he could see the whole cove stretched out below. The water rolled lazily up the beach, a gentle rhythmic movement as if the sea were stretching. The sea was still crying, but Jonah could not at first make out any words. It sounded sad, as if the ocean had captured his mother's emotions, though Jonah knew this sound was the ocean's own.

A glimmer out on the water caught his attention. At first, he thought it was the moonlight reflecting off the slow-moving waves, but then he saw it again. It moved differently than the motion of a wave, which meant it was something else. Jonah moved closer to the edge of the cliffs so as to get a better look. He didn't see anything at first, his eyes not knowing what to look for. He looked out across the sea and then back toward the shore. *There it was.* He squinted, trying to keep it in sight so he could figure out what it was. The shimmer he'd seen was a large ship with its sails out. It didn't appear to be moving yet, so Jonah assumed it was still at anchor, though it looked as if it were readying to head back out to sea.

*Come. It is time.* The voice of the sea reached Jonah, but he was instinctively aware from the lack of pull that it was not for him. *If not for me, though, then who?* he wondered. Only one person came to mind - only one person connected with a ship in this cove.

At that thought, Jonah felt a strange mixture of relief and anxiety. He knew he should be glad to see the ship leave. It would be taking Miguel with it. But there was a part of him, he realized, not ready to have the pirate disappear. He was the only chance of a father Jonah had, and that knowledge tugged at his heart.

*Not yet.* Another voice responded, and though it spoke as the sea, Jonah recognized it as the pirate. Quickly he scanned the beach trying to find Miguel. It was difficult from this far away.

*Your time is up. You must return or suffer the consequences.* Though the sea's voice was still soothing, the message was received as sharp as a cut. Jonah could only imagine what that would feel like if it had been intended for him.

The waves picked up in intensity. Jonah squinted hard into the dark and could just make out a figure far below on the beach. Miguel was standing at the water's edge, then walked in until he was full to the waist. Jonah imagined Miguel making the change from farmer to pirate, remembering the black sealcoat and boots.

*I have not completed what I came here to do,* Miguel's sea voice said. *Give me two more days and I will come to you.*

The sea churned as if a storm were brewing. Its waves rose higher with the water it pulled back from the beach. She was quiet – the ocean – as though considering the request. *I will not be denied what is mine.*

Jonah watched, as the churning of the sea intensified. Concern over what might happen to the pirate if he remained in the water wormed its way into Jonah's head. He need not have worried though, as Miguel rose up to walk upon the water itself, and climbed aboard the vessel now sitting in the cove.

*You will have what is yours and more. Just give me two more days.*

*You have tried and failed.*

*Please,* Miguel pleaded, the agony clear in his sea voice. *I will not ask for more than this.*

The sea thrashed, causing waves to beat upon the ship, rocking it. She was angry, Jonah realized. Then just as suddenly, she stopped. The water was once again calm, though the air had become thick with a dense mist. It made the hair on the back of Jonah's neck stand up.

*Two days. Nothing more.* The sea had consented.

# Fifteen

Jonah found he was exhausted when he finally returned home. It was a great relief to have sleep overcome him. For once, he did not have the nightmares. It seemed that as the sea had calmed last night, so had his dreams. It was the sun that woke him, and though he hadn't slept long, he felt rested.

Stretching, he figured he'd better head out to do the chores. As he walked past the table, he noticed a note lying there. Apparently, his ma had gone into Delmar to pick up some things. It was nice of his ma to leave him a note. A twinge of guilt pricked his conscience as he realized how hard he'd been on her lately. He'd have to tell her the past didn't matter anymore - that he was just glad they had each other.

He was only halfway to the barn when he heard his name. Jonah lifted his head and looked down the lane to see Lucas running toward him.

"Jonah! Jonah!" Lucas came racing up the long dirt drive. As he came within a few feet of Jonah, Lucas doubled over, holding his sides while taking deep, gulping breaths.

"What is it, Lucas?"

Ol' Man Wimple came to the barn door. Apparently, he'd heard Lucas' call, too. "Better come inside, boy," Ol' Man Wimple said as he took Lucas by the elbow and directed him toward the house.

Lucas pulled his arm away, looked up at the man, and shook his head. His chest heaved as he tried to regain enough breath to speak. "Can't," he panted. "You'd better come, too."

"Come where? Lucas, what's wrong? Is your mother…"

"No," Lucas interrupted with another shake of his head.

"What is it, boy? Spit it out."

Jonah glanced at Ol' Man Wimple and noticed that the man who had always been calm in the face of everything now had his forehead wrinkled in worry.

"It's Ms. Emily," Lucas finally said, now breathing more normally. "They've taken her."

"Ma?" Jonah asked. "Where? Who took her?"

"They've locked her up. There's gonna be a trial."

"Better tell us the whole story," Ol' Man Wimple said as he again moved to guide Lucas toward the door of the house.

Jonah turned away from them and ran to the barn. He didn't need the whole story. He needed to get to town and find his ma.

"Won't do no good racin' into town without knowing what you're up against," called Ol' Man Wimple over his shoulder. "Better to know, then you can make a plan. It'll take time to get a magistrate to Delmar."

"They ain't gonna wait for the magistrate. Captain Montagurell's gonna oversee it hisself."

"What the blazes would make that man see fit to do a thing like that!?!" Ol' Man Wimple snapped. He dropped Lucas' arm and followed Jonah to the barn. They would need to saddle the horses and get moving.

"It's the fish," Lucas said, "they're gone."

Ol' Man Wimple slowed his steps. "Gone?" he asked, one eyebrow raised.

"That's a load of bullcocky," Jonah snapped. "Where they gonna go?" But a lump settled in Jonah's stomach, and a dreadful sense of understanding ran through him.

"Not gone. Dead."

Jonah didn't wait to hear more. There were sure to be cries of witchcraft. And this time, he feared, they wouldn't go away. Swinging his leg up and over the back of his horse, he took off bareback, not willing to waste the time to put so much as a blanket on the chestnut's back.

# Sixteen

Delmar was buzzing with people rushing to and fro. Having thought better than to ride his horse into the center of town, Jonah had left the chestnut tied to a tree just outside the town limits, and was now on foot. It was a good thing he was, or he might never have been able to make his way through the crowds along the street. Jonah quickly scanned the area, counting the boats still resting at the docks as he did so. They were all accounted for, which meant that none of them had left yet. He looked down, and his stomach flipped in an unnatural way. The surface of the water was covered in dead fish, laying on their sides, each with one visible eye staring at Jonah, like a thousand accusations being thrown his way.

"'Tain't natural," he heard a lady whisper as she shuffled past him. "The Devil's work for sure."

He watched the general direction of movement wondering if this was where he'd find his ma, or if she was still being held somewhere else. Looking up and down the street, he realized he didn't have enough information, and wondered, belatedly, whether or not he'd be able to help his ma after all. Panic clawed at his chest as he thought of not getting to her in time.

The booming voice of Captain Montagurell rose above the crowd, "It would seem our waters have been tainted. Poisoned."

Jonah pushed forward, trying to get a glimpse of the man. Lucas had said Captain Montagurell was going to oversee things himself, maybe Jonah's ma was with him.

"These waters," The Captain continued, "which have fed our families and supplied our needs for generations, these waters to which our lives are tethered, no longer have the means to support us."

A ripple of whispered voices ran through the crowd. Jonah wished he could get closer, but it was too packed, and he couldn't push his way any further forward. He tried standing on tiptoe, tried ducking under arms, but nothing worked. However, the Captain's voice carried out over the crowd, so Jonah could hear it clearly.

"There are no more fish! They're dead. Every last one of them. Dead in their very waters. These waters are no longer safe! There is only one explanation for it all."

"Ain't no way out this time," Brigg's sneer came right next to Jonah's ear.

Jonah whipped around to see the other boy. A look of triumph clung to Brigg's features, and Jonah had the sudden urge to knock it off his face.

"I wouldn't, if I were you," Brigg said, as though he'd read Jonah's mind. "Wouldn't take much to make it two hangin's today."

The threat hung between them, enough to keep Jonah in check, though he paled at the words.

"What? You haven't heard?" A smirk crept along Brigg's face as he watched Jonah's reaction, and this time he laughed. It was a thick, dark sound, causing the anxiety already gripping Jonah to bloom into red, hot anger. The emotion pulsed in his chest like a tiny drum; a cadence signaling impending doom.

"Where is she?" Jonah demanded.

"Like I'd tell you." The Captain's son glared at Jonah. "Just you watch your back, or you'll be next. Our town's had enough of the likes of you." Brigg turned away from Jonah, toward the front of the commotion. The crowd opened just long enough to let the captain's son pass through.

Jonah started to follow Brigg, but was pushed back by the crowd as they pressed in upon themselves closing the path before Jonah could slip through. Frustration and panic surfaced, and Jonah felt his fists clamp together preparing to fight the person in front of him just to get through. But then he realized they'd have to build a gallows before they could hang his ma. That meant she wasn't with Captain Montagurell. He turned and raced off in the other direction. If he was lucky, his ma would be in a holding cell at the deputy's office. Even if they weren't waiting for the magistrate, it would take time to erect a gallows. If he were lucky, it would take half a day with all the men working together to get it built. That wasn't much time to find his ma, and for them to get far enough away.

As he ran down the road toward the deputy's, Jonah caught sight of Miguel. The man was standing on one of the docks looking down at what Jonah could only assume were the dead fish. If he'd thought he was angry at Brigg, it was nothing to what he felt now. His feet slowed as he moved toward Miguel, his hands balled in rage. "So, this is what you meant?" he yelled at the pirate. Jonah shoved his hands into the man's chest, hoping to send him into the death filled sea. Miguel wavered, but caught his balance. He turned in time to catch Jonah's hands in his next attempt to shove the man off the dock.

"The sea will have her victory in the end," Miguel solemnly

replied as he moved himself and Jonah away from the edge.

"Do you have any idea what you've done?" Jonah yelled at him.

Miguel looked up the street, his grey-blue eyes darkening, and then back at Jonah. "There's something evil afoot here." The light scruff on the man's chin began to darken as well. "It won't be long now." Then he turned from Jonah and strode off into the crowd.

Jonah hadn't understood anything the man had said. He wanted to go after him, to make him pay for what he'd done, but the sound of hammers filling the air reminded Jonah of how little time he had left to find his ma. He turned and ran down the now nearly deserted section of road.

His sides hurt by the time he reached the deputy's office, and he was breathing hard. At first, all he could hear was his own raspy breath. Then, as his breathing slowed, he heard soft crying. The sound grew louder as he moved around to the back of the building.

"Ma?" he called out. The crying stopped. "Ma? It's me, Jonah." He was no longer angry with his mother. There would be time for that later. He just wanted to get her free.

"Jonah." Panic filled his mother's tear choked words. "No, you can't be here. If they find you, too… Jonah, promise me. Promise me you'll leave at once and never come back. Find Mr. Wimple. He'll know what to do." She let out a small sob. "Please. Promise me."

"I'm going to get you out of here."

"No. You can't. You'll get caught. You have to go. Now."

"I'm not leaving you." He had been momentarily relieved to have found his ma, only to have a new wave of panic rush over him as he realized he would never be able to get her out on his own.

The clang of hammers on nails rang through the air. Jonah could hear voices, directing the work, rising and falling between the banging. It had seemed the whole town had gathered to see the construction of the gallows. He doubted the deputy himself would be there, though, as Captain Montagurell would not want his prisoner escaping. Creeping back to the side of the building, Jonah glanced in the window. Sure enough, the deputy was waiting inside, seated as near to the entrance as he could get. Even Deputy Walker seemed keen to believe the lies about Jonah's mother.

A commotion rose up among the crowd. Angry voices were yelling. *They couldn't be done already, could they?* Jonah went back to the street to see what was going on. The sea, which had been calm save for the dead fish floating in it, was now building into something wild. Waves were crashing against the docks as if to make them buckle and collapse. Dead fish were slapping against the wood, and some were landing on the shore.

Dread filled Jonah's heart. If they'd thought his mother had something to do with last week's storm, and the dead fish, they wouldn't hesitate to assume she was doing this now. He had to work fast.

Deputy Walker stuck his head out to see what all the yelling was about. The sight of the crowd moving hastily away from shore, and thus away from the nearly complete gallows as well, caught his attention. He glanced back at Emily, who, until now, he'd been ignoring. It was obvious he wasn't sure what to do. He couldn't very well leave her - Captain Montagurell would have his head. But the Captain also blame him if things were thwarted at the gallows.

As it turned out, the deputy didn't have to make the decision. Brigg had broken through the crowd and was racing toward him. "Deputy Walker! Deputy Walker!" he yelled as he ran. "You're needed at the gallows." The deputy didn't hesitate. He took off after

Brigg racing back to the other end of town.

Jonah knew this was his chance. Probably his only chance. He crept into the deputy's office, hoping Deputy Walker would have left the keys. He looked around, but saw nothing. Searching the desk yielded the same results.

Emily turned at the rustling in the office. "What are you doing here?" she called out in a hushed voice. "You can't be here. Not now. Please, Jonah, go."

"I'm not leaving you here."

"Then they'll have us both, and they'll win."

"No. I'm going to get you out."

"With what? There aren't any keys here."

Jonah kept turning around, scanning the area as if he may have overlooked the keys somehow. "They've got to be here," he said, more out of desperation than because he believed it.

"Deputy Walker wears them on his person," his ma replied. She reached her arms through the bars, and Jonah went to her. "Please, Jonah. Go. I couldn't bear it if they took you, too."

Tears slid down his face, "I won't leave you. I can't leave you."

"You must, Jonah. It's the only way."

A sound at the door made them both flinch. Emily held tighter to Jonah, as if, somehow, she'd be able to prevent them from taking her son. She knew it was fruitless, but the mother in her had to try.

Jonah clung to her as well, tears sliding down his face against the bars. He couldn't let them take her. He wouldn't. He'd fight them all the way.

"Move aside, son."

Jonah glanced up. It wasn't Deputy Walker who had come back. It was Ol' Man Wimple. "It's no use," Jonah told him. "We don't have the keys."

Ol' Man Wimple pulled out a strange piece of thin metal. "Stand watch, and let me know if they're coming back this way." He took the metal and slid it into the lock. Jonah heard scraping, and asked, "What are you doing?"

"Pickin' this here lock," he grunted back. "Now get on over there and keep a look out. Wouldn't wanna get caught now."

Jonah slid over to the door and peeked out. Giant waves were now crashing violently a good fifty feet in from shore. Dead fish slapped against the buildings, and, Jonah imagined, against the people clambering to get as far away as they could. Water sloshed against his feet.

With a clink, the lock fell open.

"Come on. Hurry," Jonah called to them as he headed out the door. He started back down Main Street, motioning for his mother and Ol' Man Wimple to follow him.

"Where ya goin'?" Ol' Man Wimple called as he helped Emily around to the side of the building.

"Out of town. Gotta get my horse."

"Not that way, ya don't."

Jonah glanced back, "I left him tied outside town. He's our only chance of escape."

"He's 'round here. I brought him in when I came."

The three of them made their way around to the back of the deputy's office. There were two horses there. One saddled ready to ride, the other, Jonah's, completely bare. Ol' Man Wimple swung up, then pulled Emily up behind him. Just before Jonah could mount his own, he heard another familiar voice.

"You might be needing these." Jonah looked behind him to see

Joseph Tanner holding out a cloth sack. "Good luck." His sad smile said more to Jonah's heart than any words. Mr. Tanner had always been good to them. He'd never believed those crazy stories, and he didn't now.

"Thank you," Jonah said as he took the sack and mounted his ride. There weren't many people he'd miss, but Joseph Tanner would be one.

# Seventeen

They took the long way out of town, looping out onto a lesser traveled trail. It was barely wide enough for one horse, so they rode single file pushing the horses at a brisk pace. They hoped that by using the trail they wouldn't be seen, allowing them time to put distance between themselves and Delmar before the townspeople realized Emily was gone.

Eventually the path rejoined the main road, and they were able to set their horses into a canter, covering ground more quickly. They rode like this for the better part of an hour, with Jonah glancing back over his shoulder. His heart hammered. He feared he'd look back to find they'd been discovered and that a mob was hot on their tails. The very thought spurred him forward, causing him to miss the turnoff of an unmarked, overgrown trail.

"Whoa, there, Jonah. Missed the turn, there." Ol' Man Wimple had already slowed his horse to a walk.

Jonah surged past the turn, tugged on his horse's mane, and, using his knees, spun his horse around. If he wasn't careful, he'd get them all caught. "Sorry," he said as he pulled up behind the other horse.

After a few minutes more, they dismounted and walked beside their horses. They couldn't afford to stop just yet, so this allowed the animals a bit of a rest. Sea grass grew thick and tall along this trail slowing them down significantly. It was also what made the trail difficult to find. Ol' Man Wimple had marked out the trail years ago, and had made sure Jonah knew about it. Now Jonah wondered if Ol' Man Wimple had known all along a day like today would come.

The trail came out on top of the cliffs overlooking the ocean. When he looked out at the sea, Jonah was surprised to see his cove down below. It was a good deal away, several miles at least, but there was nothing to block his view from up here. The ocean sang out to him, and he felt the familiar tug. He shook off the feeling.

"We'll give the horses a few more minutes, then we'll ride again. Want to get as far away as possible. Give us time to find a good campsite before dark."

Jonah nodded, but his mind was on other things. The further away they got, the calmer his nerves were. This left him clear to think through the events of the past months. As he contemplated all that had happened, Jonah found himself more and more frustrated. There had always been talk about his ma, but until recently, it was kept to hushed circles. No one was prepared, or willing, to make the accusation too loudly. There was never any proof.

*Proof,* Jonah thought, *Ha! There would never be any real proof. Ma wasn't a witch.*

"You all right, Jonah?" Emily came up beside her son.

Jonah turned to her. He had gone through so many emotions over the last few months – learning about his father, watching things build up against his mother. He both loved and hated his mother for them. But right then, as they tramped through the sea grass, Jonah couldn't put any of that into words.

"I never thought it would be this way," Emily said, as they

walked. "I never expected him to find us."

"Why didn't we leave?" Jonah asked. "Why didn't we leave when he came?"

"I don't know, Jonah. Maybe we should have. But Delmar was our home. I didn't really think he'd stay."

Ol' Man Wimple interrupted their conversation, "We'll stop here a moment. Water the horses, then be on our way." Jonah watched as Ol' Man Wimple produced a canteen. "Hold out your hands."

Jonah did as he was told, and cupped his two hands together. He held them close to his horse's mouth while Ol' Man Wimple poured water into them. His horse drank greedily, nuzzling his hands for more. Emily did the same for the other horse, and Ol' Man Wimple moved from one of them to the other in turn until he felt the horses had had enough.

"Where will we go?" Jonah asked.

"North for a bit," came the reply. "We'll lay the trail heavy, just in case someone manages to follow us this far. After a bit, there's a hard pack – a crop of sturdy rocks – and we'll double back, and head south."

"Wouldn't it be better if we just kept riding? Won't doubling back mean we'll run directly into the mob?"

"We need to make sure they aren't following us. It's the best thing to do. And anyway, we won't be coming straight back. We'll take another path."

Jonah wasn't sure. He didn't want to take any chances, and it seemed risky.

"It'll be okay," Emily told him. "I trust Mr. Wimple. Trust him with my life."

There was something in the way his ma said this that made

Jonah keenly aware there was a history between them he knew nothing about. Again, he wondered if Ol' Man Wimple had expected a day like today. It was strangely uncanny how the man seemed to be prepared for exactly this.

Jonah found it difficult to focus. He still wasn't convinced doubling back was the best idea. His mind kept worrying over what would happen if the mob caught up to them. He could never bear it if something happened to his ma. And since he didn't have any clear ideas of his own, he had to trust that Ol' Man Wimple knew what he was doing.

***

For the next half hour, they rode north, heavy footed, leaving deliberate traces to indicate they'd passed through. Once they reached the packed earth, Jonah understood why Ol' Man Wimple chose it for their turn around. The ground was hard packed clay, dried and cracked. It would be difficult to track anything across it. There were large, flat rocks lying along one side, which then grew to a crop of ragged boulders. It would not be easy for the horses to navigate the rocks safely, and would be the last place someone would think a group on horseback would go.

Ol' Man Wimple trotted on ahead, taking both his horse and Jonah's with him. They left the packed earth, and tramped along in the plants, smashing them down, leaving fresh tracks once more. He made it appear that they'd stopped for a rest just inside the shade of the trees, then brought the horses back to join up with Jonah and Emily.

"We'll be all right if they make it this far," the man said. "We'd best get going. Sun's pushing low in the sky. Not much light left." Ol' Man Wimple led them out across the flat rocks to the more dangerous expanse of boulders. "Mind your step. It'll be slow going for a while. Don't want to hurt the horses."

Somehow, they managed to step along the rocks without much trouble. Once or twice Jonah heard the scrape of a horseshoe as it slid along a rock before his horse regained its footing. They'd been lucky none of them, horses or humans, had twisted or broken an ankle or leg along the way.

Once out of the rocky outcrop, they continued into a small copse of trees. They stayed on foot, keeping their weight off their horses, and walking on fallen logs, in an effort to keep their tracks hidden. The idea was that if the mob managed to track them to the rocks, and explored the far side, they'd not immediately recognize the tracks as belonging to Jonah's party. Then, if there was no evidence to say the three of them had continued on foot, the mob would follow the only logical path; the one they'd planted going north. Jonah hoped Ol' Man Wimple was right about this.

"We should probably make camp," Ol' Man Wimple said as he brought his horse to a stop. He was watching the sky, where large, heavy clouds were gathering at an ever increasing rate. "Looks to be an ugly one."

"Do we have to?" Emily asked, her voice a little shaky. It seemed that as the shadows extended, her confidence was dropping. "I mean, couldn't we keep going?"

Like his mother, Jonah was more interested in getting to a final destination. Some place they wouldn't have to worry about the mob he feared loomed in the shadows. He knew it wasn't realistic to think that the mob had followed them all this way, especially as there had been no sound of them, but he couldn't help it. He'd feel better when the storm passed and daylight came. "I could keep going."

Ol' Man Wimple looked at the sky again. "It won't be easy when that monster hits."

Emily glanced around them, looking out at the darkening trees. It was obvious she was uneasy, and wouldn't rest much if they camped here. Jonah knew he wouldn't either; and he doubted Ol' Man Wimple would sleep at all.

"It's okay. Just so long as we keep moving." Emily said. "I'll feel better if we just get there."

# Eighteen

It turned out that a good campsite was one hidden among sea grass at the base of a large knoll. There was a small grass hut that looked as though it hadn't been used for many years. It was well protected on either side by towering cliffs, which meant the wind didn't have direct access to it, so there was not much repair needed.

They were all tired when they arrived, having spent the entire day traveling. The storm had blown in and out quickly, staying just long enough to drench them thoroughly. It had been a cold, sloppy, wet walk for the last three hours, too late in the day for any sun to dry them.

Now, as Jonah sat next to a crackling fire, he listened to the whisper of the wind through the long sea grass as it mixed with the heart-aching call of the ocean. Jonah felt a tug at his own heart, and wondered what the ocean had to be sad about. There was a lot for Jonah to be sad about. He'd just left the only home he'd ever known. For a few minutes, he hated the ocean for being able to give voice to its grief. Then he wondered when he'd started thinking of the ocean as a living thing.

An image of Miguel came unbidden to his mind and the memory of their time together at the cove surfaced. Miguel had talked of the ocean as being alive, mentioning the singing and calling of the sea. Jonah shook the thought aside. He didn't want to think about Miguel or the cove. Not now.

But he couldn't seem to push Miguel from his mind no matter how hard he tried. He saw the pirate as he came to shore that first night, saw him standing near the docks as the water turned to ice, remembered all the times he'd walked past and winked at Jonah, only for Jonah to discover something else had happened. The memory of the storm, and Miguel's excitement at its coming seemed to get tangled somewhere in Jonah's mind. Too much had happened since Miguel had come to Delmar. Too many unnatural things to be coincidental and he knew his mother had nothing to do with any of it.

A fire seemed to ignite inside of Jonah as he saw each of these events flash before him. With each one, Jonah realized, talk of Emily had increased. He had heard them whispering. He'd wondered how people could be so simple-minded. Now, he could see where people would want to blame someone.

Blame. That was it. The town had needed someone to blame. And because of that need, talk had no longer been kept to whispers. Now, he, his ma and Ol' Man Wimple were running for their lives. They'd never be able to go back to Delmar.

Anger filled Jonah like oil on a fire igniting a flame of hatred that engulfed him. This was Miguel's fault. All of it.

Suddenly Jonah knew what he needed to do. He walked the short distance to the grass hut and poked his head inside. It was dark, and he couldn't see well. A small figure lay wrapped in a blanket on what Jonah knew was a straw mat. His mother looked so small and helpless lying there. He looked around trying to find Ol' Man Wimple, but not seeing him.

"She's sleepin'. Best you ought to be, too. It's been a long day for all of us." Ol' Man Wimple had come up behind Jonah.

"I'm not tired," Jonah replied as he turned away from the hut. The older man was holding a piece of rope loosely in one hand. "What's that for?"

Ol' Man Wimple looked down. "Just checkin' on the boat. Didn't know but what I might need to replace the one that's holden her."

"What boat?"

"Got a boat stowed away in that cave over yonder." He indicated the direction with a nod of his head.

They moved away from the hut, back toward the ocean. Jonah allowed his eyes to follow the water in the direction the older man had indicated. He hadn't noticed the cave earlier. Now, as he looked, he could just make out the mouth of it tucked far back inside the cliff face. Water lapped in and out of it, so he figured it must have been a water cave – the kind you couldn't just walk into unless you were wading through water waist high. It'd be a great place to hide a boat.

"Wouldn't be much of a hideout iffin there weren't no way to escape it?"

Jonah considered the man's words. A perfect hideout wouldn't need an escape. Then again, there wasn't anything perfect about this world they were living in. An escape plan was probably for the best.

"How'd you know about this place?" Jonah asked.

Ol' Man Wimple shrugged. "'Tain't the first time someone's needed to get away," he said vaguely.

Jonah looked at him thoughtfully. His ma was some distance away asleep in the grass hut. He made his decision. "I need you to promise me something," he said.

"What you have in mind?"

"Take care of Ma. Keep her safe."

"'Course I'll do that. You and her both. Been doin' it your whole life. Ain't gonna stop now."

A small wave of guilt washed over Jonah and he was grateful it was too dark for the older man to read it in his face. "There's something I've got to do," he said.

"Ain't nothing you can do, boy." Ol' Man Wimple spoke sternly. Even in the dark Jonah could feel the man eyeing him suspiciously. "You ain't thinking about going back there, now are ya?"

Jonah shook his head and swallowed hard. It wasn't really a lie. He had no intentions of going back to the village of Delmar. There was no need. What he needed to do wouldn't take him quite that far.

"Good. 'Cause there ain't nothin' so important as for you to go and get yourself killed over."

"I'm not planning to," Jonah told him. "There's just something I need to take care of."

"Looky here, Jonah. There ain't nothing that mingling with Miguel will do but get you hurt. It won't matter that your is his son. Best you stay away from him." It was apparent Ol' Man Wimple wasn't keen on the idea of Jonah going anywhere on his own. "Why don't we get us some sleep and talk about it in the mornin'?" He must have seen something in the young man's face that told him Jonah would not be deterred because he added with a sigh, "Your ma ain't gonna like this none."

"Like what?"

They both turned at the sound of Emily's voice. The darkness shifted as she made her way toward them.

"I'm not going to like what?" she asked again.

"There's something I've got to do," Jonah said looking down at his feet.

"Jonah, nothing you do will change what has happened," his mother tried to reason.

"You don't know that!" Heat had returned to Jonah's words. The anger he felt towards Miguel was surfacing again. "Do you even know what he did?"

There was silence.

"Well, do you?" he demanded. When she still didn't speak, he continued, "It's not right, what he did. Any of it. You could have been killed!"

Emily took a deep breath and let it out slowly as though she were weighing her words. "There's so much you don't know," she began. "So much I still don't understand myself. I thought was I doing what was best for you. I should have known he'd never give up trying to find us."

"You couldn't have known," Ol' Man Wimple soothed.

"I know," she conceded. Turning to Jonah she said, "I just thought I could protect you. I thought I could keep you safe from it all."

The way his mother was speaking, Jonah wasn't convinced she fully understood that the things Miguel had done had made the rumors of her being a witch real in the minds of the town folk. He opened his mouth to say as much.

Emily raised her hand to stop him.

"I'm aware of the danger I was in. And I will always be grateful that you came to rescue me." She reached her hand out towards Jonah and gently cupped his face lightly stroking his cheek with her thumb. "You are a remarkable young man. I'm proud of who you are."

A tear escaped Jonah's eye and traveled down his cheek.

"I should have known I could never keep you from Miguel. He didn't choose the curse. Deep down, he's a good man."

*A good man? How could one even think such a thing?* Jonah didn't share his mother's sentiment. What emotion had made its way to the surface was quickly undone by the wave of anger he still felt for Miguel. He clenched his fists tightly, his jaw set in a rigid line, and glanced up at the sky. It was getting late. Every moment he wasted was an opportunity for Miguel to get away. If he got away, there would be no way to fix anything.

"I cannot make you stay here," Emily whispered. "I wish I could. I suppose I kept you away too long."

Jonah looked back and forth between his mother and Ol' Man Wimple. He couldn't bring himself to say goodbye. "Just keep her safe," he said.

Ol' Man Wimple nodded. "Be careful. And get back here just as soon as you can. We'll wait as long as we're able."

Jonah nodded. A sudden lump formed in his throat making it hard to speak. He didn't like the idea of leaving his mother behind, but this was something he knew he had to do.

"Remember," Emily said, "what's been done can't be undone. One can never go back, only forward. Don't lose yourself to this. Always remember who you are and who you're met to be."

The emotion resurfaced. Jonah could barely speak. He still couldn't bring himself to say goodbye, but he reached over and pulled his mother into a hug. When he stepped away, he brushed tears from his cheeks with the backs of his hands.

Turning to Ol' Man Wimple, he extended his hand for a hearty shake. "Keep her safe."

"We'll be fine so long as the enchantments hold."

There was a time when Jonah would have scoffed at the idea of enchantments. There may not be witches, but there sure was something else. And Jonah was right in the middle of it. He still didn't understand it, but he knew it was real. This whole nightmare adventure was real.

Ol' Man Wimple handed Jonah his knife. "Here, son. I reckon you'll need it more than me. 'Least wise I'll feel better knowin' you have it." Jonah took the gift and slipped it into his belt. Pulling Jonah in for a hug, Ol' Man Wimple said, "No need to backtrack. Just follow the ocean. You'll get there sooner."

Jonah didn't know how the older man knew where he was going, but he appreciated the tip. "Thank you," he said, then turned and walked off toward the beach. He didn't look back for fear he'd change his mind.

# Nineteen

Jonah set out to follow the ocean, walking along the shore as it wove in and out, sometimes cutting far back inland. The memory of the night before sprung to his mind. He knew he needed to reach the cove before the two days were up. The jagged path of the sea he was following was slowing him down. He feared by the time he reached the cove, Miguel would be gone.

As he came around another turn, he found himself facing a set of steep cliffs. He paused in the moonlight to consider his options. Swimming was altogether out, as he didn't know how. Walking clear around would take an extra couple of hours. Climbing the cliffs would be difficult at best, and likely impossible. He was tired from all the walking he'd done today, and his legs ached. What he really wanted was sleep.

It was this last thought that cinched his decision. He needed sleep, and though he knew he needed to get to the cove before the end of tomorrow, he also knew he would make better progress with a little rest. The cool breeze picked up, causing him to shiver. Jonah looked around for a place to rest for the next couple of hours, his eyes stopping on a cave halfway up the cliff face. It would be a good place to sleep, protected from the elements and away from prying eyes. He gathered what little energy he still had and used it to climb up to the cave.

He moved carefully, his arms straining to pull himself from one set of rocks to another. All that farm work was paying off. Fortunately, the rocks weren't really wet, and Jonah quickly found a rhythm that helped propel him from rock to rock. The sooner he got to the cave, the better.

*Stop!*

The voice stabbed Jonah's mind. He immediately stopped, hanging momentarily by one hand. He quickly reached up with his other hand for a better hold, and secured his feet directly under him on an outcrop of rocks he was just swinging over. He looked behind him. No one was there. Slowly he reached out with his left hand for another rock, then swung his leg over.

*Careful.* The voice came again.

This time Jonah recognized it. He looked down and saw he had almost placed his foot upon a rock with wet moss. In his hurried rhythm, he would have fallen. A little further up and Jonah would be past where the sea could reach. For now, he needed to be more careful. "Thank you," he called out to the sea.

Readjusting his foot, he began working his way up more slowly. He was glad to finally reach the cave, as by then his arms were shaking, and his legs were ready to give out completely. He gave one last look out to the sea, rolled over and went to sleep.

***

It was later than he'd wanted when Jonah finally woke. He hadn't counted on the fact that it would take longer for light to reach inside the cave when he'd chosen it last night. A ripple of fear raced through him as his stomach rumbled. How long had he slept?

How much of the day was lost? His stomach rumbled again, and he realized he'd have to find something to eat along the way.

Jonah groaned when he moved. His muscles were tight and sore, and his head throbbed. It was going to be a hard day, but the memory of what needed to be done drove him to his feet. He looked out at the sea below. Up or down, it was going to be slow. There was a better chance of food at the top. Carefully, so as not to slip, Jonah crawled out of the cave and began the hard climb up the rest of the cliff.

By the time he reached the top, the sun was half way to its midday arc. He'd lost far too many hours. He looked out at the sea wishing he could rest. His stomach growled, and he turned himself toward the path that wound along the cliff edge. It still cut back and forth, causing Jonah to grumble about the amount of wasted time. Being hungry certainly wasn't helping his mood any either.

After walking nearly an hour, Jonah noticed the trail seemed to converge upon another trail, the two meeting briefly and then heading off in different directions. They both headed back toward Delmar, though, and, fortunately, the grass was low enough that Jonah could see the one cut straight, while the other followed the cliff. He chose the straight path, determined to keep the one along the edge within view. This would save him time. It also provided him with bushes of berries along the way. This quelled the grumbling complaints of his belly, making it easier to concentrate.

The day passed without incident. Midday came and went, and as the sun began to dip toward the earth once more, Jonah's anxiety grew. If he didn't make it to the cove before Miguel left, there would be no way to undo all that had happened. He didn't care what happened to Miguel after that, but he hoped he'd never see him again.

A rustle of leaves brought Jonah's thoughts back around. The path had pulled up close to a copse of trees, often weaving just inside the tree line. He looked around, peering into the darkening space. Voices drifted toward him.

"They couldn't have gotten too far. We must have missed 'em."

"I say good riddance! Who cares where they went, so long as they're gone."

Jonah knew they were talking about him and his ma. He also realized he must be closer to Delmar than he'd thought. The townsfolk wouldn't like being out this long, and, just as Ol' Man Wimple had surmised, they'd seemed likely to be giving up the search.

"The Captain ain't gonna like us coming back without 'em."

"Then let The Captain go find 'em"

It was obvious these men were tired. The bitterness they expressed toward Captain Montagurrell also meant The Captain hadn't gone on this witch hunt himself. That was a relief to Jonah, as The Captain was all too good at stirring up trouble. Still, Jonah felt it best to head away from the trees, and back toward the water. He didn't want to find that his path converged with theirs further along.

Quietly, he slipped away from the trail and made his way to the path along the cliff edge. The trouble was, he was too exposed out here along the edge with nothing but the sunset behind him. He needed to find a way back down to the beach. Preferably one that didn't require climbing back down the cliff face.

The sound of the sea lapping lazily below called out to him. Part of him wanted to go to it. To lay down and let it lull him into oblivion, like it had before. He wanted nothing more than to rid his mind of the trouble, to forget it all. But he had to keep going. Before long he noticed a new path that turned away from the ridge line, toward the sea. It went a little way, and then seemed to disappear altogether.

Carefully, so as not to misstep, Jonah followed the new path. Where it disappeared, Jonah discovered there were stones that appeared more like stairs. It would be better than climbing, and he knew he needed to get out of sight on the off chance those men emerged from the trees and looked his way. He wasn't sure how sturdy they were, so he tested his weight carefully on each stone before continuing on. By the time he'd reached the bottom, the sun had set, and the moon had begun to rise.

Down on the beach, Jonah traveled more slowly. Once again, he had to follow the deep curves of the landscape. He was heartened by the thought that he couldn't be too far away now. Soon he would come around a bend to find his beloved cove. And when he did, he'd make Miguel put things right.

The moon was just a sliver in the sky now, making it hard to see. Jonah used the dark shadows around him to determine where he was. The sand shifted under his feet as he walked along, tiring him faster than if he were walking on solid ground, but it couldn't be helped.

The longer he walked, the closer to the water he drifted. It sang to him, calling him closer, but so softly Jonah wasn't aware. Soon the water was lapping at his ankles, soaking both his boots and his feet inside them. Realizing he was now in the water, Jonah considered moving back up the beach, but decided against it. Instead, he removed his boots, tied them together, slung them over his shoulder, and continued walking, enjoying the way the water made him feel.

Not knowing how far away he was, or how long it would take him to arrive at the cove, Jonah kept trudging forward. He didn't even know if Miguel would be there, but it was the only place he could think to look. Eventually his body tired, and he felt as though he couldn't take another step. Jonah sensed a new energy seep into him just at the moment when he thought to give up. It felt fluid, like the water around his feet. Renewed by this energy, Jonah surged on faster than before.

Eventually he came to a break in the beach. A rocky section lay ahead, large sharp edges pointing in all directions. He knew this was the way to the cove. It was the patch of land that separated this beach from his cove. It also kept others from ever coming too near. The rocks were slippery, and anyone who tried to walk across them would fall, the sharp edges cutting into their soft flesh. It went on for several miles this way, and so it was left alone.

Jonah hadn't thought about how he would have to cross the miles of slippery, sharp rocks. Maybe his idea wasn't all that great after all. Maybe there really was nothing he could do. Feeling discouraged, Jonah sat on a rock, the heaviness of the situation resting on his shoulders. Going forward would likely result in his death as the rocks were hazardous even in daylight, and he didn't have the energy to go back.

*Come,* the water called out to him. *Come to me.*

The soft beckoning of the sea seemed to connect with something invisible inside of Jonah. It felt alive as it tugged at him. He tried to shake it off; tried to resist the pull. "Leave me alone," he told it.

*I've been waiting, Jonah. I can help you.*

The pulling became insistent. He felt as if it would force him from the rock where he sat. Fear of being pulled under the water caused Jonah to dig his feet into the sand. He hoped if he grounded himself better he'd be able to resist whatever force was pulling on him.

*Not hurt you, Jonah. Help you. Do not resist. Come to me.*

Jonah closed his eyes, trying to make sense of the words he heard. A deep breath, then another. The salty sea air filled his nostrils, awakening his senses. He was more alert now than he'd been when he'd started out. The sea was alive. It was a part of him. It always had been. He thought he understood what it was telling him. Standing, he moved out into the water. "Show me," he said.

Before he'd even finished the words, he felt a shift in the direction of the current. His body relaxed and he found himself moving through the water as if it were propelling him onward. Feeling alert and energized, Jonah made his way around the miles of rocky shore much faster than should have been possible.

Even so, it was well past midnight when he came around the last bend. His cove lay peacefully before him. He looked up at the sky. Defeat mingled with anger as Jonah took note of the time. The sea had promised two days. He was too late.

# Twenty

The water in the cove deepened into a dark blue-green as the first grays of the new morning made their way into the sky. Jonah knew this was a precursor to the splendor of pinks and purples and oranges that would soon grace it, but he did not think of those. He needed to get to the shore to check for the longboat. It was the only way he could be sure Miguel was really gone. If it was still there, he figured he could wait by it. He knew eventually Miguel would come for the boat. He was certain the man would never leave it behind.

The sea pushed him forward, as though it heard his thoughts. As he neared the shore, Jonah noticed movement at the far side of the cove. It wasn't much, and it was hard to make out in the dim gray of the morning, but he was certain he'd seen something. It wasn't until the dense gray parted around him that Jonah realized he'd been trying to see through fog. Now, with it no longer hindering his view, he could just make out the long shape of a boat being pushed toward the water's edge. He knew without a doubt it was the long boat. And that could only mean one thing. Miguel was on the move again.

Relief flooded through Jonah has he realized he was not too late after all. Then anger surged through him. Waves splashed hard against his legs, climbing higher and higher, but they didn't seem to have the power to knock him over. Or they didn't want to. Jonah wasn't sure which. It didn't matter, though. He knew he had to stop Miguel from leaving, but he was too far away.

Miguel set his boat in the water, then walked out into the sea. His appearance shifted once again from the kindred farmer to the vicious pirate complete with his long black sealcoat, sword at the hip, and large tri-cornered hat. Miguel stepped into the boat, and rowed himself further out into the cove.

As Jonah watched the long boat glide through the water, he noticed the air in front of the boat shimmering. Slowly the large ship came into view. A magnificent mast with ten sails stood out against the now lightening sky. A sudden calm washed over Jonah. Without a second thought, he turned his attention toward the ship, moving quickly through the water.

Though he'd never learned to swim, he was no longer afraid of the water. He ducked his head under to get closer to the ship without notice, and felt the current pick up and propel him forward with rapid speed. When it stopped, Jonah reemerged to see a long line of fishing net hung over the side of the massive ship. He reached out and began pulling himself up. The rope was slippery, but not as slippery as some of the rocks he'd encountered on his way here. Still, it was hard work.

*Go.* The water whispered to him. It pushed him from underneath, raising him up out of the water. The small wave that lifted him brought him within two feet of the top edge of the ship.

"Thanks," he whispered back.

He pulled himself up the remaining fishing net, water dripping from him as he worked his way over the side of the ship. Keeping close to the wall, he slipped down and took note of his surroundings. Sails were tied down, waiting for someone to raise them. A wheel running horizontal to the deck carried a large, heavy looking chain that stretched from it over the side of the ship. Jonah figured there must be a large anchor sitting deep in the water attached to the other end of that chain.

The deck was open, save for several large masts which partially blocked his view. Large ropes, thicker than Jonah's arm, were coiled at intervals along both sides of the deck. Looking past the masts, he could make out an upper deck that took up nearly a third of the ship. That must have been the helm, as another large wheel with spokes was set vertically on it. Under that, Jonah could see a door, which he assumed led below deck.

Pirates appeared on the ship, as if ghosts from the deep were taking on bodies. There were too many of them to count, and as they materialized, they set to work heaving rope, and opening sails. Several shimmied up the masts to open sails at the top, then tossed ropes down to their counterparts below to tie off. Others gathered large poles and set them into holes in the first wheel creating a circle of spokes. Together they pushed on the poles, walking in a circle, causing the clank of metal to mix with the creak of wood as the chain wound around the base of the wheel.

Even with the hustle and bustle of the crew, Jonah knew it wouldn't be long before he was discovered. He glanced around again, looking for a place to hide. There did not appear to be much to hide behind on the lower deck. At least nothing that he felt would conceal him with all the movement. His eyes traveled the length of the great ship toward the upper deck, and came to rest upon the helm. For a moment, Jonah had the urge to go to the wheel, and place his hands securely on the spokes. He'd never steered a boat before, let alone a ship, but something inside him wanted to. There wasn't time to think about that now. He had to find a hiding place. His eyes lighted upon a group of large barrels pushed together several paces behind the wheel. If he was right, there would be space behind them. A space he could squeeze into and hide.

Keeping low to the deck, and sticking close to the railing, Jonah edged his way around the side of the ship toward the stairs leading to the upper deck. He hoped that if he didn't cause a disturbance no one would notice him. There wasn't anything to conceal him along the way, but he didn't have any other choice. He'd just have to go for it.

He paused and glanced around him making sure no one had spotted him. None of the ghostly crew, who had by now become more solid, looked his way. They were all busy adjusting sails, and rolling barrels into position for the voyage. Jonah stepped carefully along, so as not to get tangled in the rope that lay along the deck. At times he had to crawl along because the massive rope was coiled so deep that to walk through it would surely have caused Jonah to fall and become entangled.

"Hey!"

Jonah froze. His chest felt tight making it hard to breathe. He was certain he'd been spotted.

"Hey, you!" the voice yelled again.

Jonah closed his eyes tight, willing himself to be invisible. Then slowly, he turned his head in the direction of the voice. No sense dragging this out. He opened his eyes expecting to see the hardened face of the man with the gruff voice. Instead, Jonah found himself face to face with a large ship rat.

The breath that had caught in Jonah's chest erupted. Jonah slammed his hand over his mouth in time to muffle the cry, while he skittered backwards, feet slipping on the rope, as he tried to move away from the creature.

Its beady eyes bore into Jonah's as it stood up on hind legs. Then, just as quickly, it dropped to all four and scurried off toward the door that would take it below deck. There must have been a rather large hole in the door, as the creature disappeared from sight.

"Stop fightin' with that rope and get it over here," the gruff voice called out snapping Jonah back to his situation.

Jonah fumbled, tripping on the rope as he moved backward still trying to locate the pirate who had spoken, but no one was watching him. In fact, no one seemed to be looking his way at all. They were all busy on the other side of the deck. He looked down at his feet, and instinctively knew they would be coming for the rope lying there soon enough. Somehow, he managed to free himself from the massive layers, and took off running, hoping the sound of the crew moving about the deck would muffle the sound of his feet. He was determined not to be caught near that rope when they came for it.

Getting up the small set of stairs proved to be more difficult. Once Jonah reached them, he heard Miguel and another pirate talking. Their voices were heading his way. Fortunately, there was a small space behind the stairs that Jonah was just able to squeeze into. He could barely breathe, it was such a tight fit. And if anyone took a moment to look directly at the stairs as they began to ascend, he was bound to be discovered as the stairs were nothing more than boards with openings between them.

"We'll set sail as soon as she's ready," Miguel said as he approached the steps.

"But, Captain. Me thought we were staying?"

"Aye. And so we were. But 'taint no need. Ready the ship."

"Aye, aye, Captain," the other man replied. "And where should I tell the men we're heading?"

"Out to sea, Seward. Out to sea. They don't need no more than that."

"Yes, sir, Captain. Very good, Captain," came Seward's quick agreement.

They had stopped at the stairs, Miguel's foot resting on the lowest tread. Jonah felt the heat of anger in his own face. His hands caught up into fists. This was his chance. This was what he'd come for. All he had to do was come out and confront the pirate. But he couldn't seem to do it. He felt paralyzed now that he was so close to the man.

"And Seward," Miguel said turning slightly back toward the other pirate.

"Yes, sir?"

"Prepare the lower bunk."

"Sir?" Seward questioned.

"You heard me, Seward. Just do it." Miguel swung back around and moved swiftly up the steps.

Jonah, his sides hurting from the tight space he was crammed into, realized he'd stopped breathing. He took a gulp of air, his lungs pressing into his ribs. It hurt too much to breathe. He knew he couldn't stay under the stairs much longer. He needed to get to the barrels, but how could he possibly get there with Miguel at the helm? Desperately he looked for another hiding place. Anything with more room than where he was. But it was no use; the deck was too open.

Just as Jonah was thinking he'd have to give himself up or pass out from lack of oxygen, he heard a welcome sound.

"Seward, tell me when the crew has her ready. I'll be down below consultin' me maps." Miguel's feet thumped down the steps, passed Jonah, and trailed off toward the hold.

Jonah waited a few more minutes, but gave up waiting sooner than he'd have liked, and slipped out of his hiding space. He took several long gulps of air, his lungs no longer fighting against his ribs. It was now or never. He moved up the stairs, and slipped behind the barrels. *That was easy*, he thought. He should have known it was too easy.

"Anchors aweigh," came the call from the lower deck.

With a grunt, the pirates moved slowly in a circle around the horizontal wheel once again. Jonah hadn't realized they'd stopped before. But now, as the chain clanged taut, the anchor swung into view. The wind began to blow hard, filling out the sails with a crack. Then the ship itself groaned as it gave way to the power of the wind in its sails.

Miguel had positioned himself at the helm once more, and Jonah found himself staring at the captain's black boots. His heart pounded. All it would take would be for his father to turn around, settle his eyes upon him, and it would all be over.

# Twenty-One

It hadn't taken long for the ship to leave the cove and enter the open sea. Miguel stood at the helm, adjusting the direction of the ship as they traveled. His back remained to Jonah, who had long since settled down against the barrels.

Large swells rocked the boat causing Jonah's stomach to lift and drop. The unease that shook his belly reminded him of the breakfast he hadn't eaten; and as the bile rose up his throat, he was grateful there was nothing else to dispel. With each rock of the ship, the color drained further from Jonah's face. Bile rose up his throat, and he forced it back down. He knew he couldn't keep it up much longer.

"You can come out now, Jonah," Miguel called out over the winds and waves.

Jonah was feeling too sick to properly register the surprise that would have naturally overcome him.

"Best to be sick over the side than stuck behind a bunch of barrels."

Embarrassment fought with anger as Jonah realized his father had known all along that he was on the ship, and that he was seasick to boot. Adrenaline-fueled anger propelled the boy forward from behind the barrels. Then the ship rode high on a wave and plummeted quickly to the other side. What energy there had been in Jonah was quickly dispelled by the powerful urge to turn his stomach inside-out, and he raced toward the side, heaving and spewing as he went.

Nothing much came out, but his mouth tasted bitter and his throat burned from the acid that had been all he'd had in his stomach. He slouched down the railing, wrapping his arms around himself as he dropped to the deck. He would never have known one could feel so miserable on the sea if he'd not experienced it himself. Right then, he wanted nothing more than for the rocking in his stomach to go away.

Miguel's hearty laugh broke through the whistle of the wind. Jonah looked up from his place of misery, a new distaste growing inside him. How dare this man, who claimed to be his father, mock him so?

He pushed himself to standing, determined not to give the pirate another reason to laugh at him. The ship rocked violently, as if trying to throw Jonah off his feet. Jonah gritted his teeth and stared back at the pirate. There appeared to be a challenge in the man's eyes, and Jonah was angry enough to take him on.

Without warning, the ship tilted dangerously to the side at an angle clearly meant to make Jonah's feet slide out from under him. The natural thing to do would have been to grab hold of the railing to keep himself from sliding and falling. However, Jonah was too sick to realize this, and his feet did exactly what the ship wanted, and betrayed him. As they came out from under him, he slid twelve feet before the ship righted itself.

*What kind of game was this?* Jonah wondered angrily.

Slowly he got to his feet and walked back toward Miguel. The ship lurched upward, and this time Jonah tried to grab a barrel on his way down. The barrel was securely tied and didn't budge, but

Jonah missed it, and this time he went sprawling down the stairs to the lower deck.

He noticed that no one else on the ship seemed to have a problem staying on their feet. This only made him more angry. *How could anyone stand on this demon ship?* he wondered.

As Jonah looked up, his eyes met Miguel's. The pirate's beady black eyes were laced with irritation that bordered on hatred. Storms brewed within them, and Jonah knew the only way to end this insanity was to beat the pirate at his own game.

This time, as he stood up, Jonah took note of where things were around him. He moved to a position on the deck where he'd be able to grab hold of the railing when the ship lurched. Deliberately placing his feet a shoulder's width apart, he held his hands out ready and watched the pirate.

The ship rolled first to the right, then to the left. Jonah felt his body start to slide, but refused to grab the railing. As the bow rose up in the air and he reached out toward the railing, he suddenly realized he could never win if he held onto anything. His balance was precarious at best, but he stubbornly willed himself to stay on his feet. Certain he would lose his footing if he so much as breathed, and fearing he'd plummet against the railing which was now below him, Jonah pushed down on his feet, and held his breath.

The winds picked up, and with it came the rains. Drops the size of small rocks pummeled down on him. He could not see far in front of him, as the storm grew more intense and the sky around him turned black. The ship righted itself with a plunge into the ocean that sent waves splashing forcefully over the edge, drenching the deck in foot deep water that raced to find somewhere to go. The force of the water caused Jonah's feet to slip, but he managed to regain his balance before it could pull him down.

Waves as tall as the two-story townhouses back in Delmar raged on either side of the ship, but they appeared to be sailing a straight, steady course. Strangely, as Jonah became more aware of the storm and narrowed in on the details, he noticed a shift in the air around him. It felt oddly still and calm. Though the storm had not abated, and the ship continued its dangerous plunges, Jonah found he could now easily stand, even with the water that was still receding from the deck. Jonah could see the storm swirling around him, but he no longer felt the pounding of the rain, though he heard it continue to slam upon the ship.

His eyes focused on the helm and the figure he knew to be his father at the head of it. Though it was unnaturally dark, and the storm made it difficult to see very far, Jonah was able to watch his father. It was as if a tunnel of air opened and connected the two of them. He could clearly see the look on the pirate's face. The expression belied the menace the man really was. Then, without warning, the pirate's expression hardened again, his eyes narrowing in on Jonah's. A new challenge flashed in them as he spun the wheel, causing the ship to climb the monstrous swell on Jonah's right.

*What is this crazy man doing? He's going to get us all killed!* Jonah thought. He remembered the challenge he had seen in the pirate's eyes, and determined he would not let this mad man win. He couldn't. He had to make the pirate return to Delmar and put everything right – for his ma. Determination mixed with something else that Jonah could not place. He needed to beat Miguel at his own game. A foreign feeling raced through his body, and Jonah managed to channel it, securing his feet to the deck. With a force he did not know he had, he pushed his feet deep into the wood even as the ship tilted and the deck was no longer level enough for an ordinary person to stand on.

Enough was enough! He had to end this pirate madness. And there was only one way to do it.

Carefully, so as to test his ability to move forward without falling, Jonah began forcing one foot in front of the other. It was ridiculous to think he would be able to walk upright since the ship was now completely sideways in the wave. Jonah expected gravity to take control at any moment, pulling his legs out from under him, and causing his body to plummet to the other side of the ship into the vast, wild ocean. Still, Jonah knew the only way to win would be to walk across the deck without holding onto anything.

Step by step he moved. The power he felt grew stronger with each step. Jonah knew he would likely plummet to his death at any moment, but he pressed forward unwilling to accept that fate. He crossed the upper deck back to the helm where his father still stood with his hands on the wheel.

"Well done!" Miguel praised as he swung the wheel, bringing the ship back into a safe position. The storm stopped just as abruptly, and the ocean swells dropped to a roll. "I see you've found your sea legs, boy!" There was no mistaking the pride in the pirate's voice, nor the hungry gleam in his eye.

# Twenty-Two

The steady sound of rough laughter rang out around the ship. Jonah barely glanced at the ghost pirates. He didn't see what they found so amusing. Anger still sat within him, just below the boiling point. Whatever the joke, Jonah wasn't interested.

"Come along, boy," his father called to him as he let go of the helm and began to walk away. The wheel spun slowly from the lack of strong, seaworthy hands. Jonah eyed it warily. No one seemed to be going toward it. Instinct told him leaving the wheel unattended was a bad idea, but he didn't know the first thing about steering a ship.

"Never mind the wheel, boy. Seward'll grab it soon enough."

The laughter died down, and though the crew had begun to scurry around the ship once more, Jonah knew they were paying more attention to the captain and himself than to the tasks at hand. He couldn't blame them. He knew he didn't look the part – neither pirate nor cabin boy.

"Who's the rat?" an older pirate spat out the question like it had a bad taste.

"Outta line, Heckel. Back to work," Miguel ordered. Jonah thought he saw the briefest flash of anger within his father's eyes. Heckel dropped his eyes and began swabbing the deck.

Miguel led Jonah down from the bridge to the captain's quarters. He opened the door, went in, and beckoned for Jonah to join him. Jonah wasn't sure he wanted to. He had followed Miguel more out of curiosity, but now that he was being invited into the cabin his curiosity fled and he felt trapped. Part of him wanted to retreat, and he adjusted his stance ready to run.

"I wouldn't do that," Miguel said, nodding toward Jonah's shifting foot. His face had taken on the hardened look Jonah associated with pirates. His tone was no longer that of proud father, but rather of menacing mercenary.

Jonah's heart thudded hard within his chest. He couldn't remember what had made him think it would be a good idea to board the ship. What was it that had made him think he could convince Miguel to put things right? Looking at the captain now, Jonah knew there would be no convincing Miguel of anything. But what choice did he have? He was in the middle of the ocean with a maniac. There was nowhere else to go.

Three steps took him into the captain's quarters. Three steps and the door slammed shut behind him, the lock sliding into place. Surprised, Jonah spun toward the door, but didn't like the feeling of having his back to Miguel and returned his focus to the pirate in front of him. The man was unpredictable, and Jonah didn't trust him. He faced the pirate, figuring it would be better to see whatever was coming.

Miguel had taken his dagger from his belt and was actively using it to clean his teeth. "You're a clever boy," Miguel said as he shook his dagger at Jonah. "Very clever." Miguel narrowed his eyes and moved closer to Jonah. "Clever can be dangerous."

Jonah didn't know if that was praise or concern he detected.

Coming from a pirate, he wasn't sure either was a good thing.

Miguel moved away from him. "How'd you know about the ship, boy?"

"I saw it the day I first saw you."

"Yes, but how'd you know it'd be there this time?"

"I didn't."

Miguel raised one dark eyebrow and appraised Jonah. "Don't matter. You're here now. She'll be happy about that."

"Who'll be happy?"

"The sea, o'course." Miguel gave one of his hearty laughs, but when he turned back to look at Jonah there appeared a touch of sadness in his eyes.

"I didn't come for the sea," Jonah said.

"Then for what?"

Jonah had wanted Miguel to fix everything. To put the fish back, to repair the town, to fix all the damage Jonah was certain Miguel had caused. He'd wanted him to make it okay for Jonah and his mother to live in peace. But as he looked at the pirate, Jonah realized that couldn't be. The damage had already been done and could not be undone. His mother was right. You can't change the past. There was nothing to do but to move forward. His shoulders sagged at his own folly.

"Seems mighty foolish to risk stowing away on my ship if you don't want anything," Miguel said when Jonah remained quiet. His father walked over to a small writing desk near the porthole. He appeared to be fiddling with something while his back was to Jonah. "Especially seeing as there's no land in sight."

A knot formed in Jonah's stomach as the implications of the remark hit home. Miguel would have him thrown overboard!

Jonah's mind filled with thoughts of his mother. His heart ached as he thought about how she would be sick with worry for him. She had never wanted him to go near the water, and yet here he was, on a ship, with a pirate. He'd probably never see her again. He'd die without her ever knowing.

Miguel turned around, a small, silver box in his hand. "Tell ya what boy," he said, "seeing as you're my boy, I'll let ya stick around." He eyed Jonah carefully, as if trying to see something deeper in him. "For now."

The pirate's long stare made Jonah uncomfortable and he dropped his eyes to the box in Miguel's hands. It looked like a woman's fancy jewelry box. However, a woman's jewelry box in the hands of a pirate didn't make much sense to Jonah. He knew pirates liked treasure, lots of it. He suspected they'd steal just about anything if given the chance. Given that the box was silver, Jonah figured the pirate might have pilfered it for its value. Still, to keep the box on the ship? That didn't fit with pirate tales. And the way Miguel handled the box indicated it had sentimental value, but he knew pirates were not sentimental. Which meant only one thing. The box was important, and its value was not in the silver.

Miguel looked down at the box as if just remembering it was in his hands. "It's more than a box, boy," he said, the gentleness of his father returning. He turned and returned it to the desk where he locked it in one of the drawers.

"You'll be bunkin' here with me," Miguel said.

Jonah, whose back was still just inches away from the locked door, glanced around him. The space itself wasn't too bad. It was well lit with oil lamps, and two hammocks, one above the other, hung to one side across from the desk where Miguel currently stood. There was a small circular table in the center of the cabin, between Jonah and Miguel. On it lay several rolled scrolls, and a map spread out on top. If it wasn't for the pirate captain, Jonah thought he might not actually mind this room.

"You'll be bunkin' here with me," Miguel repeated, this time swinging around with a feather pen dripping with ink. "So long's you do as you're told, there won't be any trouble."

Jonah wasn't sure if he should take that as a threat or be comforted that the captain wasn't planning his demise just yet. Neither thought made his jelly legs feel any more secure. What he needed was time. Time to figure out just what he was going to do now.

Miguel sat down on the small stool in front of the desk. Jonah could hear the scratch of a pen across the pages of a large book. He wondered what Miguel was writing but didn't feel brave enough to ask. Suddenly, he felt very tired. The last few days had finally caught up to him, and despite his reservations of spending his nights with the pirate captain, Jonah found the hammock inviting. He slowly made his way over to it and was soon sleeping soundly.

# Twenty-Three

The next few days were uneventful. Miguel would wake Jonah, and for a few minutes over breakfast, Miguel seemed like a caring father. But as breakfast would come to an end, there would be a shift, and the pirate would be there again; vicious and cruel. Sometimes Jonah thought he saw a bit of a struggle during the transformation, but he could never be sure. He enjoyed those few moments in the morning but learned quickly to do his best to stay out of the way for the rest of the day.

Jonah spent his time mostly doing menial things, like swabbing the deck. It was hard work, and Jonah found he tired easily. A few minutes at the rail with the fresh salt water spraying up around him was all it took for Jonah's sore muscles to be ready to go again. After several weeks at sea, Jonah had filled out nicely, the muscles he'd built at the farm now perfectly defined.

The ghost crew never again directly mentioned Jonah, accepting that the Captain had taken the boy on, though it seemed to Jonah most of them weren't too keen on having him around. There was a general sense of meanness that lingered about the ship; and it was not uncommon for members of the crew to mutter and cross themselves when they passed by Jonah. The sign and treatment weren't uncommon to him, though when he'd been on land it had generally been reserved for his mother. Now, as the pirates performed the sign, Jonah wondered why they felt the need to protect themselves. After all, they were pirates – the most feared beings on the sea.

"Never you mind them," Seward had told him once. "They's just superstitious."

"Most seamen are," Jonah had replied trying to shrug it off.

"Aye. Indeed they are." Seward had considered Jonah then. "But pirates – there's a bunch as seen a thing or two. Superstitious by nature, they be. Experience has taught them not to tempt the fates."

The first mate had left him to ponder the meaning of his words. It did not escape him that Seward hadn't explained what superstitions the crew feared, or how Jonah played into it. He generally kept his distance, avoiding the roughest of the crew whenever possible.

It wasn't as if he was planning on sticking around, though he'd already been on the ship for longer than he'd intended. Part of him was still hoping he'd figure out a way to convince Miguel to right everything back at Delmar. As impossible as he knew it was, Jonah also believed that if anyone could do it, it would be the pirate who had caused the trouble in the first place. But the longer he was on the ship, the less confident he felt about the results.

As the days turned into weeks, and the weeks turned into months, Jonah found a certain camaraderie with a select few of the ghostly crew. He was fascinated by the way they worked together during the day, then spent the evenings telling tales of adventures so fantastic Jonah could not tell truth from fiction. It was these moments that lifted Jonah's spirit, lightening the mood and allowing Jonah to feel a part of something bigger. It was exhilarating.

Every night after the tales had been spun and Jonah returned to the cabin, he'd find Miguel sitting at the desk. The pirate would remove the silver box, and, with his back to Jonah, do something with it. Then he'd scratch away in the book before the two would turn in.

"What are you doing?" Jonah ventured to ask one night. Though normally the angry pirate at this time of night, Miguel occasionally had nights where he teetered between father and pirate. Tonight was one such night, and Jonah had been around him long enough now that he dared to ask the question.

"Ship's log, boy," the pirate snarled back.

Jonah hesitated at the gruff voice before asking, "Ship's log?"

"Shoot, boy, you ain't meaning to tell me you don't know what a ship's log is?" It was the softer Miguel who responded. The one Jonah was being to recognize as the father he'd always wanted to know.

Jonah wasn't sure if he should admit that he didn't know what a ship's log was, uncertain if that would tip Miguel back to the angry pirate he normally was this time of night.

"See here, boy, every good captain keeps a ship's log. A record, see, of all the goings on of the day."

"Like a journal," Jonah said, happy to have something to relate it to.

Miguel gave a hearty chuckle. "Aye. Like a journal." He turned back to his work. "Don't you ever let me catch you messin' with it, though."

The edge had returned to Miguel's voice, and Jonah took it as his cue to slip into his hammock. It rocked lightly as the boy stared at the ropes of the hammock above him unable to drift to sleep right away. In his mind, Jonah considered the need for a ship's log and curiously wondered what the log would tell of the adventures such a ship full of ghostly pirates might tell. As his mind rolled over these thoughts, it turned to the silver jewelry box. Jonah didn't see how the silver box related to a journal. He glanced over at the man scribbling away. The harsh tone of his words was still fresh, and Jonah decided he'd pushed enough for one night and left the matter alone.

Jonah found himself very much awake. His thoughts roamed over the comings and goings of the ship. It roamed over things which seemed, to him, to be so very strange. In fact, he decided, there really was nothing normal about this ship. Not the crew. Not the captain. And certainly not about himself being on board. A strange tickling sensation began to creep over him. He wanted that log, certain now, that it held more than just daily happenings. He wanted to see what secrets it held. He wondered if it held answers – though to what questions, Jonah did not yet know. And, as he finally started to doze off, Jonah determined he would find a way to read it despite the warning Miguel had given him.

His eyelids grew heavy as these thoughts swirled through his mind. They gathered and spun, sinking deep into the haze that was somewhere between wakefulness and sleep; and they hung as if suspended from some great puppeteer ready to perform, or perhaps transform.

***

*He stood on an island, the hot sun hanging high in the sky. The sand underfoot was so white it glittered like diamonds. Jonah bent down and scooped some in his hand. It was hot against his skin, and he let it trail through his fingers back to the ground.*

*Straightening, Jonah noticed the palm trees in the distance. There were only a few, and spaced several feet apart, so their shadows did not reach one another. Sweat dripped down Jonah's brow. He wiped it away with the back of his hand. The shade of the palm trees looked very inviting, so Jonah began walking toward them.*

*After a while, he stopped and surveyed the area again. The palm trees did not appear to be any closer. The water was crystal blue, and if not for the ebb and flow of the ocean, would be perfectly still. Where were the birds? Where was the breeze? The gentle lap of water was the only sound. Was the island enchanted?*

*With that question in his mind, Jonah realized it was indeed an enchanted island. There was no other explanation for what was happening. No other reason why he seemed to be able to walk forever and never come closer to any of the palm trees and the relief they would provide. There was no other reason for the air to be so still.*

*The heat was intense, and Jonah could feel his skin burning. His whole body ached for relief. He turned and walked into the crystal water, expecting relief, but instead found himself in a warm pool. It did not cool his burnt skin, though it did not seem to make it worse. He looked out, away from the island, and noticed a ship in the distance. He wondered if the ship was coming toward him, and if it was, if it was friendly.*

*"'Tis the ghost ship, lad."*

*Jonah turned toward the voice at his right, and saw a shimmer in the air.*

*"It cannot come here, so it sits out at the mouth of the cove, uncertain where to steer."*

*"But why?" Jonah asked.*

*"It is forbidden. The Island chooses who can come and who can go."*

*"Why am I here?"*

*The air stirred, and the shimmering began to take on stronger light.*

*"You are here to learn. There is much you need to know."*

***

"Wake-up, Boy!"

Jonah groaned and shifted in his hammock.

"The day won't wait," Miguel's voice prodded.

As Jonah opened his eyes, a deep forceful throb pounded against his skull, causing him to cry out. He closed his eyes tightly, trying to shut out the pain.

"Bad night, son?"

The dream sprang back to Jonah's mind. The island, the enchantment, and the shimmering air. It had seemed so real. He shook his head to try to clear it. "Yeah. I guess."

"Looks like you've got a powerful headache. Let's get something in yer stomach there and see if it helps."

Jonah didn't feel like eating. He just wanted to return to his hammock, but he figured once his father turned into the pirate captain again, he wouldn't have the luxury of that option. He swung his legs over the hammock and let them dangle there for a moment. His father brought him a mug of something warm, and he sipped at it. It tasted like spiced cider, but Jonah could not place it with surety. After a few sips, he made his way to the small table and began to nibble the bread and cheese provided. He was surprised to find that eating and drinking helped tremendously; and by the time they had finished he was feeling nearly as good as new.

"Tell me how you met my ma?" Jonah ventured.

Miguel set his mug down. A faraway look came over him, softening his features even further. "Your ma was an angel. I knew the day I met her I wanted to live the rest of my life with her." He blinked and looked more clearly at Jonah. "She was the prettiest girl around for miles. The first time I saw her was at the schoolhouse. Her family had recently moved to the area, so she was new to us. She outshone all the regular girls, and right then I knew she was the one. So I set my books on the seat beside her. She pretended not to notice, though I reckon she was watching me even then from the side." Miguel chuckled softly to himself.

"Did she feel the same?"

"Don't know, for sure. She wouldn't let me court her right away. It was torture watching her go walking out with those other blokes. But I was persistent. In the end, I think that's how I won her over."

"Did she know? You know…. about…."

"Naw." Miguel shook his head sadly. "I didn't even know. Sure sorry it turned out the way it did, but can't says as though I would have done anything differently had I known. Your ma was one of a kind."

There was a twitch at the corner of Miguel's left eye. There wasn't much time left with his father this day.

"I wish I could have known you then," Jonah said feeling the longing that penetrated deep within him for the loss of a father.

"Shall be a good day," Miguel sneered, and Jonah knew the pirate was back. "Yes, a good day! I can feel it in me bones!" He turned toward Jonah with a wicked grin. "You'll see, boy. Today'll be a good day!"

# Twenty-Four

The day was bright, and the water calm. It seemed like every other day to Jonah, but the captain was making it clear he did not believe this was an ordinary day. He kept checking his time piece, glancing upward at the sky, and checking the sails. The ghost crew had taken their cue from him and were scurrying around the ship as though there were too many things to accomplish.

"Watch it, boy!"

"Better get back to the cabin with those."

"Bring me more rope."

"Outta the way!"

The ghost crew was as snappy as the captain, and it seemed nothing Jonah did was quite good enough. He was always under foot and in the way. It was troubling to Jonah, who had only just managed to get a sense of how things ran from day to day. As it turned out, the day was anything but ordinary, and yet Jonah could see no reason for it.

"Straight ahead!" came the call from the crow's nest.

Jonah squinted ahead but could not make anything out.

Miguel took out his telescope and placed it against his eye. "Aye! There she is!" There was great joy in the way Miguel said it. A greedy excitement only a pirate could have.

Jonah's stomach sank. He didn't know what they were talking about, but he didn't like the sound of it either. A feeling of foreboding sank heavily upon him, and he found himself wishing he wasn't on the pirate ship.

"Now we'll see what you're really made of!" Miguel said, a gleam in his eye.

The pit in Jonah's stomach doubled in size.

"'Tis excitin', ain't it, boy!"

"What's exciting, sir?" he dared to ask.

"Wait and see. Wait and see." The pirate's eyes glittered with excited malice, increasing the dread that was growing within Jonah.

Throughout the next hour, Miguel kept checking his telescope. He'd rattle off a simple command, and then look again. Jonah tried to keep himself busy, but there was nothing for him to do. Miguel would not let him leave his side, so Jonah stood with the pirate at the helm feeling completely useless and inadequate.

By the end of the hour, Jonah could just make out a speck on the water. He doubted it was land, as he knew enough to know that the man in the crow's nest would have called out "land ho" long before now. Which meant it had to be something else in the water; and there was only one thing that would be this far out at sea. It had to be another ship.

His stomach sank down into his feet as the feel weight of realization hit him. He was on a pirate ship. Even he, with his limited knowledge of ships, knew what pirates did. Jonah hadn't considered that being on a pirate ship might mean he'd have to experience pirate life firsthand. At least not the part that included plundering other ships. In fact, he hadn't considered much of anything before he'd decided to board this ship. He'd been impulsive, foolhardy, thinking he could confront Miguel and make everything right again.

"Ready the ship!" Miguel called out.

Jonah couldn't see anything else left to prepare. He'd watched the men scurry around all morning, racing along the deck, up and down the ratlines, and back and forth through the hull. He suspected there was little left to do now but to light the fuses and set off the canons, although even he knew they were too far away for that.

"Frigate, sir?" Heckel called back.

"Indeed!"

The ship burst to life with a flash of movement. With all the commotion, Jonah hoped he might be able to steal away. He was not looking forward to what was sure to come. When Miguel next lifted his telescope, Jonah began taking slow steps back away from him. He was just reaching the steps to descend to the lower deck when Miguel spun around.

"Don't you go nowhere, boy! You won't wanna miss this show. T'aint no better view than right here!" There was excitement ablaze in the pirate's eyes.

Jonah had no choice but to stay. He made his way back to Miguel's side.

"Atta boy!" Miguel sneered.

"Ship's ready, sir!" Seward announced a moment latter.

"Very good." The red gleam in Miguel's eye blazed like fire. He turned back to the ship and called out, "Stand ready!"

Every pirate on the ship stopped what he was doing. Every one of them stood perfectly still. Their solid forms shifted, shimmering in and out, as they became the ghost wisps Jonah had remembered seeing that first day. Then Miguel stood with arms open wide as he'd done when he'd changed from pirate to farmer and back again.

He tipped his head back. Salt water crashed up along the side of the ship. Larger and larger came the waves. Water rushed under Jonah's feet. And still Miguel stood, head tipped high, arms open wide. Strangely, the water was not retreating off the ship. It was pooling at the pirate captain's feet.

Once the water reached a foot deep, Miguel finally opened his eyes. A fierce, piercing look speared through Jonah, making him feel cold to the core. Miguel thrust his arms down, and the water rose up around him. It circled him like a cyclone. Jonah could feel the spray as it came around. And then, as suddenly, Miguel forced the water away from him. It collapsed, like a lost waterfall, drifting off the upper deck, down along the lower, and back out to sea.

As the water raced back to join the ocean, the great ship shuddered. It groaned with a sound like tormented sailors, the ghosts of which haunt the deep. The ship shook so violently Jonah was certain it would break apart. He braced his feet against the floor, hoping it would not split right between them, and waited for what he was certain was inevitable doom.

Wind swirled around him as it built up pressure. The ship pushed in against itself, becoming long and narrow. Like Miguel had done the first time Jonah had seen him, the ship was now changing into something else.

The groaning stopped, and the ship's speed increased significantly. Jonah could feel the rush of the wind as it cut through the water. The speck in the distance was quickly growing larger, and as it did, it began to take shape. It was indeed a large ship, and they were gaining on it much faster than they should be able.

Looking around him, he saw the narrowed ship was no longer the beautiful pirate war vessel it had begun as. It was now a vessel designed for speed. The ship had become a frigate. The pirate crew would overtake the other ship before the sun began to set.

# Twenty-Five

It took less than two hours for the frigate to reach the merchant ship. The difference in their traveling speed made it seem as if the brigantine was waiting for them; though Jonah was certain that if they had any idea who was on this frigate, they would have made all haste to get away. As it was, the merchant ship was sailing at its normal speed, no doubt laden with trade goods.

As the frigate came up alongside the brigantine, it shuddered violently as it made tremendous transformation back to its original form. Ocean water surged upward all around the ship, masking the transformation. Ghost pirates shimmered just beyond the realm of this world, waiting to be called back to their ship. The frigate, like the pirate ship had done before, groaned with a torturous sound as it pushed its way back to its full size. It rose up, out of the water, to tower over the unsuspecting ship.

Jonah noted the shock on the faces of the merchant's crew as they took in the transformation. If Jonah hadn't seen it happen before, he wouldn't have believed it either. Shock quickly turned to fear as realization of the pirates spread. Before they could sound the warning, cannons from the pirate ship exploded into the side of the brigantine, breaking the hull wide open.

Ghost pirates materialized into solid form, springing into

action. Many jumped aboard the merchant ship along with their captain. Swords met swords. Pistol shots rang out, filling the air with smoke. More cannons were fired; and more of the merchant ship's timber exploded into the air.

Miguel pulled his own sword out and used it to motion the crew forward. "Come on, then," he hollered as he leapt over the rail of the helm to the lower deck, grabbed a loose rope and swung onboard the now helpless merchant ship.

Jonah was too terrified to move. He stood watching it all unfold before him, as helpless as the merchant's crew. He thought he was going to be sick as he saw a sailor topple over the edge of the ship with a sword stuck through his stomach. Just as the man fell forward, a pirate grabbed the hilt and pulled the sword free. He grinned a wicked, blood-thirsty grin, thrust his sword up in the air toward Jonah as if in salute, and turned back toward the battle.

Jonah turned away and vomited.

When he'd come aboard the pirate ship, he had only hoped to make things better for his mother. He'd had no idea what being here would really entail. Now he was stuck in the middle of a bloodthirsty battle. His stomach heaved again, insisting that the last of its contents join the rest on the upper deck. Jonah obliged, then crawled to the barrels where he'd hidden before. He pulled his knees up under his chin, and for the first time in several years, Jonah cried.

The noise of the attack continued to boom around him. Bits of wood flew near, landing on the deck and splashing in the water. Bloody screams filled the air as more lives were cut short. Gun powder and smoke clouded everything. The scent swirled around Jonah burning his nostrils.

Eventually, boots sounded on the deck as pirates returned from their looting. Their voices were filled with loud laughter as they recounted the glory of their attack. The commotion forced Jonah to pull himself together. He wiped at his face with the back of his hands. It wouldn't do for the pirates to see him crying. It would only add to the mounting frustration of having Jonah on board the ship.

And then there was the captain to face.

He hoped Miguel hadn't noticed his lack of appearance among the chaos of the attack itself. He was certain that if Miguel noticed, it would only add to the anger Jonah was sure the mean pirate felt toward him. Maybe Miguel, the pirate, would turn his cruel, merciless character on Jonah and force him to walk the plank. The thought terrified Jonah.

He decided to wait until things settled down some before making his appearance. Having not been part of the carnage, Jonah knew he would have nothing to add to the string of vile remarks. If he was lucky he'd be able to slip below to his bunk without being noticed.

"Better getcha outta there afore the Captain gets back." The sound of Seward's voice startled Jonah. He hadn't realized anyone knew where he was. "No need to look so surprised. You ain't the first young rat to take cover during an attack."

The information was a surprise to Jonah. It had never occurred to him that anyone else on a pirate ship might not be hungering for a bloodbath. Pirates were pirates after all, and wasn't that what pirates did?

"Come on, then," Seward said holding his hand out toward Jonah.

Jonah took the weathered hand fully preparing to be pulled out and shamed. What choice did he have? He'd already been found out.

But when Seward led him out from behind the barrels, Jonah was surprised, and relieved, to find the other pirates not paying him any attention.

"Don't worry 'bout them," Seward said, "they don't care what you're up to right now. They're just happy to have had a little excitement. Doesn't happen as often as ya might think. Come on, now."

Seward led Jonah back to the cabin. Jonah was reluctant to go inside. Once again it seemed Seward could read his mind. "Don't worry, boy. Captain ain't here just now."

Jonah cautiously peeked into the cabin. Sure enough, it was empty. Jonah was grateful for that. Hopefully he'd have some time before Miguel came back. As much as he didn't like the pirate, there was a part of him that wanted his father to be proud of him.

"Seward, do you think…you know… that you could teach me?"

"Yup. We'll start tomorrow."

"Why are you doing this?" Jonah asked him.

"Been around a time or two. You're not the first one I've trained, boy. Tain't any shame in needing a little help." The pirate's weathered face was soft around the eyes. There was no judgement or malice. Just a general grandfatherly kindness, if a pirate could be grandfatherly. It felt strange amid the chaos of the pirates.

Seward left Jonah with his thoughts. His emotions were all over the place, and he had a foul taste in his mouth that was more than the bile left behind from his vomit. He didn't approve of the pirate life, but he was glad to know he'd be learning to defend himself. It would never do to be on a pirate ship without some skill in that department. And maybe, just maybe, he might earn the respect of his father.

# Twenty-Six

The dream started almost immediately.

*The strange, enchanted island came out of the fog racing toward Jonah until he thought it would hit him. Instead, Jonah found himself on the burning sand once again. The heat was so intense. The shady trees were off in the distance just as before. Once again, he felt the desire, the need, to reach their shade. But like before, when Jonah tried to walk toward it, he never got any closer. The trees were always just as far away.*

What's the point? *Jonah thought.*

*"Why do you ask?" The voice from before was back. Jonah turned toward it and found the area next to him shimmering.*

*"I didn't actually ask anything," Jonah said testily.*

*"First lesson: just because you keep it in your head does not mean it has not been said." The light took on strong, firm lines. The shimmering became an intense glow.*

*"Why am I here?"*

*"I told you before. You're here to learn."*

*Jonah was annoyed. He'd had a long day, and now he was stuck in that weird dream he'd had before. He wasn't in the mood for games.*

*"You brought me to this place, to this heat, why? To have me burn up? The only shade around is under those trees over there, and yet there is no*

*way to get to them. What's the point? Why bring a person to this waste of an island only to taunt him with what he cannot have?" Even in his dream, Jonah felt his irritation clearly.*

*"There is nothing here one cannot gain if he only tries." The glow fell away leaving an old man standing before Jonah. His grey beard was so long it nearly brushed the sand, and he leaned against a tall staff, though it was apparent this was not from a need to hold himself up. "Lesson number two: don't expect anything worthwhile to come easily."*

*A light breeze danced across the beach. The low waves of the ocean rushed up the sand tickling Jonah's bare feet. Though the water wasn't cool, there was a sense of relief from the scorching heat, then the waves retreated.*

*"Look out there," the old man said pointing his staff out toward the horizon. Jonah's eyes followed the direction of the staff. "What do you see?"*

*At first Jonah didn't see anything on the water. He squinted trying to see something further out. There was a thick fog rolling in toward the island; and amid the fog there was also a speck. A dark, unshapely speck. It really wasn't identifiable, but Jonah knew it must be a ship as nothing else would be out in the vast ocean.*

*"Fog mostly. A ship maybe," he told the old man.*

*"It's the* Mary Margaret. *Do you know what ship that is?"*

*Jonah shrugged. He had never paid much attention to the names of ships coming in and out of port back in Delmar, and he knew there were many more in the numerous ports around there as well. The ship really could have been any one of them for all he knew.*

*"That, dear boy, is your father's ship."*

*Those words hit Jonah like a stab at his gut. He didn't know why that knowledge should affect him the way it did. He hadn't paid attention* to the name of the ship he'd been sailing on for the past several weeks; and he wasn't particularly fond of the ship or the people – could you call them people – on it.

"It sails on as though on an aimless mission, but it is not so aimless. Sit and watch."

Jonah sat with the old man on the beach watching the ship a long time as it moved through the fog and closer to the island. At the point that Jonah could finally make out the full shape of the ship, he noticed a change in the fog. It had been rolling in like ordinary white fog, gentle and smooth, but now began to swirl in grey strips, like a series of ropes tying themselves together.

"What's happening to the fog?" Jonah asked.

The wizard stood. "The island's enchanted. The Mary Margaret's not allowed here. Your father searches far and wide for this island. The fog is forming a barrier to prevent him from coming here."

Jonah looked at the old man leaning on his staff. His eyes were a cloudy grey, as if storms were always rolling in them. He was looking out at the fog with an intent glare which was oddly familiar. "Who are you?" Jonah asked.

"I am Sachlavar, keeper of the island."

"Are you doing this? Are you controlling the fog?"

"Now there are some decent questions," Sachlavar said. "No. I am not. Could I? Yes, I suppose I could if it were necessary, but it is not. I told you, the island is enchanted. It knows how to take care of itself."

Jonah considered this. He had witnessed enchantments aboard the Mary Margaret and even back at Delmar, thanks to his father. Why not an enchanted island? Because the whole thing was too fantastic – supernatural – and Jonah knew he was dreaming. Then again, anything could happen in a dream.

"You're not dreaming," Sachlavar interrupted his thoughts. "Not really."

"You read minds?" Jonah asked incredulously. "Of course you do," he answered himself.

Sachlavar shrugged. "It's a curse, really, but it has its perks."

Jonah didn't know what to make of the wizard or the situation he was in. Nothing about this made sense, so it had to be a dream. But what if it wasn't?

"What do you want with me?" he asked.

"To teach you." Sachlavar turned and began walking down the beach. "Come."

Jonah wasn't sure why he decided to follow Sachlavar. It might have been the curiosity of the old man. It might have been that he really wanted to know why his father's ship could not come to this island. It might only have been because somewhere in his mind he believed it was just a dream, but even in a dream it was better to be doing something than standing around doing nothing. The only thing he knew for certain was that he felt compelled to follow the man. It seemed the further away the old man went, the stronger the urge was to follow him. He could continue to sit and stare at the now grey wall blocking his view of the Mary Margaret, or he could follow Sachlavar.

He only took five steps before he found himself walking beside Sachlavar. The wizard kept walking as if Jonah had been beside him all along. Jonah glanced behind him and found the spot he'd been at before was quite a distance away. It should have taken a lot more than five steps to catch up with the old man.

Together they approached the shady trees, which Jonah gratefully noticed were getting closer. When Jonah had first seen them from a distance, they had looked more like palm trees. Now, as they approached, they appeared more leafy than ordinary palm trees. They were unlike any trees Jonah had ever seen.

There was a small table laid out with marvelous foods in the shade. Two wooden chairs positioned next to next to the table. Sachlavar motioned for Jonah to take one. The canopy of the trees shut out the heat of the burning sun, and the gentle breeze that lingered made the little oasis feel perfect.

"Go ahead, help yourself," the wizard told Jonah gesturing to the food before him. "You'll think better on a full stomach."

Jonah's stomach growled as he looked over the meat pasties, fruits, and pies. He hadn't seen food like this since before he left Delmar. A plate appeared in front of him and he began to place food on it. The meal tantalized his taste buds and nourished his belly, exactly what he needed. The more he ate, the more food appeared. He wished he could keep eating, but like all stomachs, his was eventually full. Jonah was certain he'd never eaten so well in his whole life.

It wasn't until he leaned back in his chair that he realized Sachlavar hadn't taken so much as a bite. Immediately his mind went to the worst possible reason the old man would not have eaten with him. Poison.

Jonah's face paled as he asked, "Why didn't you eat?"

The old man chuckled softly before answering. "Don't worry, it's not poisoned. Wizards don't need sustenance like humans. We're immortal."

"Do you ever eat?"

"Not often." Sachlavar motioned at the table. "Have you eaten all you desire?"

Jonah patted his stomach wishing he could eat more. "My stomach couldn't hold another bite. It was very good. The best I've ever eaten."

Sachlavar smiled. "Since you've had your fill, we best get down to business. We haven't much time left." With that, he raised his staff, and the *food disappeared leaving a plain wooden table before them.*

"Do you know where you come from, Jonah?"

After their conversation on the beach, Jonah was taken back by the normalcy of the question. "Sure. Delmar," he replied.

"It is good to know where you grew up, but what I meant was do you know your heritage?"

Jonah thought for a moment. His mother was from an old fishing port, but Jonah didn't know its name, or even where it was located. He only knew she'd grown up in one because she'd mentioned always living by the sea. Her family was a mystery to Jonah as he'd never spent any time with them. He didn't even know their names. As for his father, all he knew was that he was the strange man who had shown up out of the blue one morning, and turned out to be the disconcerting pirate, Miguel. Somehow, he didn't think that this lack of information was what Sachlavar was interested in.

"Well?" the wizard asked, eyebrows raised slightly.

Jonah didn't want to admit that he didn't. He didn't want to look stupid in front of the wizard, though he didn't know why that should matter if this was only a dream.

"It's not a dream, Jonah," Sachlavar interjected reminding Jonah that his thoughts were not his alone to hear. "Heritage is important. Knowing it is valuable."

Jonah considered his words before replying. "My ma came from some fishing village, but I don't know anything about it. Or about her family," he added. "When she moved to Delmar, she never talked about anyone from her past." Jonah suddenly felt guilty. He should have pressed his ma for information over the years. Now he felt like he was missing something; and he felt embarrassed for the connection to Miguel, who apparently wasn't allowed on this enchanted island.

*"And your father? What do you know of him and his people?"*

*"Nothing. Not really," Jonah admitted. "I only met him a few months ago. Even then I didn't know he was my father. Not for many weeks after." Jonah thought back over those months, the strangeness of it all and the unexpected revelation on the beach. "I really don't know much. I know he's a pirate." Jonah didn't add that he'd seen his father change into that very pirate, or that he'd witnessed his whole ship transform as well. There were some things that, even in a dream on an enchanted island, Jonah couldn't bring himself to share. Things which should be impossible but weren't.*

*"Your father is indeed a pirate. A very powerful, and strange, pirate. Among our people, he is known as the Pirate King. A unique individual with the power to control the ocean and all things related to it. You have seen this power?"*

*Jonah nodded.*

*"The night is growing old, and morning will be upon us soon. We don't have much time. Come. There is something I need to show you before you go."*

*Sachlavar and Jonah stood up from the table. As the wizard raised his staff, the wind picked up in a circular motion, and a strange tickling sensation crept over Jonah's skin. Like a blanket, the wind wrapped tightly around him, lifting him into the air, and then all became black.*

*The whirring in his ears told him he was still conscious, but it wasn't until the sound stopped and the wind died away that Jonah saw he'd been transported to the mouth of a cave. He was standing 100 feet above the ocean on a ledge that jutted out over the water below. The cave was set back and looked ordinary from where Jonah stood.*

*Sachlavar appeared beside him. "This cave houses some of the most well-kept secrets of all the world. Only a select few ever have the privilege to come here. Fewer still have the privilege of entering inside and learning* its secrets. With secrets comes great responsibility."

"Why am I here?"

"This is your heritage. This cave holds the secrets of your family's past."

"I don't understand," Jonah said just as the air around him began to shiver.

"We are out of time. You must be going now." The wizard became transparent, the glow returning as the air began to shimmer. "You will understand in time. For now, be careful. Don't do anything rash."

"Wait!" Intrigue had ignited curiosity, and it felt wholly unfair that Jonah wouldn't have the opportunity to explore the cave.

Without warning, Sachlavar disappeared as the ledge dropped out from under Jonah, causing him to descend into a dark mist.

# Twenty-Seven

Jonah woke with a start. Sweat laced his forehead. The throbbing headache was worse this time. He held his head in his hands, hoping for some relief, but there wasn't any. Light poured in through the porthole, and though it was not a large hole, it felt as though the whole room was blinded with light.

The door banged open. "Where were ya, boy?" Miguel stood framed in the entrance with his sword still securely in his hand.

Jonah blinked trying to place what time of day it was, or even what day it was. He looked at the pirate wondering what he should say.

"Ya missed a good show!" The pirate's eyes narrowed in a menacing way. "You weren't hidin' away, were ya boy?" The nasty way Miguel spoke to him gave Jonah the impression there was no right answer. Instead of saying anything, Jonah rubbed his still throbbing head.

"Head hurtin'?"

Jonah looked up to meet Miguel's eyes. He saw the struggle between father and pirate flash through them. It was fleeting, and the pirate won, but Jonah was certain he'd seen his father surface briefly. He nodded hesitantly.

"No time for that. Buck up!" Miguel said, slapping Jonah on the back causing his head to throb harder. "We've work to do!"

Jonah had no choice but to go back out on deck. It took a great deal of will power not to reach up and cradle his head as he stood.

"Well, boy," the pirate snapped prodding him in the back with his sword to get him moving.

Jonah flinched, but managed to quicken his steps so as to avoid another jab in the back. There was no telling when that sword might run him through instead of hurrying him along.

Up on deck everything appeared as it always was. The ghost pirates, no longer shimmering flecks of light, were busy tending the ropes and sails. Seward was at the helm steering the ship in some direction unknown to Jonah. They were in the middle of the vast blue ocean with nothing in sight once again. There was no evidence of the carnage and destruction that had last greeted him.

Miguel pushed Jonah toward the bridge. "Time to earn your keep, boy," the pirate said with a rough chuckle. Jonah knew better than to question the captain, so he made his way to Seward.

"Dismissed," Miguel told Seward as he took over the wheel.

Seward nodded and half bowed. He gave Jonah a sympathetic glance as he turned and made his way to the lower deck.

"It's time you learned the important parts of commanding a ship, boy."

Jonah had no idea why the captain would want him to learn how to command a ship. He looked at the pirate, and once again saw the struggle between father and pirate. Maybe that was it. Maybe it was the father coming out. Or maybe this was what Seward meant about training him. He certainly hoped not. Spending more time with the pirate version of his father was not something Jonah wanted to do. He glanced at Seward but saw no hint of an answer there.

For the rest of the day Miguel instructed Jonah in the finer points of steering a ship. It seemed simple, but when Jonah took the wheel and Miguel let go, Jonah found it difficult to control. The ocean tried to pull the ship with the current, but Miguel insisted Jonah keep the ship in a straight path, cutting directly through the natural flow of the water. Jonah was certain this was madness and that no other ship would have been able to accomplish such a task.

It didn't take long for his arms to ache. His grip was deathly tight, and his knuckles were so cold from the spray he was sure they were frozen in place. Although the muscles in his hands and arms screamed and burned, Jonah didn't dare relax his fingers for fear the wheel would pull him over. About the time he thought his muscles would give out, Miguel took hold of the wheel.

"Enough for one day," Miguel told him as he took over. "Dismissed."

Jonah stepped away and rubbed his arms. They were too sore for Jonah to care that Miguel hadn't offered him any praise. As he walked back toward the lower deck stairs, Jonah realized even his legs hurt. They felt like jelly from standing and holding the wheel for so long. He had known his arms hurt, but he had no idea, until he started walking, that it had taken every last muscle in his body to keep the wheel straight, and the ship on course.

Looking forward to a reprieve, and not caring that his stomach was growling, Jonah headed toward his bunk in the captain's quarters. He was nearly to the door when Seward stopped him.

"You did well today."

"Thanks," Jonah replied, too tired to really care.

"Where ya headin'?"

Jonah looked at the door to his bunk.

"Not thinking 'bout beddin' down now, are ya?" Seward questioned.

"Actually, yeah." He wouldn't have dared to give that reply had it been Miguel, but there was something about Seward that made Jonah feel he could be himself.

"Did you forget about our training, lad?"

"Thought you said we weren't startin' till tomorrow."

Seward chuckled and smacked Jonah on the back, causing Jonah to wince. "No time like the present. Grab a bite in the galley and meet me below on the gun deck." Seward let out another hearty chuckle as he headed down the narrow passage.

Maybe he didn't like Seward after all.

He wasn't thrilled with the new instructions. His body hurt, and he wanted nothing more than to sleep. The thought of his hammock was tempting, but he feared he might offend Seward. In the end, he decided it was best not to offend the one person who didn't treat him like scum for being on board the ship.

# Twenty-Eight

The gun deck was aptly named as it had line after line of cannons. Each was positioned near an open hole in the side of the ship, which stood several feet above the water line. The cannons were held in place with large, thick ropes to keep them from rolling; and stacks of cannonballs lay waiting beside each one. There wasn't much space left after all that.

"I see ya made it," Seward called out from the far side of the deck. It was dark now, and Seward had lit several lanterns hung at intervals along the ceiling. "Ready to start yer training?"

Jonah didn't know what he was getting himself into, and wasn't sure if he should say yes or no. He was still tired, and his body still ached, though having stopped by the galley, he was no longer hungry. Having convinced himself to come, he nodded his head in the affirmative.

"Good. Good."

Seward turned around and grabbed a couple of swords from a space in the wall. Turning back around, he tossed one of the swords to Jonah who jumped out of the way. The sword clattered on the floorboards.

"Bad form, Jonah. Bad form. First lesson, never let your sword hit the ground." Seward positioned himself in the combat stance, sword extended, knees slightly bent. "Now pick it up," he growled.

This was a new side of Seward. One Jonah hadn't seen before and it frightened him enough to spur him to action. He picked up the sword and found it was surprisingly heavy. Or at least it felt heavy with Jonah's weakened muscles.

"Stand like I am, boy."

Jonah tried to lift his sword outward like Seward. He bent his knees a little and felt them start to buckle. His sword drooped in his hand.

"Now that's a sorry picture!" Seward said with a hearty laugh.

If Jonah hadn't been so tired, he would have been angry. He was certain he was a sorry sight, probably would have been without the sore muscles. Still, he didn't have the energy to be mad.

"En garde."

Jonah tried to mimic Seward's stance. He raised his sword to the ready. His arm started shaking. He reached up with his other hand, placing both hands on the hilt to steady it, but the tip continued to droop.

"That won't do," Seward said. He dropped his sword arm and walked over to Jonah. He set his sword against one of the cannons and began to help Jonah properly position his arm. Every time Seward would position Jonah's sword arm and let go, Jonah's arm would shake and the sword would droop. No adjustments to Jonah's stance or his balancing arm helped.

Finally, Seward stepped back. "Can't train tonight, boy. You're as floppy as an eel." Seward looked Jonah over. "How long'd Captain have ya at the wheel today?"

Hours. Lots of hours. The sun had been just past midday when he'd started, and it was past supper when he'd stopped. Granted, he hadn't held the wheel the entire time, but he figured he'd held it most of the time. "Most of the afternoon, sir."

"'Twas yer first time!" Seward swore and shook his head. "Ain't been so long as he can't remember," he muttered, then swore again.

"Wait here," he told Jonah as he headed back across the deck.

Jonah was too tired to argue. He slumped to the floor where he was, sword resting beside him. He leaned his head against one of the cannons and closed his eyes. The dark was welcoming, enveloping him like a blanket. He must have dozed off, because the next thing he knew he had woken to the feeling of something wet and slimy against his skin. He jerked his arm back, immediately sorry he did as his muscles screamed at him.

Seward leaned over him.

"What are you doing?" Jonah demanded, forgetting his decision not to offend the man.

"Helpin' ya. Now hold still." Seward took a slimy green plant in his hands and began wrapping it around Jonah's upper arm.

"What is this stuff? It looks like seaweed."

"It is."

Jonah looked at the seaweed now being wrapped around his arm. It was cool and slimy against his skin. He couldn't imagine how this would help him.

Seward must have sensed his thoughts because he began to explain. "The seaweed will help your muscles heal faster." He continued to take strips of the plant and wrap them around Jonah's arms. "Just a little pirate magic."

Pirate magic. Great. Just what Jonah needed. He'd seen what pirate magic could do and never had he seen it benefit anyone. He jerked his arm away. "How's this supposed to help?" he demanded, pointing at the seaweed gingerly with his other hand.

"It'll strengthen your muscles, help them recover." Seward reached out and took Jonah's arm back. He continued to layer seaweed wraps around Jonah's arms, all the while shaking his head, muttering to himself.

"What?" Jonah asked.

"Huh? Oh. Nothing. Never you mind."

Once Seward had finished wrapping Jonah's arms, he began to wrap Jonah's legs. It was strange, but the cool feel of the seaweed did seem to make his muscles ache a little less.

Seward finished and sat back. "Your father shouldn't have pushed you this far. You're lucky, ya know."

"What makes me lucky?" Jonah asked, pondering for a moment how Seward knew Miguel was his father.

"Seaweed only helps those with the power. It don't do a fig for normal people. This will help you heal faster."

"I haven't got any powers," Jonah spat out, a hint of anger at the edge of his voice. "And what makes you think he's my father?" The fact that these things would allow him to heal faster with the aid of the seaweed didn't factor into his emotional outburst.

Seward blinked. "I told ya before, boy. I've trained many in my day." The old man gathered up the fishing basket he'd carried the seaweed in and stood. "I've known your father since the day he was chosen. The power's there, Jonah; it chooses who it wants. Your father was chosen." Seward shook his head. "No matter now. Let's get you settled. Can't have you going back covered in seaweed."

Jonah's mind filled with questions. First Sachlavar, now Seward. He'd not considered before that his father had a past worth exploring. Or that there might be someone willing to tell him. He opened his mouth trying to find the right words to form a question, but there were just too many swarming him at once.

"Never you mind, now," Seward said in response to Jonah's unspoken questions. "I'll answer your questions, boy. Just not tonight. You need to rest. We'll leave ya down here for tonight."

Seward helped Jonah to a corner of the gun deck where a couple of gunny sacks were laid out. "It tain't much, but it'll do till you're better."

Jonah wanted to argue, but another wave of exhaustion ran over him. "Thank you, Seward."

"Me pleasure, boy."

# Twenty-Nine

Jonah's sleep was fitful. He felt like he was floating underwater. His body seemed to drift along, his shaggy hair floating around him, and his muscles no longer ached. It seemed to him that his lungs ought to be burning, that he ought to be trying to breathe, gulping down tons of water, and drowning. And yet he floated along, not needing to breathe, not feeling any pain.

*Everything around him sparkled from the sunlight that streamed down through the crystal-clear water. It had the same enchanted feel as the island he'd visited in his earlier dreams. Jonah drifted along, waiting for something or someone to emerge and tell him where he was, and why he was there.*

*After a time, a pink bubble appeared beside him, small at first, then growing larger. Jonah watched as it expanded, growing increasingly more pink, until it was the size of himself. It drifted along beside him, apparently caught in the current just as he was. Over time, the dark pink began to fade as it became more and more translucent. Eventually the bubble burst, throwing tiny pink bubbles out into the water around him.*

*Why did the bubbles have to be pink?*

*"Would you prefer green?"*

*The tiny pink bubbles immediately changed to green.*

*Jonah blinked. Where the large bubble had been, a mermaid now floated. Her golden hair was glittering with jewels as it drifted out around her, and her tail glistened like emeralds. Jonah had never seen anything so beautiful. As she gently swam along beside him, keeping pace with the current so as not to move ahead or behind, he had the vague notion that mermaids weren't real. Which meant he had to be dreaming again.*

*"Who are you?" He asked, surprised to hear his own voice under water. "And how am I speaking under water?"*

*"I am Meranna," she said in a singsong voice that blended perfectly with the water. "Sachlavar sent me."*

*Jonah remembered the wizard quite well. He felt certain there was more the old man wanted to tell him, but their time had been cut short. Thoughts of the cave came to his mind. There was something significant about the cave. Something about his heritage.*

*"But how am I breathing?"*

*"All who have pirate magic can."*

*Pirate magic. There it was again. That's what Seward had called it.*

*"But I don't have any magic."*

*Meranna gave him an exasperated look. "Of course you do! If you didn't, you wouldn't be here."*

*Jonah shook his head, preparing to argue. The look on Meranna's face told him it would be fruitless to do so; and since this was only a dream, Jonah figured it didn't matter anyway.*

*"I'm…"*

*"Jonah," Meranna finished for him, "I know." She moved slightly ahead of him now, reaching back to take his hand. "We haven't much time."*

*"How come I'm here with you, and not on the island with Sachlavar?"*

*Meranna gave him a look of disbelief. "You couldn't go there like that," she said pointing at him.*

*Jonah hadn't realized the seaweed was still wrapped around him, the ends of which danced along in the current. He must have looked quite the sight — a green mummy unraveling in the deep. Embarrassment washed over him causing his cheeks to flare to an unattractive red.*

*"Come on," Meranna said, "follow me." She let go of his hand and swam away from the current.*

*Try as he might, he couldn't seem to get himself turned around and so Jonah continued to drift along with the current. He didn't actually know how to swim. His mother had never let him near the water before. The one time he'd been in the water he'd managed to make it to the ship, but that hadn't been him. He hadn't swum. The sea had done all the work. Now he was stuck in an underwater current, drifting further and further away from the only one who seemed to know why he was here in the first place. And the sea wasn't helping him this time.*

*Panic leapt through him as he made this realization. If only he knew how he'd done it before. He attempted to turn his body the same direction Meranna had gone. But once he'd managed it, he wasn't sure how to move past the current. Jonah watched as, off in the distance, Meranna moved her tail up and down in the water, her arms at her side, gliding through the water as if there were no current. He didn't have a tail, so he pulled his legs together, placed his green arms to his sides, and tried to move his legs up and down mimicking the motion of the mermaid. He was barely able to hold his own against the current but didn't actually advance far enough to make any significant progress. Jonah tried again. This wasn't like holding the wheel and having the ship cut through the current. Then, the wind and sails had done most of the work. He'd only had to hold the ship steady. Jonah felt the current pushing and tugging on his body, making any progress he might have made obsolete.*

*Meranna was beyond Jonah's view when he looked up again. Even if he could figure out how to move through the current, he had no idea where he was going. He gave up, letting the current move him forward again. This was a dream, after all, and so in the end it wouldn't matter where he ended up.*

*Suddenly Meranna was in front of him. "What are you doing?" she demanded, placing her hands on her fish-hips.*

*"Thought it'd be fun to ride the current for a while," Jonah snapped back sarcastically.*

*"You don't have time to play around," Meranna said, the sarcastic remark obviously lost on her. "Come on," she said, grabbing him by the wrist and pulling him forward a bit, "we're running out of time."*

*Jonah yanked his arm back. "Time for what? Why are we always running out of time?"*

*Meranna pointed to the seaweed hanging off Jonah, "That won't last. In order for it to do its job, we have to be there before you run out of time," she said in an exasperated voice. "And you won't sleep forever.*

*It was as if Meranna expected Jonah to know all this. He suddenly felt embarrassed, as if he'd let her down. He shook off the feeling, though, reminding himself that this was all new to him. Whatever it was that everyone else seemed to know, he hadn't learned it yet. And, he reasoned, this was all just a dream. Which, he realized, Meranna also seemed to know. So then why did it feel so real?*

*"Where are we going?" he asked.*

*"The Shark's Lair. Now come on."*

*At the sound of Shark's Lair, Jonah was more than happy to not let the seaweed do whatever it was that seaweed was supposed to do. He reached up and started to unwrap a piece. "I am not going to any shark's lair."*

"Stop!" Meranna grabbed his hand to prevent him from unwrapping his arm. "Don't unwrap it. Once it's on, you can't unwrap it without doing more harm."

"I don't care. It can't be any worse than going into a shark's lair."

"You can't unwrap it, Jonah. Please." Meranna said. Her manner had shifted, and she seemed nervous now. It was as if she were pleading with him, and Jonah felt a sense of joy that he might cause concern to the mind of this beautiful creature.

He paused and looked into the face of the now very distraught Meranna. He hadn't thought the mermaid was capable of feeling anything, but, apparently, he was wrong. He stopped trying to unwrap the seaweed. "Well, I'm not going into any shark's lair. That would be stupid. I'm not interested in letting any sharks close enough to eat me." Even if this is a dream, he thought.

At that Meranna let go with a burst of laughter that tinkled through the water like little glass beads bouncing off each other. "No sharks will eat you!" she said. "Come on." Again, she took him by the hand and started pulling him through the water.

Jonah wasn't sure about this, but the mermaid was no longer upset, and he liked it when she was happy, so he let her lead him along. After a few moments, Meranna let go of him and kept swimming.

"Meranna, wait!" Jonah called after her. If he'd been smart, he would have just let her go by herself, but he wasn't thinking about that anymore.

She was back in less than a minute. "What? We have to hurry."

"I, um," suddenly he was embarrassed again, the uncomely red creeping back up his neck. "I, well, I've never…"

Meranna's eyes grew wide with disbelief. "You can't swim?!" she said indignantly.

Jonah couldn't meet her eyes but shook his head. "No."

*"How can you....?" She started to ask, seemed to think better of it, and stopped herself. "Come on, I'll take you. You can tell me later." She reached out and took his hand once more.*

*Tell her what, Jonah wondered. Why he can't swim? That was easy enough. "My mom..." he started.*

*"Not now," Meranna cut him off. She had pulled a pearl out of her hair with her free hand and handed it to Jonah. "You'll need this."*

*"What is it?"*

*"An air pearl, of course." She glanced over at him as she started to swim along pulling him behind her. "Don't tell me you've never heard of an air pearl?" She rolled her eyes and explained as they moved forward. "It'll give you the air you need while we're traveling." She glanced over her shoulder and saw him nearly lose the pearl to the swift current they were cutting through. "Hey, careful! Don't lose it! You need it!" she chided. Once Jonah regained a firm grip on the pearl, Meranna continued her explanation. "Humans can't go as fast or as deep as mer-people without consequences. Not even ones like you."*

*"Like me?"*

*Meranna gave him a look that said she didn't believe he didn't know. She felt that he was mocking her and chose not to answer his question. Instead she shook her head and said, "Look, since I have to bring you with me, you'll be going faster than your body can handle even with the pirate magic. The only way to survive will be to put the pearl in your mouth. It will provide the air you need to keep from going unconscious," she told me. "Or worse."*

*"Worse?"*

*"Just put it in your mouth!"*

*Jonah raised the pearl to his lips. A thought occurred to him, and he brought it back down as he asked her, "Wait, I don't have a pearl now, but*

*I'm still breathing. Why can I breathe now?"*

"I told you — pirate magic. It's part of being…" here she hesitated. "Well, it's part of being you." She seemed hesitant to say more about it. "Please, time is running out. There will be someone to answer all your questions later. Just put the pearl in your mouth."

Had this not been a dream - a very real dream, but a dream none the less - Jonah would have pressed Meranna further. As it was, he recognized that some things just couldn't, or wouldn't, be explained in dreams, so he let the subject drop. Still, it felt real enough that he figured he ought to take precautions. After all, dying in a dream was still dying, right?

Meranna picked up speed, and Jonah decided it was probably best not to argue. He popped the pearl in his mouth, tucked it into his cheek so as not to swallow it, and allowed his mouth to adjust to the smooth feel of the thing as it sat there taking up space. After a few seconds, the smooth surface became broken at irregular intervals with little bumps pressing outward. They tickled the inside of his mouth as they popped lightly; then his body immediately felt a surge of energy as the oxygen now released made its way to his bloodstream. It felt amazing, and he wondered how long it would last.

Later, Jonah would remember moving through the water, cutting through the current as if it were never there. He would remember picking up speed, and then the crystal-clear waters getting darker and darker. He couldn't remember anything after that, though, and now he wondered if the water had gotten darker, or if he simply blacked out.

Regardless, he found himself now being pulled at a much slower pace now. He felt for the pearl in his cheek, and discovered it was missing. He hoped he wouldn't need it now, because he had no idea where it had gone.

The water around him was still crystal-clear. The light above shone less intensely. Before them was an underwater cave. Two currents seemed to fight with each other at the mouth of it; one trying to get in, the other trying to get out. Neither seemed to be going anywhere, creating a strong water barrier that kept everything out. It reminded Jonah of the fog rope protecting the island.

Meranna stopped just before the double current barrier and let go of Jonah. "Hurry. He's expecting you."

"You're not coming with me?"

Meranna's expression was sad. "No, Jonah. I can't. Only you can go in there."

Jonah didn't like the idea of entering this unknown cave by himself. He looked at the cave, wondering who was waiting for him on the other side.

"Go on, Jonah. You don't have much time left."

Jonah looked down at the unraveling seaweed, now mostly shredded save a few thin pieces. They were still attached - barely.

He wasn't ready to enter the cave. "I haven't told you why I can't swim," Jonah said lamely. He was stalling. Going into the cave, the Shark's Lair, especially alone, didn't really appeal to him even if Meranna had said no sharks would eat him.

"It's okay, Jonah. You need to go. We'll meet again." Tiny pink bubbles started coming closer and closer to Meranna, dancing around her. They collided together as they mulipled, encasing Meranna in one large pink bubble, just as she'd first arrived. The large pink bubble drifted quickly away, and Jonah was left alone at the entrance.

# Thirty

Jonah spent several minutes trying to muster the courage to enter the Shark's Lair. He looked down at his arms and legs. Green strips hung from them like strings. What could possibly go wrong? he thought. He considered taking the seaweed off and not entering the cave. After all, it's only a dream. But what if it wasn't a dream? He weighed his options. Meranna told him no shark would eat him. She also told him not to unravel the seaweed. She hadn't told him why. Not exactly. But the look on her face had convinced him to leave it alone for the time being.

*The water around him began to roll. It was a slow, gentle roll sending bubbles dancing around him. The water was also darkening, losing some of its crystal-clear appearance. The bubbles came faster, some growing larger. The light continued to recede. Still more bubbles came, rolling upward. Jonah could see them popping at the surface. It reminded him of water boiling over the fireplace back home.*

*Boiling water!*

*Panic propelled Jonah forward, where he struggled with the double current barrier. It was like trying to move through the pigpen after a big storm had come through. Jonah felt like he was stuck in the muck, trying to work his way through to the fence rail. The few steps it would normally have taken felt like miles as he fought through it. But he kept going because the cave was the only place that didn't appear to be boiling.*

*Eventually he broke through and tumbled into the cave. As he did, he saw the water turn into a steady stream of fast bubbles making their way to the surface. The towers of bubbles were fascinating to watch, and Jonah would have stayed lost in their show if he hadn't felt the movement of water behind him.*

*He turned around and saw nothing. The cave itself was dark, and it took some time for his eyes to adjust. In the meantime, stirrings in the water around Jonah continued to cause him to turn in all directions trying to locate whatever was making the water move. The hairs on his arms would have stood up if not strapped down by the seaweed, and fear prickled along Jonah's spine. He was keenly aware that he was now in the Shark's Lair, and desperately wished he wasn't.*

*Something brushed passed him.*

*"AAAAHH!" Jonah screamed, startled and unsettled by the movement.*

*A bump to his legs caused him to try to jump, resulting in more of a flailing motion that didn't get him any further away. Another bump, this time to his chest, sent him spiraling in a backward somersault. He was just getting level again when another bump hit his side, sending him sprawling out in a rather sad version of an underwater cartwheel.*

*Jonah was not having fun. He could not even get his body righted again before the next hit came. He was losing control, and worse, he was starting to panic. Fear gripped his chest, tightening like a fist around his heart. Pain seared through him, and he suddenly felt paralyzed, though he wasn't sure if it was from the fear induced panic, or his sense that his efforts were useless. Whatever the cause, he was stuck, being rammed from first one direction, then another. The bumps came faster and faster. Jonah was certain there was no escape and began to succumb to the feeling of helplessness.*

"Zarsish! Stop that!" The sound of the voice bounced around the cave. The bumping stopped. The water went eerily still. Jonah watched it apprehensively, not convinced the danger had passed.

"Jonah's our friend," came the voice again. "He needs our help."

Sachlavar materialized in front of Jonah, his long, white robe floating around him. "Don't mind Zarsish. He just likes to play." A small shark, about the size of the wizard, swam into view. Sachlavar ran his hand along its side. Zarsish swished his tail back and forth, reminding Jonah of a giant dog with razor sharp teeth.

The wizard looked at the mouth of the cave and watched the racing bubble towers. "We haven't much time, lad. Come along. Let's see what we have." Sachlavar turned and moved past Jonah deeper into the cav., Jonah couldn't help but notice how the long strands of silvery-white hair and beard drifting aimlessly around Sachlavar looked a lot like tendrils smoke. He almost laughed at the idea of smoke in water but choked it back when Zarsish brushed his leg as it swam past.

Jonah waited until the wizard and his shark were well in front of him, then he started slowly forward.

"You'll have to come faster than that if we're going to have time to fix you up properly," Sachlavar called back to him.

Although he could not swim, Jonah discovered that he could walk inside the waterfilled cave. Strange. But dreams were like that, he remined himself. The seaweed trailed around him falling off his arms and legs. Glancing back, he could see that the water had lost all its crystal clearness. Something told Jonah that the changes in the water had something to do with his lack of time. He picked up the pace, keeping just far enough behind the shark so as not to be able to reach out and touch it. He didn't like being that close to the shark even then but figured he had better keep up if the wizard was right.

*It didn't take long before they came out into a cavern full of sparkling rock. The water no longer filled the space completely, and Jonah followed Sachlavar to the surface. In the center of the room was a crystal table, as clear as if it had been polished. It stood on a small island of rock that rose just a foot out of the water. Light bounced around the room, though Jonah could not detect where it came from.*

*"Come over here. Quickly, quickly," Sachlavar said as he strode out of the water and moved next to the table.*

*Jonah hesitated, watching Zarsish swim around the room.*

*"You don't have time to waste. Come on now. Zarsish won't bother you. Come on. Hurry up."*

*There were two things Jonah had learned. One was that he couldn't move very fast through water — at least not by himself. And the other was that when Sachlavar said there wasn't much time, Jonah had better prepare to wake up with a headache. He didn't know what would happen if Sachlavar didn't get to do whatever it was he needed to do while Jonah was here with his seaweed on, but he did know there wouldn't be much time to find out.*

*Jonah looked at Zarsish once more. The shark was on the other side of the cavern. Jonah did his best to run through the water to the crystal table where Sachlavar was waiting for him. It was difficult, as movement underwater always is, and Zarsish ended up pushing Jonah the rest of the way, bumping him playfully along. Jonah didn't find it very comforting.*

*Sitting on the crystal table were four items. A round, smooth, blue oval stone, a dry eagle's feather, a piece of pink coral, and a silver box, much like the one Miguel had shown him when he'd first come aboard the* Mary Margaret.

*"Each of these items has special value. You will need them all during the journey ahead of you."*

*Jonah reached out his hand, still wrapped in shredded seaweed, to pick up the blue stone.*

*"No!" Sachlavar commanded. "You must not pick them up yet. You must earn them. Every one of them."*

*Jonah shook the seaweed dangling from his arm. It was really beginning to annoy him now that it was unraveling every which way. "What about this stuff? Can I take it off yet?"*

*The wizard looked Jonah up and down. "Oh. Yes, yes. There's no need of that now."*

*Sachlavar waved his hand over Jonah and the shredded, tangeled seaweed began to unravel itself. As he watched, Jonah could not help but wonder about Meranna and her serious concern that he not take it off and that he was running out of time. "Why couldn't I take it off before?" he asked.*

*"You mean the seaweed? Ah well, you could have."*

*"But Meranna said something bad would happen."*

*"She was right."*

*"I don't understand," Jonah said.*

*"In order for the seaweed to do its job, you must first come into the cave. Its powers are not activated unless it comes within these magical walls. If you had removed the seaweed before entering the cave, the seaweed would have left burns along your skin. Scars would form that would never go away."*

*"How is that possible? You just said the power doesn't work unless it's inside the cave."*

*"For someone like you, Jonah, the dormant power within the seaweed begins to react on contact. It cannot complete the process without being inside this cave, but it reacts with your own powers. It's this reaction that causes the burns."*

"Does Seward know this? Did he even know it was possible for me to come here?"

"Seward knows enough but does not have knowledge of all. He serves his purpose well."

Everything about this experience was too fantastical. He knew he was dreaming, but there were too many coincidences, too many strange connections to ignore them all. One thing stood out more than the rest. "What do you mean, people like me? You said it. Meranna said it. What do you mean?"

Sachlavar looked hard at Jonah. "You mean you don't know?"

Jonah shook his head.

"Surely you must know something. At the very least you must have suspected." Sachlavar went back to directing the magical unwrapping of Jonah's legs. Then said to himself, "It doesn't make sense. They never come unless they know something."

"Look, Mr. Wizard…"

"Sachlavar."

Jonah rolled his eyes. "Sachlavar. I don't know what's going on here. All I know is that I go to sleep, and the next thing I know I'm talking with you."

"Well, that makes it more difficult indeed," the old man said.

"What's more difficult?"

"Ummm? What?" said Sachlavar distractedly. "Oh, nothing. Nothing. Don't you worry." Having removed the last strand of seaweed, the wizard stood up and looked at Jonah. "All will make sense soon enough. We haven't the time to get into it now." He turned back toward the table and lifted the eagle's feather, dry despite the damp air around them. "You have learned to steer the ship. That is good. For learning this important skill, you have earned the eagle's feather." He handed Jonah the feather.

"Great," he replied sarcastically. "What am I supposed to do with it?"

"The eagle's feather holds great power, as do all these items. The feather will provide you strength when you feel you have none. It will grant you wisdom so long as you seek it. These are the two greatest gifts you can have at this time."

Jonah turned the feather around in his fingers. It looked rather ordinary, and he wondered what he was to do with it. Where should he keep it? It wasn't as if he could tuck it in his hat and not have it be noticed. Then Jonah remembered this was a dream, and he wondered if, when the time came and the dream dissolved, he would even have to worry about what to do with the feather.

Just as he was wondering about it, the cave gave a great shudder, and the streaming towers of bubbles Jonah had seen outside the cave broke through causing a great disruption in the water around him. Water raced through the cavern, filling it completely. The bubbles followed, violently tossing Jonah around. Zarsish took off in a flurry of whipping tail.

"Remember your heritage." Sachlavar's words bounced around the cave as he faded into brilliant light and exploded into a million tiny pieces. The colors penetrated the bubbles turning the violent balls into a rainbow of deathly proportions.

All of a sudden Jonah's lungs hurt. They burned and ached for the need to take a breath. The bubbles continued to jerk him about, making it nearly impossible to figure out which way was out. He knew he couldn't hold on for long, and with his inability to swim, he was desperately aware of the danger he was in. His chest squeezed tight as panic welled up within him. The need to take a breath grew in intensity. Jonah knew he would either have to take that breath of water or pass out — either way the result would be the same.

Just as he was about to surrender to the urge, he remembered the *feather in his hand. He gripped it harder and thought,* If ever there were a time when I needed strength, it is now. I need the strength to endure. To not take a breath, and to be able to swim to safety.

*An immediate reaction occurred. Jonah was swept away, as if on a current all its own. His lungs stopped hurting, and he felt himself propelled at such a rapid rate, he was certain he was already dead. Then, as suddenly as it began, it ended throwing Jonah upon the shore, exhausted, barely holding on to the feather, and consciousness left him.*

# Thirty-One

Jonah awoke on the hard floor of the gun deck. His head ached, as it always did after these dreams - if they were dreams. This last one had seemed far too real for Jonah's taste. He still remembered the feel of the bubbles on his skin, and the panic of not being able to swim. His muscles were cramped, and he stretched them out in hopes of some relief. He yawned and stretched his arms back over his head. It wasn't until he'd dropped them down again that he realized he no longer had seaweed wrapped around them. Maybe that was a dream, too, he thought. He couldn't be sure of anything right now. Except that as he stretched, his muscles no longer hurt.

Looking around, Jonah took in the lines of cannons, and recalled Seward's attempt to teach him sword fighting the night before. "Ugh! Seward must think I'm worthless," he said to himself as he recalled his inability to even hold the sword. A wave of frustration ran through him. He might as well have been back at Delmar for all the good he was here. Maybe, if he was lucky, Seward would overlook his ineptness and give him another chance.

Pale light was making its way through the gun ports in the sides of the ship. The pirates were probably making their way to the galley even now. Jonah's stomach growled, making him keenly aware it was breakfast time. He wondered if Miguel was looking for him; then figured he'd better head back up. It wouldn't do to have the pirate angry with him.

As he pushed himself from the floor, Jonah noticed an object on the ground. He picked it up and held it in the light. It was a magnificent eagle's feather. *Maybe it wasn't a dream after all,* he thought, turning it over in his hand. He shook his head. *Nah. Must be a coincidence.* But just in case, he tucked it into the inner pocket of his vest.

Jonah dropped to the ground when the door at the far end of the deck opened. The sound of heavy boots thumped along the floorboards toward him. Jonah wasn't sure if he was supposed to be down here. Seward had left him to sleep, but he felt certain Miguel wouldn't have allowed it if he'd known. And if it were the rest of the crew, there was no telling what they might do. Jonah wasn't keen on getting mixed up with more trouble. Quickly he made his way behind one of the big guns in hopes of shielding himself.

"Another one's coming," a deep, gruff voice said.

"Not like that's new or nothing. One always does," came the reply.

"Maybe so. But not like this one," returned the first.

"Whatcha mean?"

"'Tis a bad omen, that one."

"The boy? Ain't nothing, but a land rat. Shouldn't worry yerself over 'im," the second said.

"'Tain't a good sign, I tell ya. 'Tain't good a'tall."

Their steps continued to move among the cannons, in and out, as if they were stopping to check them. Jonah needed to find a way around the cannon. He needed to figure out how to get to the other end of the deck without being noticed. Jonah wasn't sure he'd receive a kindly welcome and wasn't interested in finding out. It didn't seem likely he'd be able to get past the men unnoticed, though.

Jonah peeked around the end of the cannon. The two pirates had stopped near a pile of cannonballs. Jonah watched as they each lifted one and carried it back toward the front of the cannons. Now with their bodies facing Jonah, he could see that the biggest one was Heckel. Jonah pulled back quickly, hiding himself again as they loaded two of the big guns. He listened as the balls were dropped into the barrels and rammed down tight, his heart thudding with each pound of the iron rod. Heckel had never shown Jonah any kindness, and had made his distaste for Jonah known well enough.

"Don't know whatcha's worked up over. Jonah ain't…"

"Don't say 'is name! 'Tis bad luck!" Heckel snapped.

"You don't take on with such superstitions, now, do ya?"

"'Tain't no superstition. Mark my words, with that name, the boy's cursed."

Jonah lay flat on his stomach and peeked out at the pirates. They proceeded to work their way down the line, picking up a cannonball, walking around to the front, and loading each. It was obvious they intended to load all the cannons. Which meant that Jonah was trapped.

"Well, then, whatcha plan to do?"

Heckel shook his head, then dropped his voice. "Just you be sure whose side you're on when the time comes. One way or another, I'll be cap'ain. And the boy will be the first to go."

Jonah felt sick to his stomach. He shuddered to think what would happen to him if he were found now. He knew he needed to get out of here and fast. Looking around him, Jonah made a quick mental picture of his surroundings. Breathing deeply, he watched the pirates' movements. With the two men preoccupied, it appeared this might be Jonah's chance to move closer to the door. He watched them load another cannon and then move to the next. Heckel had his back to Jonah, while the smaller one moved around to the front of the barrel. Jonah knew that as they worked to load the cannons, neither would be looking his way.

Swiftly, he moved from behind the farthest cannon, ducked under its barrel and positioned himself against the next one. He knew he'd have to work his way up along the cannons one at a time, making his way past the men. The pirates would move from one side of the ship to the other, loading each cannon on their way back down toward Jonah. This made the first few movements relatively easy, so long as he timed it so the sounds of the ramrod covered his own steps. Things would get trickier as he got closer to the pirates since the two men were moving back and forth among the rows of cannons working their way to the back of the deck.

"Twon't be so easy. The captain had him up at the helm yesterday. You know what that means," Heckel said.

"That don't mean nothin'," replied the other.

The pirates continued to work steadily lifting and lugging cannonballs back to the next set of cannons, then loading, stuffing and ramming them down the barrels. It was a rhythmic pattern, and Jonah worked out his own pattern of duck, crawl, slide, hide as he moved from one cannon to the next in their direction.

"Captain don't have no one at the helm lessen he has a reason. Don't need no extra helmsman. He's a trainin' the boy. That's what."

"How's that?" the smaller one asked.

"Ain't no captain make a boy stand at the helm eight hours at his first. Ain't no captain force him to steer straight with a hard current pushing aside. Don't like it. Boy's not ready. Too young. Ain't no boy that young been trained afore either," replied Heckel.

The work paused as the second pirate asked, "Never?"

"Never. Just ain't been done afore." The larger one hefted the cannonball into the barrel. It slid down, scraping along the inside until it could go no further. The ramrod was lifted, jammed down the barrel until it found the ball, and the burly pirate started banging away at it. "No brat's gonna take my chance. Not this time. I've waited too long – centuries – for this chance. I ain't gonna let no one take that way. 'Specially not some cursed land rat."

Jonah caught his breath and froze. He didn't understand what they were referring to, and he didn't understand how someone could have waited centuries for anything. But with everything he'd experienced since the arrival of his father on the beach that first day, he wasn't about to question that now.

The pirates finished loading the cannon and began to move closer to Jonah. He pulled back. In listening to them, he'd forgotten to keep moving. Now their boots came toward him. Jonah had neglected to time his movements so he could cross behind the pirates when they turned. Now, he'd be exposed. All the pirates would have to do was turn around and they'd see him.

Sinking back against the base of the cannon, his heart beating so loud he was sure the pirates could hear it, Jonah closed his eyes and prepared himself to dive past and race for the door. He didn't like it, but it was the only plan he had now.

A deep breath. The sound of boots moving closer. It seemed to play out in slow motion. Jonah opened his eyes. The beating of his heart was so loud it vibrated in his own ears drowning out all other sounds. He saw weather worn boots just under the barrel of the cannon he was resting against. He shifted position, readying himself to race past.

Thump, thump, thump. The blood rushed past his ears.

Clump, clump, clump. The boots came closer and closer.

Heckel was just stepping past the end of the barrel of the cannon Jonah was hiding beside. One more step, a turn of his head, and Jonah was a goner. He didn't have time to decide if he might be able to slip between the base ends of the cannons, sitting butt to butt in their lines. It was now or never.

Jonah jumped up, causing a small commotion. Heckel started to turn in Jonah's direction when a familiar voice rang out. "What's taken ya so long? Captain sent ya down here to load them cannons an hour ago." The pirate's head snapped back around toward the door.

The boy skidded to a halt, grabbing hold of the cannon to stop his forward motion. As he did, a small thud resounded. It wasn't much, but it was enough for the pirate to react. As he did, Jonah ducked under the cannon barrel, not wanting to be seen, and hoped he'd get passed by before he was noticed.

Seward's familiar voice came to his rescue once more, drawing the attention of the pirates back toward the door. The only problem was that Jonah needed to get through that door.

"Captain wants ya on deck."

"We ain't done down here," Heckel replied.

"Yeah," echoed the second, "we ain't got all 'em cannons filled."

"Loaded, ya knucklehead. We ain't got 'em all loaded."

"I'll finish up down here," Seward growled. "Captain wants to see ya. Get going."

Jonah had managed to get behind another cannon. This time

as he approached the base of the cannons, he laid himself flat and tucked himself into the cramped space between the cannon butts where they just met but didn't rest against the base. As long as Seward kept talking, the pirates shouldn't look his way.

Heckel muttered insults in a low voice as he led the way to the door. They exited, and Seward shut it behind them. He went to the nearest pile of cannonballs as if nothing had happened. He grabbed the first, went to an empty cannon and started the process of loading it. Where two had carried the ball before, Seward was able to do it alone. It made Jonah glad that Seward was on his side. At least, he though Seward was on his side.

"You can come out now. They won't be back down for some time yet," Seward called out.

Jonah tried to wiggle his way out, trying to reverse what he'd done. His feet moved, even his legs moved a little, but he was wedged in tightly. He didn't budge. He had compressed his lungs as he'd forced himself into the small space, and now he realized he was only taking small shallow breaths. His head began to spin slightly. He tried to call out, but it hurt too much to get enough air.

Seward continued loading the cannon. When Jonah neither replied nor appeared beside him, Seward turned around to look for the boy. The kid's bare feet stuck out from under the butts of two cannons. They were dirty and had someone been in a hurry it would have been easy to overlook him. Going toward him, Seward tried again. "You plannin' on staying under there all day? Did ya forget you've got training still ta do?"

The boy didn't respond. Everything in front of him had gone blurry, and his head hurt from the lack of oxygen. Without a response from Jonah, Seward grabbed hold of the boy by both feet and began to pull.

"Got yourself into a bind, didn't ya?" Seward remarked as he tugged. The older man braced his right foot against the base block, while pulling with all his might. Jonah slid backward half an inch. Not enough to free him though. "How'd ya get yourself in here anyway?" Seward wanted to know. He figured if they were having this much trouble with his body, Seward couldn't see how the boy had managed to get his head through.

It took some more tugging, and eventually Seward realized the boy had gone through between the two ends where there was more space but then managed to wedge himself off to the side, where there was very little space. As he came to this conclusion, he tugged Jonah's now limp body to the side, and worked him back through, head and all, where the boy's body then took over and began to breathe more naturally.

"Had us a bit of a scare there, boy," Seward said as Jonah fluttered open his eyes. "See'n as you're back with us, I better finish up here." He went back to loading cannons.

Jonah was amazed to see Seward was able to work twice as fast the as the other two pirates. It wasn't until Seward was nearly finished that Jonah finally thought to question why the cannons were being loaded.

"No ship, 'specially a pirate's ship, is worth a fig without a belly of loaded cannons," came Seward's reply. "Can't be caught unprepared, now can we?"

Jonah had never thought about it before, but as Seward said it, it kind of made sense. How else would they be ready for a surprise attack? It really had taken a long time to load all those cannons. Even if everyone were able to work as quickly as Seward, it would take too long to get ready on short notice.

"I see yer better," Seward said, coming up to Jonah.

When Jonah gave him a puzzled look, Seward pointed to his arms. "No seaweed."

Jonah looked at his arms and legs. He vaguely remembered Seward being on the cannon deck with him last night. Vaguely recalled Seward wrapping him in seaweed. And then there was the dream. When he'd woken without the seaweed, he assumed he had dreamt that Seward had wrapped him as well. "That was real? You actually did that?"

Seward laughed a hearty laugh. "Indeed, boy! Indeed!"

A thousand questions whirled around Jonah's head. There was so much that didn't make sense. So many things he wanted answers to. "How? What?" Jonah began.

Seward shrugged. "Don't rightly know, boy. You probably know more than I do. I just train people like you. It's my job. But I don't know all the details."

"That's what Sachlavar said, or something like that." Jonah rubbed his head. "Why does everyone keep saying that, "people like you"?"

"Don't you know?" Seward asked him in return.

Jonah shook his head.

"Strange," Seward said, as if speaking to himself, "never had one's not known what he was a'fore." To Jonah he said, "That's a question best saved for Sachlavar. Alls I can say is you're special, Jonah. Can't say as I can 'splain it all. But you're special." He looked at Jonah hoping the kid would understand him. "My job is to train you this side. Sachlavar's in charge of everything else. Ask him next time you see him."

"So, he's real?"

Seward gave a hearty chuckle. "That he is. It all is."

A strange uneasiness settled in Jonah's stomach. He'd seen and experienced some really strange, at times revolting, things since he'd come aboard the *Mary Margaret*. Jonah realized part of him had still been hanging on to a small thread of hope that it was one terrible nightmare. *Guess I won't be waking up from this one.*

The queasiness gave way to genuine concern as a thought struck Jonah. "Why doesn't the crew like me?"

Seward finished loading the last canon. He dusted off his hands and paused to consider Jonah. "They're jealous. You've something they can't ever have."

"What's that?"

"Integrity. And power."

Seward helped Jonah over to some barrels where the two sat down.

"I don't understand."

"Yer heritage gives ye power. Tain't like any other. Somethin' they can't ever have."

"Sachlavar mentioned my heritage, too."

"I'm not surprised. Heritage is important. Important to know. Important to understand."

Jonah gave thought to the words Seward had said. He would need to learn about his heritage – about where he came from.

"Best get started," Seward interjected as he got up and went to the far side of the deck and opened a hidden case in the ship. It was here that the swords had been stored. He pulled them out and tossed one to Jonah. Instinct took over and Jonah caught it without trouble. As if he'd done it all his life, Jonah positioned the sword and his feet ready for a fight, then let his sword arm drop.

"Wait. You said they were jealous because I have power *and* integrity. What did you mean by integrity?"

"Well, yer didn't come here to become a pirate, now did ya? En garde!"

Seward had shifted his stance and called out before Jonah could ask another question. For his part, Jonah quickly brought his sword back up bringing his body back into ready position.

"Very good, boy!" Seward called out.

Though the initial praise was appreciated, the ready position was where Jonah's natural instincts ended. When Seward moved to lunge or strike, Jonah found he had no idea what to do. He tried to dodge, or to parry, but Seward would easily disarm him, sending his sword flying to the floor. After each attempt, Seward would stop and instruct Jonah to retrieve his sword. Every time Jonah did; and every time, no matter what Jonah did, Seward relieved him of his sword again. The earlier praise felt like a mockery amongst such continued failure.

It didn't take long for Jonah to become frustrated, ready to give up. Seward often laughed when Jonah misjudged a move and went too far past. Not being able to hang on to his sword, and having Seward constantly laughing grated on Jonah's nerves.

After nearly an hour of the humiliation, Jonah retrieved his sword yet again and stood with the tip pointing downward. "I thought you were going to train me," he accused. Anger prickled over him.

"This is training," Seward said with a hearty chuckle.

The sound of Seward's laughter grated against the emotion building within Jonah. "How is this training?" he yelled. "All I do is raise my sword and you knock it out of my hand."

Seward's voice remained calm, and merriment continued to glint in his eyes. "Knowing what not to do is just as important as knowing what to do," Seward said. "And the best way to learn anything is to do it."

Jonah didn't like Seward's response. How could doing something he'd never done, and going at it all wrong, possibly benefit him? The only thing he seemed to have learned was how not to hang onto his sword. He was pretty sure he could have figured that out entirely on his own. "I don't think I've learned anything doing this," Jonah complained. He sat down on a barrel of gun powder and let his sword fall in front of him. His anger turned inward and disappointment with himself took over. "I'm no good at this. I'll never figure it out. I don't even know why I'm doing this."

Seward sat on another barrel near him, laying his own sword across his lap. "Yer learned more than ye realize, Jonah."

"But I didn't do anything."

"Ye didn't repeat yer mistakes. You learned what didn't work, and ye didn't repeat it. That's more than most figure out."

Jonah didn't reply.

"Look here, boy. Instead of doing the same thing over again, ye tried something different. That's more than many learn at all. Don't be so hard on yerself. Trust me. Tomorrow will be better."

Jonah wasn't convinced. He kicked his feet against the barrel in a dejected way. All he'd wanted was to make Miguel undo everything he'd done in Delmar. Instead, here he was on a pirate ship, sailing who knew where, learning things he never thought he'd need. In no way did he feel he was completing what he'd come here to do. And to top it all off, he wasn't making any progress in being able to impress his father. It all felt like a waste.

He thought about his mother. It was good that Ol' Man Wimple was with her. She'd be safe with him. Jonah hadn't planned on being gone this long and now wondered why he hadn't listened to her. They'd tried to warn him — both of them. Now it seemed, in trying to help, he had only made things worse. He wondered how his mother was doing and if she'd been able to return to the village. It was a ridiculous thought, he knew, but he tried to convince himself it was true so he wouldn't feel so guilty about leaving her.

"Better get ya some grub a'fore the captain calls for ya," Seward said, interrupting Jonah's thoughts. "Wouldn't do for ya to not have your nourishment a'fore you take the wheel again."

Jonah cringed at those words. He remembered his aching body from the day before, and the seaweed wraps Seward had given him. He didn't know how Seward had done it, or what the deal with the seaweed was, but he was glad it had worked. "Thank you, Seward."

"What for, boy?"

"For the seaweed. I don't understand it, but thank you."

"'T'weren't much. Just doin' me job."

# Thirty-Two

Just as Seward had suggested, Miguel had called for Jonah shortly after the meal. The afternoon leading late into the night found Jonah steering the ship once again. Unlike the day before, though, Jonah hadn't fought the wheel to keep the ship in position. He felt like his arms had become stronger overnight. The light sea spray had felt good on his face, as had the wind in his hair. The only thing that seemed to trouble him was the constantly shifting current. Sometimes it was unbelievably strong, other times just a light change. His job had been to keep the ship sailing straight, no matter what else happened. It wasn't the part about keeping the ship straight that bothered him. It was the actual changing of the current. He knew it wasn't normal; and yet, it was just as real as everything else. Unnatural was normal for this ship.

"Can you feel it, boy?" Miguel asked. "Can you feel her power?"

It was the pirate asking, so Jonah took a moment before replying. He had learned it was important to weigh his words before he spoke. The pirate could be easily provoked and the delicate balance Jonah had been developing could be just as easily undone.

"The sea or the ship, sir?" Jonah finally replied.

"Ah, so you can." The pirate clapped him on the shoulder. "'Tis good to know the difference."

"The one is greater than the other. The other but a shadow of the first."

Jonah considered these words as he stared out into the darkness. The pull of the ocean, it's ability to shift and change, the renewal of energy he'd felt from the sea spray, all of this resonated within him - a knowledge deep within, an awakening of something.

"The sea is the stronger of the two."

"Aye. She is the source."

They stood together at the helm, the pirate's hand still resting on Jonah's shoulder. For the first time since coming on board the *Mary Margaret* a feeling of belonging washed over Jonah. He glanced at Miguel. There was something different about the pirate's eyes. Pride, maybe? Acceptance?

***

For several days Jonah spent his mornings in training with Seward below on the canon deck, and his afternoons at the helm. He was learning quickly with Seward, discovering ways to move his body, arm, and wrist to effectively parry, while getting in solid lunges and thrusts. He became quick on his feet, able to shift easily, moving agilely, and not lose his balance. His counterstrikes were better than his offensive ones, though, and Jonah knew if he was going to impress the captain he would need to work on that.

Jonah realized that impressing the captain had been his objective from the moment he first asked Seward to train him. This was more than just survival for Jonah. He wanted the captain to be proud of him. He wanted to make his *father* proud. With this knowledge, his approach to each challenge shifted. He stopped focusing on the unnaturalness around him and embraced it. It was the reality he was in now, and he was determined to conquer it.

At the helm, he learned to ignore the changes in the water, no longer hesitating or wondering if he had somehow turned the ship. He had learned to calculate direction from watching the sun and the stars. His confidence grew, as did his muscles. He had filled out and looked more like a man than a boy now.

On this particular night, Jonah stood at the helm under a star filled sky. He was enjoying the breeze on his face, and the roll of the water as the ship cut through. Miguel had left him to steer the ship himself, having decided Jonah was now capable of ignoring the changes the magic brought on. So, for this night, Jonah had the helm to himself; and he found he really liked it.

With the clear night sky, Jonah guided the ship without concern for anything below. It was an easy straight course, so he allowed his mind to wander. His thoughts ran over the time he'd been on the ship, what he'd seen and what he'd learned. The fact that he still hadn't mastered the attack in sword fighting bothered him. It wasn't because he couldn't do it. He just wasn't the type to seek after violence. Jonah credited his mother for that. Her kind nature, and her insistence that they never cause problems, had influenced him. Regardless, he knew he would have to double is efforts to master an offensive attack if he were to secure his father's respect.

As his mind wandered over this, he was reminded that he was here on this ship because of her. It wasn't anything she had done. He'd come here to make Miguel right the wrongs he'd committed against her and against the whole town of Delmar. It was the only way Jonah knew of to give his mother back the life she knew. Was it too late to make a difference? He'd been on the ship for two months and accomplished nothing of the task. It seemed time was running out. Jonah knew he had to impress the captain to have any chance of convincing him to help. Jonah also knew he would have to put all his energies into his sword training to make this happen.

Irritation washed over Jonah, and he gripped the wheel tighter, his knuckles turning white with the force of it. Determination clung to him, its claws digging deep into his soul. Had he been able to see himself at that very moment, Jonah would not have recognized the boy at the helm. Instead, he would have seen a younger version of the pirate father he hadn't been able to decide to love or hate.

The sound of "ship off the portside" rang out from the crow's nest. Almost immediately a darkness crept over the sky as clouds rapidly choked out the stars. The current shifted in a violent manner as if attempting to attack the ship. Jonah barely took notice, steering the ship effortlessly through the maddening current, gaining in strength. His blood began to grow hot, a sensation of boiling rolled through his body. With eyes sparking red as embers, and his muscles twitching, Jonah heard, from his own mouth, the command, "Ready the ship!"

Ghost pirates in solid form filled the deck moving from sails to ropes and back again. Their forms shimmered as they morphed into the wispy versions of themselves. The ship shuddered and groaned. A rush of adrenaline ran through Jonah's body. His eyes became wild, and his heart thudded in excitement. The ship began its transformation, changing as it had before, into the frigate.

Miguel came above deck and looked around at the din of activity. "Who gave the command?" he demanded in a deep, cutting voice.

"The boy, sir," came the reply from one of the shimmering ghosts.

Miguel looked up, past all the pirates, his eyes coming to rest on Jonah. He made quick time as he walked across the deck and swung himself up to the helm. His eyes were shifting between the grey-blue of father and the fierce red of pirate. The rapid change would have been unsettling to Jonah weeks before, but now it merely irritated him further.

"Just what do you think you're doing?" the captain growled.

"Steering the ship, Captain," Jonah spat back in a voice that now sounded menacing and gravelly.

The pirate captain tipped his head ever so slightly and narrowed his eyes. The fierce red was gaining more control. "This is *my* ship, *boy!*" he growled. "*I* give the commands."

"40 knots and gaining," came the call from the crow's nest.

Miguel took his eyes off Jonah and looked out in front of the *Mary Margaret.* By now the sky was black, but Jonah followed the captain's gaze. Jonah was thrilled to find he could make out shadows in the dark. A small part of him, somewhere in the back of his mind, recognized that this was not possible; yet he could do it just the same. Excitement flared. It was the same excitement Jonah could now feel rolling off the captain's shoulders. When Miguel turned back to Jonah, there was no longer any conflict in his eyes. The red had taken over.

"Man your stations," Miguel commanded. Then turned back to Jonah before taking off to join the orderly chaos below. "I've got my eye on you, boy. Remember that."

Out in front of them Jonah could see the rush of the current coming in, strong and sideways. The *Mary Margaret* stayed steady under Jonah's control, while the other ship struggled, and turned to match the current. Jonah knew it was a fear of being destroyed, or overturning the ship, which made the other captain choose to turn. The lone ship was no match for the pirate king and his magic. It was now making a steady course toward the *Mary Margaret*, helping to close the gap. And with the *Mary Margaret* now a frigate, the pirates were making excellent time.

The pirates raced forward under the cover of darkness to meet the unsuspecting ship. As they had done before, the pirates brought the frigate alongside the ship. There were shouts from the crow's nest on the brigantine, as well as from the deck, as the sailors finally noticed the frigate in the water beside them. Anchors were dropped, and sails slackened to slow the vessel.

Without warning, the frigate shuddered and began to expand. Jonah's excitement rose. The unsuspecting ship, now within range and without hope of escape, would have no chance against the mighty *Mary Margaret*. Jonah gave a menacing laugh.

"Fire cannons!" Jonah and Miguel bellowed at the same time. Miguel swung around, sword in hand, and glared across the ship at Jonah, but Jonah had come into his own. Miguel, the pirate king, no longer frightened him.

The *Mary Margaret* shook as her cannons were fired. Orders were given, and commands to continue firing came from both Miguel and Jonah. The mighty galleon shuddered uneasily as multiple cannons were fired at the same time.

The crew of the sea stranded brigantine scurried about on deck. Gunfire shot out across the inky sky toward the *Mary Margaret* but was lost in smoke and water. The cannon balls from the mighty galleon, however, found their mark, sending large splinters of the lone brigantine high into the air. Holes were blasted into her side, and the vessel began to fill with water. The ship would not be going anywhere but down.

Ghost pirates had already materialized. They secured the sinking ship, drawing it alongside the *Mary Margaret*. Soon they would be boarding the broken vessel, seizing anything of value, and killing anyone who got in their way. With the ship sinking, time was limited. They would need to be quick, though Jonah felt certain it wouldn't matter if the *Mary Margaret* were pulled down as well. Something about the power she possessed, he knew, would allow her to remain unharmed.

Jonah secured the wheel, leaving the helm in preparation to board the now defenseless brigantine. He swung over the railing, dropping down to the lower deck of the *Mary Margaret*. Adrenaline raced through his veins. He drew his sword, and amid the clouds of smoke, charged forward. He was determined not to be left behind.

Landing on the deck of the sinking ship, Jonah immediately went to work attacking and parrying as he fought off the crew. He had no idea what it was he should be looking for but was enjoying the rush of the fight before him. Slashing his way through the crowd, Jonah made his way across the deck. There were few men still below, and Jonah did not hesitate as he swiped his sword back and across cutting his way through them as they tried to find an escape. Blood dripped from his weapon as he made his way to the captain's quarters. Anything of unusual value would likely be kept there.

He pushed his way into the room. The ship groaned loudly and began to tip heavily to portside. Since Jonah had the ability to maintain his balance no matter what angle the ship, the tilt of the boat did not affect him. The girl in the room, however, stumbled to the side and grabbed ahold of a plank in the wall to steady herself.

The adrenaline slowed, and Jonah found himself questioning why a girl would be in the captain's quarters. His head began to hurt as he felt the struggle begin. Part of him wanted to rush forward and run his sword through the girl. Just another body on the ship. A smaller part of him seemed to be holding him back, insistent that the girl need not be run through. The sword in Jonah's hand moved forward and back in strange jerky motions.

At that moment, the girl turned, a sword in her own hand. She appeared startled to see Jonah and raised her weapon toward him. Jonah responded in kind, the pirate side of him pushing forward, eager to fight. The other part of Jonah, however, noticed that although the girl held up the sword, it was apparent it was much too big, and much too heavy for her. It was obviously not her own; and likely, she'd never been trained on it.

Jonah slashed his sword through the air just in front of the girl. A menacing grin covered his face as she pulled back away from the tip. She held out her sword again, as if to cover herself with it. She still had one hand on the wall to her right. Jonah knew this would make her less agile. His grin broadened. He pushed forward a little more, and the girl took a step back. She still held the sword in front of her, but now Jonah was certain she didn't know how to use it.

*Easy prey*, he thought. Then immediately another thought, *Defenseless. That would make you a coward.* The grin on Jonah's face wavered, as did his sword.

The girl took that moment and lunged at him. His reflexes kicked in, he countered, disarming her and knocked the sword from her hand. The boat groaned and cracked as it tipped further to the side. The girl lost her footing and fell to the floor. Jonah glanced at the shift in the ship. The girl scrambled on hands and knees past him. He spun around jamming his sword down into the floor, catching the girl's sleeve. She tried to pull her arm away, but it was stuck. She gave several hard tugs on her sleeve. A small rip started, but it wasn't enough.

Jonah leaned down over her. She moved her other hand, tucking it under her body. Jonah put his foot on her back, pressing her into the floor. "What's a girl doing on a ship like this?" he growled at her.

She shook her head in disgust, refusing to answer. He grabbed her hair and yanked her head back.

"I asked you a question," he growled in her face.

"What do you care?" the girl choked out, defiance etched on her features.

"Maybe I don't," Jonah said as he pulled his sword out of her sleeve, kicked her over, and pressed his foot down on her chest with just enough force to make her uncomfortable.

She moved her arm, shoving her fisted hand into the pocket of her oversized trousers, and removing it again.

"Then again," Jonah said nudging her pocket with the tip of his sword, "maybe I care a great deal."

At that, the girl shoved Jonah's leg and rolled out from under him. She managed to get to her feet before Jonah recovered from the unexpected move but didn't make it very far before Jonah had her by the hair, his sword at her throat. "I wouldn't do that again," he hissed in the girl's ear. He felt the urge to slit her throat; to be done with her. Girls were said to be bad luck on a ship, and this one appeared to prove the saying true.

The ship heaved, and water began to pour into the captain's quarters. It wouldn't be long now before the ship was pulled under, taking everything and everyone left on board with it. It was time to go. The only thing keeping him from leaving was the curiosity of what the girl had in her pocket. If she'd risked her life to be aboard this ship, and then to come here to get it before the pirates could find it, Jonah felt it must be quite valuable. He wasn't about to let whatever it was get away. He knew he should just cut the girl's throat, grab whatever it was, and be on his way. It would be fastest.

A voice fought its way into his mind. *She's defenseless.*

Another voice fought back. *'Tis her own fault for being here in the first place.*

*Maybe it's not.*

The second snarled. *Doesn't matter. A pirate shows no mercy.*

A pounding throb crept up from the base of Jonah's head as the two voices battled one another for dominance inside.

CRACK!

The brigantine split at the seams. Water poured into the room rapidly filling what was left of the cabin as the ship slid further into the sea.

*Slice her now!* the menacing voice commanded.

*NO!* the first voice said more forcefully. *There's no time.*

*Then take her prisoner!* the second said in desperation.

Jonah shook his head to clear it and did a quick check of his surroundings. Water was now up to the top of his boots. He didn't have time to figure out which voice would win the argument. Panic overcame him pushing both voices to the back of his mind. He dropped the sword to his side and pulled the girl by the arm. She twisted, trying to get loose, but his grip was too tight.

"Stop fighting," Jonah hissed. "You see that water? The ship is breaking in two, there is no escaping it if you stay here."

The girl continued to struggle. The fire in her eyes made it clear she was a fighter. She would not give up easily.

"Let me put it this way," Jonah sneered at her, "you can stay here and go down with the ship, or you can come with me."

She quickly looked around at the water sloshing up her legs, and when Jonah tugged her again, she followed.

Together they trudged their way out onto the deck. The *Mary Margaret* was still beside the sinking ship, though no longer connected and beginning to pull away. It would change form again soon, giving it the ability to make a fast get away and avoid the downward pull the sinking ship would create as it went under.

"Hurry," Jonah said.

They raced to the side of the sinking ship which was tipped more on its side than level. The girl began to fall behind, unable to walk on the tilted deck the way Jonah could. He pulled her along and watched as the *Mary Margaret* began its transformation back into a frigate.

"We'll have to jump," Jonah told the girl. Her eyes grew large and she started to back away from the railing shaking her head. Jonah turned to look at her. "We have to do it now or we'll lose our chance."

Jonah pulled the girl back to the railing. Her face was now white, and fear was evident in her eyes. She was not cut out for this kind of thing. Jonah felt the irritation of a seasoned pirate. He grabbed her by the waist and thrust her up on the railing in front of him. She waved her arms wildly, not well balanced. For himself, Jonah was steady, agile, and swift. He wrapped his arm tightly around the girl. Then, in one fluid motion, he was up on the rail and springing off toward the pirate ship with the girl screaming all the way.

# Thirty-Three

The Mary Margaret was completely transformed, and the frigate was now well on its way. The screeching of the demolished ship being sucked under the sea rang through the air. Jonah had managed to spring himself and the girl onto the deck of the frigate, tumbling over and over as they landed. The girl hadn't moved since, only groaned.

Jonah was just getting himself to his feet and putting away his sword when he heard Miguel bellow, "What in the blazes?"

Ghost pirates moved to the side as the pirate captain stomped his way to the center of the commotion and right up to Jonah. The exhilaration of the plunder had given way to a certain exhaustion, and Jonah was wise enough to be frightened of Miguel's flaming eyes.

Miguel looked Jonah up and down. It was apparent the pirate captain was angry, and any love the man might have had for Jonah was long since gone. "Treason has only one punishment," he sneered.

"Treason?" Jonah dared to ask.

"Mutiny. Treason of the sea."

"But I didn't..." Jonah began.

Miguel lifted his sword up to Jonah's chin. "Oh, but you did."

Jonah lifted his chin away from the blade, and Miguel pushed the tip lightly against Jonah's skin. "Death for traitors," he hissed.

At the sound of "Land Ho!" Miguel spun around so quickly his sword sliced through the ghost pirates nearest him. It did them no harm, of course, as they were ghosts, part of the magic that seemed to be everywhere on the ship. But the action slowed the crew, making it difficult for them to move out of the way of their captain.

"Where?" Miguel yelled back.

The man in the crow's nest pointed to the west. Miguel slid his sword back into position at his waist and whipped out his spyglass. It took only a moment for him to expand it and put it to his eye.

"What about him?" Heckel complained.

"Take away his sword and throw him below," Miguel commanded without turning around.

Heckel stepped forward, a broad menacing grin plastered on his face. Two other pirates stepped forward with him. "Your sword," Heckel demanded.

Jonah cringed inwardly. He hesitated, his hand hovering just above the hilt. The fire he'd felt before flared deep inside and started to push its way outward. The urge to draw his sword and fight grew within him.

Heckel's two henchmen had come up beside Jonah, and just as Jonah's fingers touched the hilt of his sword, they grabbed his arms. Heckel smashed him over the head with the butt of his gun. Jonah's fingers relaxed, his body swayed, and everything went black as he dropped to the deck. The last thing he saw was Miguel's face in his own telling him, "There can be only one captain, boy. One. And I am that one."

# Thirty-Four

Jonah woke with a headache. He was in a musty, dark space and the weight of the air pressed against his lungs. He slowly blinked open his eyes, expecting the bright light to worsen the pain in his head. There was little light, however, where he'd been thrown. He sat up slowly and felt the straw underneath him. A thin trickle of light reached him from a crack in front, and slightly above, where he sat. As his eyes adjusted to the darkness of the space, he slumped realizing he was in the hull of the ship.

The stench wasn't as strong as Jonah imagined it should be, though the air was stale and sour. He'd learned that punishment was rarely anything less than death, and that was usually dealt with swiftly. Pirates rarely kept prisoners, so the area was not used often. What little stench there was, was certainly old, and that was enough to roll Jonah's stomach.

A scuffle to his left caused Jonah to turn. Squinting his eyes he could make out a huddled mass in the corner furthest from him. A mass the shape of another human being. It took him a few minutes to recall what had landed him down below in the first place. He groaned as he remembered the girl he'd dragged back with him.

"They put you down here, too?" Jonah asked, rubbing his head to try to lessen the throbbing.

The girl stopped moving. "After they knocked you out, the captain had more important things to deal with. Didn't seem to have time to deal with me. For now, they've stuck me down here, to deal with later - when they decide your fate." She went back to scuffling around.

"So, they'll kill you, too?"

"I'm not sticking around to find out."

Jonah got up and moved closer to her. "What are you doing?"

The girl looked up. "More than you."

Jonah moved took a another step.

"Stay away! Don't come near me," she said. She paused long enough to make sure Jonah wasn't moving toward you, then went back to work.

Jonah moved back to the other side of the hull and sat back down. "I'm sorry," he said.

She stopped. "What?"

"For getting you into this. It's my fault you're here."

"Well, I'm not sure I had much choice," she said referring to the sinking ship. She continued to fiddle with something in the straw.

"Depends on what method they choose to kill you, I guess," Jonah said.

"What do you care? You were going to slit my throat back there."

The image of the scene flashed through Jonah's mind as though he'd witnessed the event instead of living it. He felt his stomach somersault as he cringed at the memory. "Sorry. I don't know what came over me."

"What came over you? Are you serious? You're a bloody pirate, on a bloody pirate ship, and you don't know what came over you?" She was no longer searching through the straw. Her body was turned toward him. Though he couldn't make our any of her features, Jonah imagined she was staring at him with one of those indignant looks his mother might have given him when she didn't believe what he was telling her.

"I'm not a pirate. I've never done anything like that before."

"Well, you certainly fooled me."

Flashes of the previous night engaged Jonah's mind. He winced inwardly and wondered what had changed to cause him to behave like that. The carnage he left in his wake… it made him sick to think about.

"What's your name?" he asked, wanting to dislodge the flood of memories.

There was a pause, as if she were weighing the wisdom of sharing that information. "Cora," she finally said as she went back to work.

"Jonah," he said, indicating himself.

Cora didn't appear to care. She was busy moving her hands among the hay on the floor and didn't so much as grunt in his direction.

"What are you doing?" he asked, shifting his position so he was now leaning toward her.

"I told you. I'm not sticking around here." Cora pulled her hands out of the hay and held them up before tossing something to the ground.

"Hey, your hands are tied together."

"No kidding, Genius." Cora snapped as she sat back. She blew hair out of her face. "That's why I'm doing this." She lifted a small sharp rock with her fingers and showed it to Jonah.

Jonah came closer, squinting to get a better look. The rope between Cora's hands was a bit fuzzy. She'd been trying to cut through the ropes by rubbing it back and forth across the stone.

"How's it working for ya?"

She huffed and lifted her wrists up so he could see them better. "You tell me," she snapped. It was obvious she hadn't made much progress. For all the fuzz, there wasn't any part of the rope that was fraying yet.

Jonah hadn't been tied. It seemed strange that she would be tied and he wouldn't. "Why didn't they tie me up?" he asked more to himself than to Cora.

"Beats me. Maybe because they'd knocked you senseless. It wasn't like they had to worry about you for the last two days."

"Two days?"

"Yeah. At least I think it was two days. I don't really know as there isn't much to go on down here. But if meals and quiet are any indication of cycles on a ship, then, yeah, two days."

As if to confirm the fact, Jonah's stomach grumbled. "Wow. Two days," he said. He reach up and rubbed his head again.

"Out cold."

"Here," Jonah offered, remembering that Cora was tied and down here because of him. "Let me help you."

Cora eyed him suspiciously. Jonah didn't blame her. He'd threatened to kill her, dragged her to this pirate ship, got her locked up, and had really done nothing to prove he could be trusted. What Jonah knew that she didn't was that something strange had happened to him. He hadn't been himself.

"How much harm can I do?" he said. "It's not like I have a sword."

That seemed to appease her a little. Either that or she realized he had a better chance than she did at succeeding. She handed the piece of rock to him, then held up her hands making the rope taut between them. Jonah took the rock and began to saw back and forth on the rope. It was slow going, but he made better progress than she did by herself.

"You seem different," Cora said with a little hesitation.

Jonah paused in his sawing and looked at her. He shrugged. "I am different." Turning his attention back to the work at hand, he tried to ignore her as he sawed at the rope. He really wasn't interested in talking about it. It wasn't as if he understood it himself. What he had done the night before was not something he would have normally done. Ever.

"How come, do you think, they didn't tie your hands?"

Jonah paused in his work and looked at his hands. He shrugged. "I don't know. Maybe like you said, I was out cold."

Cora rolled her eyes. "Not likely." She huffed and shifted from a crouch to kneeling. "Probably wouldn't do any good if they did."

"What do you mean?" Jonah went back to work sawing the ropes.

"You're like him, aren't you?"

The question surprised him coming from her. He wanted to ask her who she meant, but he knew. He kept sawing.

"Did you know?" she pressed.

"No." Though as he thought about it, he should have suspected. After all, Miguel was his father.

"Was that your first time?" she asked more tentatively, like she as afraid she might provoke him.

He nodded, still not looking at her.

"How's it work?"

Jonah stopped, and finally looked Cora in the eyes. It dawned on him that he didn't know anything about this girl; yet it was obvious she knew something about him. Well, maybe not him, but about his father or his father's kind. The idea of the change didn't seem to shake her. Oh, sure. She'd been scared enough on the ship the night before, but she seemed to understand that this – whatever this was – was real. It was almost as if she was familiar with the idea of it. "I don't know," he told her, shaking his head as he went back to working on her ropes.

"You threaten him, you know."

Jonah paused, the rock resting against the rope. He blinked, as if he wasn't sure what he'd just heard.

"It's true," Cora continued. "He wouldn't want to kill you if you didn't threaten him. It's not how it works."

His eyes narrowed. "What do you mean?"

Cora bit her lip.

"You know something about all this, don't you?"

Instead of answering him, she asked a question of her own. "How long have you been training?"

"A few weeks, maybe a month. I'm not really sure."

"Which is it, a few weeks or a month?"

Jonah shrugged. "I don't know exactly." To be honest, Jonah wasn't certain how long he'd even been on the ship. Some days he felt as if he'd always been on the ship. It was difficult for him to reckon time.

"Don't you keep a log or something?"

"A log?"

"Yeah. Like a ship's log? Or something?"

Jonah thought of the book Miguel wrote in every night. He hadn't ever considered keeping one himself. "Umm. Nope. Nothing like that."

Cora blew out some air. "Okay. Unless we can steal the actual ship's log – which is highly unlikely given our current situation - we'll have to assume a month. Doesn't give us much time."

"What do you mean, give *us* much time." Jonah finally broke through the ropes and Cora shook them off. She rubbed her wrists gingerly. They were red and raw, but the damage was minimal.

She looked at Jonah, determination evident in her eyes. "There's still hope, but we've got to get you to the island."

# Thirty-Five

"How do you know about the island?" Jonah asked. "For that matter, how do you know about Miguel?"

"You mean the Pirate King."

"Yeah, whatever."

"I've heard stories," she hesitated, "about him." She paused as though deciding what to tell him. "My whole life I've heard them. In some ways it didn't seem possible, but…" she shrugged.

"What aren't you telling me?" he demanded.

"Nothing. It doesn't matter. We just need to get out of here." She began pushing things around again, sweeping the straw with her hands and her feet as she crawled along.

"What are you doing now?" he asked her.

"Looking for something I can use to get out of here."

"You won't find anything." He knew the hull wasn't used for much. It was mostly just an open, dark space.

Cora rapped on something wooden. "What about these?"

Once again Jonah moved closer to her, following the path she'd made through the straw. As he got closer to her and the other side of the hull, he could make out the shape of crates against the outer wall of the ship.

Cora paused in her work and turned her head toward him. "Do

you know what's in them?" she asked indicating the wooden crates.

"No."

"Then how would you know? Maybe there'll be something useful inside." She turned back to the crate and tugged at the top. When it didn't budge, she banged along the edge trying to get it open.

Jonah figured it was pointless. Even if she did manage to get one open, which he doubted, it wasn't likely she'd find anything to help them escape from where they were. He was certain they were locked in the hull. Likely, there was only one set of keys on board the *Mary Margaret*, and Heckel would have them. Feeling like there was nothing they could do to prevent the inevitable, he sat back and watched as Cora fought with the crate in front of her.

"You could be doing something," Cora called out with irritation.

"I am," Jonah replied. "I'm watching you."

Cora snapped. He could feel the change even in the darkness. He was sure that if he could have seen her face clearly, she would be glaring at him. "You do realize that if we don't get out of here it's certain death for both us?"

Jonah didn't reply. He'd rather not think about the inevitable. In every way he had failed. He had failed to avenge his mother, failed to gain the pride of his father, failed to make everything right in the world. And he'd even become the thing he hated most about his father, though he had no idea how that had happened.

"Fine. Don't get out of here. What do I care?" Bitterness and frustration tinged her words. She went back to banging on the crates, pausing only long enough to pull at them some more. "I don't know what Saclavar was thinking?"

That got Jonah's attention. "Saclavar? The wizard?"

"Yeah," Cora grunted as she pulled on another crate lid. "Who else?"

"Wait." Jonah scooted forward. "Did Saclavar send you? Was that ship just a ploy?"

Cora stopped moving. "Umm, not exactly," she said uncomfortably. She regained her confidence, though, as she added, "but I'm sure he wouldn't be impressed."

"This is too weird," Jonah said, rubbing his head again. The ache had lessened but trying to think hurt, causing the pain to flare back up.

"He doesn't actually know I'm here," she said quietly. "I mean, he probably knows I'm here now because I'm here with you, and he knows everything about you."

"That's not creepy or anything." The idea of someone knowing everything about him gave him the willies, but it seemed to make sense.

Cora came over and sat down beside him. "Look, I'd overheard him talking about you. I just, I don't know, thought maybe I could help."

"Help? By coming out in the middle of the ocean and nearly getting yourself killed!"

"I didn't nearly get myself killed," she retorted. "You nearly killed me!" She got up with a huff and went back to her crates.

He could hear her grunt as she pulled against the crates, slamming her boot into the side as she did so. Irritation flooded him. She was right. He was the one who almost killed her.

"What can I do?" he asked irritably.

"The same thing I am," she returned as she finally managed to pull the top off the first crate. "Unless you think feeling sorry for yourself is going to help you."

It wasn't that he didn't want to get out. He didn't want to die, and he hadn't accomplished what he'd come here to do. He hadn't managed to even ask Miguel to make things right. And now, here he was, a complete disappointment to his father. He'd thought he would be able make him proud. Disappointment in himself gave way to despair as he acknowledged the situation he now found himself in. Nothing he did could undo what had been done. At least not for him. But maybe, just maybe, he could do something to make sure she was okay. After all, it was his fault she was in this mess.

"Look, Cora, I'm sorry about all this." Even with her hands untied, Jonah didn't see how she was going to get out of this mess - how either of them would.

"I'm not giving up," she said. "And neither should you."

Jonah watched as she went back to work rummaging around inside the crate. Wood shavings spilled out over its sides, and, when she didn't find anything useful, she moved on to another. Jonah followed pulling at the lid of one of the crates himself. Together they worked through two more crates. It took a lot of time to get each one open.

The yelling and stomping of pirates above caused both Jonah and Cora to look up at the ceiling. Jonah held his breath. Since they couldn't make out the words, they had to guess what was happening by the sound of the boots.

"Doesn't sound good," Jonah said.

The voices sounded angry. Jonah was certain, by following the direction of the sound of the boots, that the pirates were headed toward the doors that would bring them below deck. That thought was enough to yank Jonah from his wallowing misery. He wasn't ready to die. If only he had a sword, he would feel like he had a chance to fight his way out.

"You find anything yet?" Jonah asked Cora. Panic had crept into his voice. He turned to look at her when he asked the question, knowing it was fruitless.

Cora quickly dropped her hand from her pocket, shook her head, and started pulling at the next crate lid with more urgency. The motion triggered something in Jonah's memory. He searched back in his mind and remembered her on the ground in the captain's quarters of the sinking ship.

"What were you doing in the captain's quarters?"

Cora stiffened.

Realization dawned on him. "You were searching for something."

She hesitated, her hand moving back to her pocket before dropping back to the crate.

"And you found it." An idea formed in Jonah's head. "What's in your pocket?"

"Nothing."

"I saw you in the captain's quarters. I was there." Irritation made its way into Jonah's voice again. "You put something in your pocket. Something you didn't want me to see."

Yelling and stomping traveled across the deck above. They both paused and looked at the ceiling following the sound.

"If it was important enough for you to risk your life retrieving it, it just might buy our way out of here."

The thudding of boots coming down the stairs indicated the pirates were just moments away.

"Come on, Cora. What is it?"

"There isn't time for this," Cora said, clearly not willing to give up whatever treasure she had. Her hands were frantically tearing apart the crates in front of her, but to no avail. "They'll be here any minute; and I, for one, don't plan on being here when they arrive."

"And just what are you going to do?" Jonah snapped at her. "You've got nothing but a bunch of straw! That won't stop them from tearing you limb from limb, or making you walk the plank."

"That's better than being hung out for the birds," Cora snapped back. She'd turned toward him in her own anger. Jonah's eyes had grown large. "Oh, don't tell me you don't know what I'm talking about. Boy, have you got a lot to learn." She came closer to him. "They've charged you with mutiny. Most likely they'll put you in a cage and leave you hanging out for the birds to peck to death. No food. No water. Scorching sun. The birds will come. And they'll pluck your eyes out first. That is, of course, if they don't decide to keelhaul you first. Maybe they'll do both. Don't think they'll go easy on you, 'cause they won't!"

Jonah's stomach flopped uneasily. He suddenly felt very ill.

The sound of boots had grown louder, and now stopped. In its place was the sound of angry yelling.

"Or, if you're lucky, they'll just shoot you. Either way, what I've got in my pocket won't save you. It's only useful if we get away from this ship."

The door burst open and Cora turned away to hide herself among the crates. Jonah didn't have the luxury of crates. He was too close to the door, and too big to be able to hide. No matter where he was, they would see him.

"Open the door!" Heckel bellowed from behind the door. Keys rattled and clanged as they dropped to the ground twice before the door was unlocked.

Jonah stood just back away from the door and watched as several large burly pirates pushed their way into the hold. Though he didn't know them all by name, Jonah recognized them. They were Heckel's cronies, which meant Heckel must be somewhere nearby. He searched the pirates looking for his nemesis.

Those pirates who had entered first, now came to a stop forming two lines with a path down the middle. The remaining crowd parted, and Heckel thumped his way down the stairs to stand in the doorway. Jonah was grateful that, for the moment, the darkness prevented the pirate from seeing him. Heckel reached back and grabbed a lantern. He held it up shining the light across the darkness towards Jonah. A length of cord loosely hung from his other hand as he glowered at Jonah.

The anger Jonah had been feeling seeped out of him like blood from a dying man. His heart plunged to his feet. A cold, hard knot formed in his stomach. He was not ready to die. But without his sword, he had no idea how to summon the strength to fight someone like Heckel, let alone all the rest of the pirates. He was greatly outnumbered, and outarmed.

Jonah felt his body stiffen in preparation to fight. He knew he didn't have a chance, but he couldn't convince his body that dying was an option. Heckel stepped forward blocking any chance for Jonah to slip past and escape. The big pirate raised the cord, looping it in preparation for tying it to the boy. Jonah got the feeling Heckel would have used it as a noose, stringing him up right there, if given the chance.

"Turn around, boy!" Spittle flew into Jonah's face as the man bellowed his instructions.

Turning around was a bad idea. Jonah was certain the moment

he did Heckel would pull a knife and slit his throat. The pirate was out to get him one way or another. Probably no one would even care. He was charged with mutiny. The only sentence for mutiny was death. Jonah was sure the pirates wouldn't care if that death happened before the actual trial.

"I said, turn around!" Heckel leaned in close enough that Jonah could smell the man's fish breath.

Jonah began slowly to turn.

"Hands behind your back!"

As he put his hands behind his back, Jonah's eyes settled on Cora. She had tucked herself in among the straw, probably hoping she wouldn't be remembered. Guilt washed over Jonah. He was to blame for her being here in the first place. She didn't deserve this.

He kicked his leg back connecting with the pirate nearest him. Swinging around, he raised his fists. *There's no way this will be a fair fight,* he thought as is jabbed his left hand toward the nearest pirate's midsection and immediately followed it up with a wild swing to his jaw.

With a yowl, more surprise than hurt, the pirate called out, "Get him! Hold him fast!"

Ducking punches while swinging his fists wildly, Jonah managed to connect three or four times before his own feet were swept out from under him. He landed hard on his face, the wind completely knocked out of him. A boot pressed in hard on his back, while his arms were yanked behind him.

Rough cord pulled tight around Jonah's hands. He was grabbed roughly by his shoulder and pulled to his feet. A jerk to the ropes at his hands pulled him backward and made him stumble right into Heckel's grasp. The burly pirate slipped his arm around Jonah's neck in a chokehold, causing Jonah to lose his breath. "Not so important now, are ya, boy?" The stench of the man's breath would have knocked Jonah out if his hold wasn't already doing just that.

"Let him go!"

Heckel swung around, dragging Jonah with him. The boy was rapidly losing consciousness. Images swam in and out of his sight as his eyes tried hopelessly to keep up. The lack of oxygen pressed heavily against Jonah's mind, his lungs burned, and his knees were weak. He couldn't hold on much longer.

"I said, let him go." The voice was fierce, if not loud.

"On whose orders?" Heckel demanded.

"The captain's."

Heckel's arm tightened slightly before it slackened, and Jonah's legs gave out. His head throbbed and his vision swirled as he collapsed onto the floor.

Hecklel stepped over Jonah. "'Tis the captain who charged this here boy with mutiny."

"Aye. And 'tis the captain who decides his fate." Seward had stepped around Heckel and was now helping Jonah to sit up. "The captain sent me to fetch the boy to him. You are dismissed."

Heckel glowered at Seward. "'Taint how it works," he growled. The big man turned to the other pirates in the hold. "What say ye? Do we wait for the captain, or is it death as is fittin'?"

The pirates in the hold turned to one another. None was willing to go against the captain; to do so would be mutiny. But they were reluctant to go against Heckel as well. The one was in front of them now, but the wrath of their captain was such none was willing to challenge. The pirates looked to one another, but not a one spoke.

"Death can wait an hour more," Seward said as he hefted Jonah up.

The pirates parted, making a clear path for the first mate to help Jonah out of the hold. Death had been delayed. But as Jonah made his way past the pirates, he wondered if it might have been better if Heckel had killed him then.

# Thirty-Six

It didn't take long for Jonah to regain his legs. The headache that accompanied the full return of his senses, however, pounded relentlessly. He was not in any hurry to see Miguel. Nothing good could come of this meeting.

"'Twon't be as bad as all that," Seward said, as if reading the boy's mind. "He ain't in his right mind, if ya know what I mean."

Jonah didn't know if Seward meant Miguel the pirate, or Miguel the father. On this pirate ship, it might be the latter, but any sane person would have considered the pirate more out of his mind.

"He charged me with treason," Jonah said. "A delay in my death sentence doesn't change the outcome." As he had in the hold, Jonah wondered if it would have been better to have let Heckel kill him down below. Torture and birdcages really didn't appeal to him.

"Give him a chance," Seward said. "There's more to the captain than whatcha see."

That was certainly an understatement. Miguel could shift between an everyday farmer and a pirate, his entire appearance changing with him. He could be kind and patient one moment yet draw in massive storms the next.

They came to a stop in front of the large oak doors of the captain's quarters. Seward thumped heartily upon the door three times, then untied Jonah's hands. "No need for this now." He raised his fist and again beat against the door three times. There was the sound of wood scraping against wood - probably a chair sliding backward. Heavy steps followed - the sound all too familiar to Jonah – and the door swung inward revealing a very disheveled man.

Jonah barely recognized the man before him. Miguel's hat was missing, his hair in long tendrils of tangled knots. It was greasy, and therefore shone in the pale light. His shirtsleeve was torn, and his trousers were smeared with blood. The tie at his waist had come loose, leaving his shirt to flutter in an unflattering way. The lines in the man's face were etched deeply, though the bags under his eyes were swollen and black. It looked like the pirate had been roughed up in battle and hadn't slept in days.

"Come in. Come in," the pirate said in a very tired voice as he turned and walked back into the room.

This wasn't the pirate or the father Jonah had come to know. This shell or a man seemed fragile – broken. Jonah leaned in close to Seward. "What's wrong with him?" After Miguel had sealed Jonah's fate, Jonah was surprised by the twinge of concern he felt for the pirate.

"Been havin' himself a bit o' a fight. A battle, as it were."

"Well, don't just stand there. Bring the boy inside," the captain bellowed.

"Come along, Jonah," Seward said as he led the way into the cabin.

Jonah came in slowly and glanced around. The whole room looked as if it'd weathered a storm. The great map table was flipped on its side, its compass rolling around, unable to gain north. One of the hammocks hung limply by only one rope, swinging with the rock of the ship. Bottles of rum had been smashed – shards of glass scattered everywhere. The only thing that seemed to be right about the room was the little desk by the windows. It was upright, the ink and quill set to the left, the ship's log open in the center.

"What happened here?" Jonah asked before he could stop himself.

Miguel looked around him as if seeing the mess for the first time. His shoulders slumped, the appearance of a defeated man. It seemed he had no fire left in him.

"I have delivered the boy, Captain, just as you ordered."

"Thank you, Seward. You may go."

Seward gave Jonah an apologetic look. "Do not worry, Master Jonah, all will be well."

*Master Jonah?* Seward had never called him that before. *What had he meant by it?*

Jonah watched as the man he'd considered a mentor left, closing the door behind him. He was now alone with the man he knew was his father, but this man in front of him was unfamiliar. He neither appeared the great and fearsome pirate, nor the more gentle but demanding father. It was as if something had broken within him.

"I believe we have a trial to attend," Miguel said, a slight edge to his voice.

The knot that had formed in Jonah's stomach doubled. The man before him may not have looked like the fearsome pirate, but he certainly maintained the same agenda.

"Mutiny is a troublesome thing, boy. Troublesome indeed." The pirate turned to look at Jonah. His face was aged and drawn. "Indeed, we cannot overlook such behavior onboard ship. It would do no good. Send the wrong message."

The bitter taste of bile found its way into Jonah's mouth. What was the point of being rescued from one killing party, just to turn around and be offered to the next. Though he'd been prepared to fight to his death, Jonah now found that having his death put off, extending the time he had to wait knowing it was coming, was much worse.

"But Seward, well, Seward doesn't think it was mutiny. Says it ain't mutiny 'less one knows what he's about." The pirate spat, as if the very idea tasted foul. "So, tell me, boy," the pirate came close to Jonah, "What made ya do it?"

"I… I… don't know," Jonah stammered. He had a hard enough time remembering what had happened. Knowing why it happened was something he couldn't even begin to grasp. One moment he had been enjoying his time at the wheel, and the next he was fighting his way across a foreign ship, slaughtering anything that moved. His stomach lurched that the memory.

"Must be cause you're me boy," the pirate said thoughtfully, rubbing at his chin. He had picked up a pistol and was now waving it around in the air. "Powerful magic, that."

Jonah wasn't comfortable with the direction of the conversation – or the gun. He was used to his father showing up now and again, usually first thing in the morning, but mostly, he was used to the pirate. The vicious, mean, nasty pirate. The one that seemed both to want to kill him and train him. This man who stood before Jonah now was neither. It was as if something had broken through and cracked the man right in half, then tried to piece him back together again, and it didn't go so well.

"Train the boy," the pirate was muttering. "Prepare him. Bring him to her. I did all that. Mutiny it was. Not his fault. Can't control.

Too much power. Must be stopped."

Clearly the captain had lost his mind. The fact that Jonah's fate lay squarely with the man before him didn't bode well. But maybe, if he were careful, the situation would lend itself to an opportunity for escape.

"The code doesn't care whose fault it is. Mutiny cannot be tolerated. Even if it was done without knowing." The pirate's voice has steadied. It was clear the pirate was debating with himself, and it seemed the pirate side was winning. That made Jonah even more uneasy.

The man swung around to face Jonah. "Tell ya what, boy." His head hung heavily to one side, "Don't do it. You need him." The pirate shook his head and righted its position. "Don't try to stop me."

"I wasn't… I didn't…" Jonah stammered.

"Not you, boy!" he bellowed.

Jonah looked around him wondering if he'd missed someone. There wasn't anyone else in the room. The pirate had definitely cracked. This could not possibly end well.

Just then the door slammed open. Jonah swung around to see Heckel standing in its frame, his men just behind him. He looked over the Captain, a smirk coming to his lips, greed clear in his eyes.

"What do ya think you're doing!" Miguel bellowed. "Get out!" For a moment it sounded like the pirate king was back.

Jonah never thought he'd have felt relieved to have the pirate king around. But with Heckel so close, it was good to see the captain had someone else to dispel his displeasure on. Besides, this unstable pirate was starting to seriously scare Jonah.

"We's some unfinished business," Heckel sneered. He had

unsheathed his sword, and now held it point down. The gleam in his eye did not leave. If anything, it hardened into a challenge. The man must have been insane to challenge the captain. "We's done had us a vote, see. The boy dies."

Miguel's left eye twitched, and his head jerked. "I'm the captain. I give the orders 'round here."

"Then ya'd best be getting' on with it. Some of the men here, see, thinks you may be gettin' soft. Ya must honor the code. And the code says ya honor the vote."

With his eye still twitching, the captain took a couple jerky steps forward, placing himself between Jonah and Heckel. "I know the code," he growled.

The men behind Heckel shifted, becoming impatient. Jonah wondered what it was that Heckel had said or done to convince these men to go against their captain. Now that they were here… Jonah looked back at the windows by the desk. Could he get there before Heckel made his move? He didn't think so, but he had to try. Take steps slowly backward so as not to draw attention to himself, Jonah managed to get within an arm's length of the desk before he froze. He was not surprised by the verdict, only by the sound of regret that came with it.

"The boy will die."

Heckel stepped forward. Miguel stopped him. "But I will choose the terms." Conviction had returned to Miguel's voice and posture. This time Heckel took a step back. Miguel glanced around, retrieved his sword from the overturned table, and raised it above his head. "Now get out of me quarters!" he bellowed.

# Thirty-Seven

Heckel and his men didn't wait to be told again. They turned and tried to push their way back toward the main deck, tripping on one another the whole way. It seemed the return of the pirate king was enough to remind them of their place, and to send them scurrying back to position.

Miguel had taken quick stock of the mess, then bellowed for Seward, whom he ordered to clean it up. The fierce red eyes were burning, and Jonah wasn't sure if he should be frightened by them or elated that the crazy split personalities were gone. It didn't matter though, as his fate had been sealed.

Jonah leaped onto the desk, desperate now to get out of the room. This was his last chance. His only chance.

"T'won't do you any good," Miguel told him. "Them windows are sealed tight."

As Seward scurried around the cabin righting furniture and sweeping up broken glass, Miguel retied Jonah. "Sorry, son," he said, "I didn't mean for it to be this way." There was just enough change in the pirate's voice for Jonah to recognize his father in it. His mind ran back to Delmar when he'd first met the pirate. There were times when the man had seemed genuine and kind. But there had been those other things as well – all the unnatural things that had set the town against his mother.

Jonah swung around, anger welling up, and faced Miguel. Looking into the face of the fierce pirate, he nearly lost his courage. The image of his mother came to his mind, and he clung to it for strength. "When you first found me on your ship, you asked why I had come."

Miguel raised an eyebrow. Whether in interest or amusement Jonah couldn't tell.

"You told me once that you'd come to Delmar to find me and my mother. That you'd loved us all this time. But what you did in Delmar ruined my mother. Turned the people against her. You destroyed her!"

The pirate blinked, the red glow in his eyes shifting.

"It wasn't enough for you, was it? You couldn't just leave us alone. You destroyed her – twice!"

The red fire was out, replaced by the smoky haze Jonah had known at the cove. "I didn't…"

"The freak ice, the storm, the fish, the tidal waves!"

"That wasn't me," Miguel said.

"Don't deny it! I saw you! I was there when you turned the water to ice."

"Oh, well, yeah, I did that one. Just a little joke. That Montagurrell needed to be taught a lesson."

"And it nearly killed my mother."

"I made sure it didn't."

"I know," Jonah relented. "I saw that, too. But do you really think the townsfolk believed it was a freak of nature? And what about that storm, huh? There wasn't anything natural about that at all."

"Actually, that wasn't me."

"Of course it was you! We'd never had a storm like that in Delmar before."

"You did that, Jonah. I may have encouraged it a little, but it was all you." When Jonah continued to look at Miguel in puzzlement, Miguel continued. "All I did was awaken your senses. It would have happened anyway, I just accelerated it. With your senses open, you're tied to the ocean, and thereby, the storms."

Jonah didn't understand any of what Miguel was saying. It didn't make sense. He certainly never felt powerful enough to do anything like that. And he never would have brought something like that to Delmar. The risk to his mother would have been too great.

"And the fish?"

Miguel's expression darkened. "That wasn't me, either."

"Who else then?"

Miguel raised his hand to cut off the boy. "I'm not sure who, Jonah. It may have been the ocean herself."

Jonah deflated a little. "Why would she do that?"

"As a warning to me."

"Ah, Captain, sir?" Seward interrupted. "The men."

Miguel glanced toward the door. A commotion of angry voices could be heard. The spark that had left Miguel's eye was back. The red flame ignited once more.

But Jonah wasn't finished. "Isn't there anything you can do? You can't just leave ma to fight this alone."

The pirate's red eyes flared. "Oh, she isn't alone, boy. She never was." He grabbed Jonah roughly by the shoulder and shoved him toward the door. "Get a move on. They's awaitin'."

With a solid kick to the door, Miguel forced Jonah out onto the open deck. The light was bright, causing the young man to blink in discomfort. Miguel shoved him forward, making him stumble to his knees. Frustration turned to despair. The only reason Jonah had come aboard this ship was to help his mother. He'd failed her at home. And he failed her now.

"And what have we here?" The captain said.

Jonah jerked his head up. Struggling between two of Heckel's men was Cora. They must have gone back below and brought her up. She was tied with her hands out in front of her and had a gag in her mouth. She was doing her best to make things difficult for the two men. But they were strong, supernatural beings, and they simply hefted her up between them and dragged her kicking body forward.

"Let her go! She hasn't done anything!" Jonah was surprised to hear his own voice. His conscience dug deep. Cora would never have been on this ship had it not been for him. He couldn't let them hurt her. Jerking forward, Jonah tried to escape Miguel's hand. The pirate was surprisingly strong, given the unruly state he was in.

"Hold up, son." Jonah barely heard the captain speak. He gave a violent shrug, Miguel dropped his hand, and Jonah turned to see what the pirate had in mind.

Miguel put out his hand to stop the progression of the pirates and stood in front of the girl. He looked her over as if considering her. Then a look of recognition crossed his face, and he leaned in, his nose nearly touching her own. "And just what are you doing on my ship?" he hissed.

Cora scrunched up her nose as though she'd smelled something foul. It was probably Miguel's breath. Pirates weren't great about hygiene as a matter of principle, but Miguel was especially ripe today.

"What. Are. *You.* Doing. On. My. Ship?" He demanded with more vehemence.

Cora glanced in Jonah's direction.

"Aah, yes. The boy brought you here," Miguel said as he moved around her. "And what would this sea rat want with you?" At this last question, Miguel turned to Jonah.

"I just… she was…" Jonah stammered. He thought about telling the pirate about whatever she was hiding in her pocket, but something restrained his tongue. In truth, he'd only brought her along because he'd not been able to kill her. That would not go over well with the pirate king. "I don't even know her," he finally said. Maybe that would make them go easy on her.

"Plank. Plank. Plank," came a low chant. It began to build as more pirates took it up. "Plank. Plank. Plank."

Miguel turned to the crowd. His glowing red eyes were wavering. The twitch was back in his left eye, and his head jerked involuntarily. "It's the plank you want?" He asked the crowd.

"Aye!" came the reply.

"What say ye, boy?"

Jonah didn't know if Miguel meant for his own death or for the girl's. Maybe, if he agreed to having Cora walk the plank, he'd be accepted as one of the crew again. Jonah looked at the pirates around him. Heckel's sharp glare cut right through him. The burly pirate would never let Jonah live. He tried to swallow the lump growing in his throat.

"Father," he said. It was the only thing he could think of that might grant him some mercy.

Miguel leaned over to Jonah. "Father, now, is it?" He spat. "A dutiful son would not embarrass his father. You're no son of mine."

The pirate stood straight again; the tick in his eye increased. "Throw them overboard!"

# Thirty-Eight

Jonah was yanked to his feet and forced to follow Cora. Several pirates had prepared the gangplank, while others held the struggling girl. She twisted and turned, throwing her weight around while Heckel tried to tie a blindfold on her. He cursed when she managed to kick him in the knee.

Eventually, he gave up. "Let her watch as the sharks tear her apart," he sputtered, then shoved her on the plank.

Cora stood on the plank as it bounced lightly under her. She didn't have her arms to help her balance, though her fingers were nimbly trying to work out the knots behind her.

"Now, none of that," Heckel said as he climbed on the plank behind her. He pulled out his sword and pressed the tip of it into Cora's back. Jonah had to give her credit. She barely winced, not letting any sound escape her lips. She did, however, move forward.

"You can't do this," Jonah found himself saying. A hand immediately clamped over his mouth. He tried to fight back, but being tied, he couldn't do much. He opened his mouth as far as he could under the hand, and bit down.

"Whatcha gotta go and do that for?" Seward yelped.

Jonah was momentarily taken aback. He hadn't expected Seward to be part of this. Maybe he should have. After all, Seward was part of the crew. Part of this cursed ship. But Seward had been Jonah's mentor. Had helped him when no one else would. Jonah tried to pull away.

"Now hang on a minute, Jonah," Seward said. "Things ain't often what they seem."

"Oh no?" Jonah countered. "So, Cora's not really walking the plank. I'm not really sentenced to die?"

"Well, no… I mean yes, she is, and you are."

"Then I'd say they're exactly as they seem." Jonah could feel the anger build within him. He recognized the boiling sensation as it started to creep through him. "I never should have come here."

"Now, don't go sayin' that. 'Tis a good thing you came."

"Jump. Jump. Jump."

The chant broke through their conversation drawing Jonah's attention back to the gangplank. Cora had reached the end - the tip of Heckel's sword only an inch from her back. The plank bounced heavily with the added weight.

"Jump down, sweetheart, or be pushed."

Cora glanced over her shoulder at the pirate and the sword still wavering behind her. Her eyes swept to Jonah's, then she turned back and jumped.

"No!" Jonah yelled and fought against Seward's grip. He couldn't believe she'd gone over. "You can't let her die," he said to Seward. "It isn't right."

Seward shrugged. "Nothing I can do. But you…"

The first mate didn't get the chance to finish. Four of Heckel's men had surrounded Jonah, pulling him forward. Jonah looked up to the quarter deck where Miguel stood. The pirate's jerky head motions had become more pronounced. The pirate king looked down at Jonah but said nothing.

"Ain't no land rat gonna usurp me," Heckel growled, his face inches from Jonah's own. To his own men he said, "Bind him well. Don't want anythin' happenin' to this one."

A burlap sack was secured and placed over Jonah's head. Cords were wrapped tightly around the sack, squeezing Jonah's body uncomfortably. The air inside the sack was thick, and heavy making Jonah panic. He tried to pull away, but there were too many hands. They bound his legs and attached a rope between the cords on his feet and wrists. Jonah felt his legs buckle as they tied something else to him. He figured it must have been a cannonball, given its weight. There would be no plank for him, he realized, as they were making certain there would be no chance of survival.

Tears streaked down his hot cheeks as he thought about his mother. He should have listened to her all those years. Should have stayed away from the cove, away from the water, and never, ever have gotten on this ship. She wouldn't have wanted him to risk his life for her comfort. Now she'd never even know what had happened to him.

# Thirty-Nine

Water seeped in, first cooling the air in the sack, then filling it up. The cords between Jonah's wrists and ankles tightened as they soaked up the ocean. The lead weight of the cannonball dragged his body forever downward and prevented any chance of buoyancy. They really needn't have tied him up. He would have drowned anyway, given that he couldn't swim. Was it really necessary for him to suffer more?

Red hot rage boiled inside him. Anger at himself. Anger at his father. Anger at the pirates. It rolled inside him, waiting to be unleashed. The ocean bubbled around him, pressing itself against him.

*This would be a fine time to dream,* he thought.

*Use the ocean.* A watery voice floated to him. It sounded familiar, but Jonah couldn't seem to place it. The pressure of the water as he sank deeper made his head want to explode. His lungs burned. He couldn't keep his mind focused.

*Call to her. She'll help you.*

If it were possible, the world seemed to get blacker. Jonah was losing consciousness. If he were going to do anything, he would need to do so now. But what could he do? He couldn't make his brain work.

In the recesses of his mind, Jonah thought he heard the sound of something heavy above him. Like something being plunged deep into the water. The current shifted, wrapping itself around Jonah. Bubbles pressed against him, tickling the little exposed skin he had. The cord holding him seemed to release; bubbles racing away. His body drifted, becoming lighter.

Just as Jonah's mind went black, he broke the surface. His body held in place by the unseen current. Then he felt someone slap his face. He tried to pull himself back.

"Jonah. Jonah. Wake up!" The voice sounded far away, and Jonah only wanted to sleep. "Come on, Jonah." He was slapped again. This time he sputtered, and as he came to, began to flail. He managed to hit his rescuer.

"Ow!" Cora yelled. "Stop flailing around!"

Jonah stopped moving, and found he was able to stay above water. The pressure pushing up from underneath told him the ocean was holding him in place.

"Cora!" He exclaimed through a raspy, scratchy voice. "How did you… Why are you… I saw you go over."

"I got lucky. They never searched me before sending me over. I had the ocean stone. Course I didn't know it'd actually work," she said.

"Wait. Back up. The ocean stone? What is an ocean stone?"

"Umm…"

"It's what you stole from that ship, isn't it? It's what you hid in your pocket."

"Yeah. It's an important magical relic. Lucky for me, I guess." Cora had let go of Jonah was treading water near him. Her body bobbed up and down with the ocean. "I saw what they did to you.

How'd you get out? There's no way you could have gotten out of that yourself. Unless," a cloud of fear crossed Cora's eyes. "No, you said you hadn't…"

"I didn't do it," Jonah cut in not liking the expression on her face. "I thought you had. Though how you would have gotten those cords undone is beyond me."

Cora shook her head. "It wasn't me. I didn't do anything to help you."

"Not even with your ocean stone?"

She shook her head and chewed her lip. There was an uncomfortable moment as the realization hit him.

"You hadn't planned on helping me."

Embarrassment shone on Cora's face.

"Doesn't matter," Jonah said tartly. "I can't really blame you. Not after what I'd done." He knew it was his fault Cora was here in the first place. "I'm sorry I got you into all his."

Cora looked uneasily at him.

"What?" Jonah asked.

"Nothing. Just…" Cora obviously beginning to tire. She bobbed less high, and her arms were moving more slowly.

Jonah waited, watching her. She shifted uncomfortably under his stare, gave a hard kick and briefly brought herself higher out of the water.

"I saw them throw someone else overboard, too."

The news surprised Jonah. There hadn't been anyone else in the hold. Who else would they have thrown over?

"After they threw you over," Cora gasped between slaps of ocean against her face, "there was a pretty big commotion. Lots of guns were fired. Bunch of hypocrites if you ask me, throwing you off for mutiny."

"What are you saying?"

"Someone else was in the water."

A strange uncomfortable sensation prickled over Jonah. "Who?" he asked.

"The captain."

The memory of the watery voice rushed back to Jonah. It had been familiar. It made sense. "He told me how to get free," he said quietly. "Maybe he knew what they were going to do all along."

"He's one of them, Jonah. You can't trust him."

"He saved my life."

"You don't know that."

"Yes, I do. It was him. It was his voice."

It was clear Cora was uncomfortable with the way this conversation was spinning. "We can't stay out here forever. Eventually even your strength will fail." Cora was already showing signs of exhaustion. It was apparent she wouldn't be able to keep her head above water much longer. Already she was bobbing underneath the surface. "We have to get to the island. We'll only have a small window once I summon it." She dipped under the water as she reached underneath, fumbling with her clothes. When she brought her head above again, she held a flat stone the size of a small saucer in one hand, and a small golden compass in the other. The stone was translucent blue, catching the light and spraying it outward in various patterns of color.

"He gave up his ship to save me. I can't leave him."

"You don't even know where he is!" Cora said. She slipped under again, her body obviously tired. Her waterlogged clothes weighed her down more, no doubt expending her energy faster.

Jonah wasn't tired. The ocean current had been holding him up. He hadn't needed to expend any energy. Reaching out, Jonah grabbed hold of Cora and pulled her up so her head was above water. He watched as the light danced across the ocean's surface around her. It was mesmerizing and reminded him of something. "Maybe I don't. But I know someone who does." He let go of Cora.

"I can't," Cora started, beginning to flounder again. "Please, Jonah, we have to go now."

"Go ahead. Summon your island. I'm not going with you." Jonah moved further away from Cora in the water. "You're tired. You won't last much longer. Don't worry about me. I know what I'm doing." Jonah tried to believe his own words, and hoped he was telling the truth.

Reluctantly, Cora raised the compass and flicked it open. A brilliant light rose out of it. She placed the stone in its path, and as the light penetrated it, she turned the stone in a slow circle until its light broke open revealing an island. Jonah recognized the enchanted sand sparkling in the distance from his dreams.

He paused in the water. "So, it's real."

"Yes, Jonah. It is. All of it. Please. Come with me."

The island looked peaceful, and the idea of resting on it was very inviting. But Jonah was his mother's son. If there were any chance Miguel had a part in rescuing Jonah from his watery grave, then Jonah had to try to find him.

"I'll be okay. You'd better get going."

"You're sure you won't come with me?"

"I'm sure."

Cora gave Jonah a sad smile and turned toward the island. Her tired arms dragged through the water as she began to pull herself toward the oasis. It didn't look as though she'd make it on her own. Jonah didn't want to be responsible for another person's demise.

As the thought came to him, he felt the push of the current holding him up in the ocean. Miguel had told him he could control it. Quieting his mind, Jonah tried reaching out to the ocean.

*Go with her. Take her there.*

Immediately, Jonah felt a shift in the current around him. He felt the ocean surge toward Cora, and he watched as the water lifted her up and carried her to shore. Relief flooded his heart. Exhilaration ran through his veins. He had done it.

# Forty

*F*nd *Meranna. Need help.*

Jonah waited for the ocean to respond, but unlike the obvious help it offered Cora, the ocean did not appear to have heard him.

*Please.*

Not knowing what else to do, Jonah began swimming in the direction of the ship. The *Mary Margaret* was gone, of course, but it was the only place Jonah could think of to begin looking. There was no sign of Miguel. No indication that he'd ever entered the water. The murky memory of the watery voice floated back to him again. He knew he'd heard Miguel. It was the same voice he'd heard the pirate use when he spoke to the ocean.

*That's it,* he thought. If Miguel's voice had been able to carry to Jonah, there was no reason why Jonah's voice couldn't carry to Miguel.

*Miguel. Where are you?*

Though he listened attentively, there was no return answer.

*Miguel. Answer me.*

*He cannot hear you.* Jonah shivered. This voice was familiar as well. It was the voice of the ocean herself.

Anger erupted inside him. *Where is he? What have you done with him?*

*I have done nothing.*

*You cannot leave him to die out here.*

*He belongs to me. I can do with him as I like.*

Jonah felt frustration growing inside him. He recalled Miguel telling him the ocean only wanted to please him. This was not pleasing him. Why would the ocean do something against him now? Another thought entered his mind. When he'd listened in on Miguel's conversation with the ocean, it was obvious the ocean was in charge. Yet, Jonah had seen Miguel control it, like when he turned her to ice. But there was one thing more prominent in that conversation, and Jonah grasped at that now.

*You told him to bring me to you. He did as you required. You owe him for that.*

The ocean waves sprang up violently, crashing around Jonah. He slipped briefly below the surface when the ocean's supporting current dropped him. But he was no longer afraid.

*I owe him nothing! He belongs to me.*

*But I do not. I came to you willingly. I have the power to walk away.* Jonah didn't know how he knew this, but he felt it was true. *Give me Miguel, or I will leave you forever.*

The ocean quivered beneath him, then all went silent. The ocean was as smooth as glass, as if it had stopped breathing. Then, slowly, Jonah saw the stream of bubbles. The pink bubbles swirled as they traveled, coming closer together and colliding to form one large bubble. When it popped, Meranna was before him.

"She'll not talk to you now," Meranna said in greeting.

"I'm not worried about that. I need to find someone."

"The Pirate King. I know."

"Will you help me?"

"It is very risky. He is not well."

"But you know where he is? And he's alive?"

"I suppose one might say that. But he won't be much longer. You've made the ocean very unhappy with your request."

Meranna swam around Jonah. "You seem to have learned the way of the water."

"The way of the what?"

"You've learned to swim."

Jonah hadn't noticed, but he was treading water on his own.

"It's part of your powers. You are one with the ocean."

"Not at the moment. She's mad at me, remember?"

"We haven't much time." Meranna turned and dove, breaking the smooth-as-glass surface.

*Hold on, Miguel. I'm coming.*

Jonah followed Meranna. He swam less gracefully, but he was able to hold his own. The deeper they went, the more difficult it became. *A little help would be nice*, he told the ocean. She didn't oblige.

They were deep under water when Meranna turned back to find Jonah. "Here." She handed Jonah a pearl from her hair. He recognized it as a breathing pearl and popped it in his mouth. Immediately the crushing pressure that had been building against his skull lessened. Apparently, it helped with that as well as oxygen.

"He's over here. Not in good shape. Doesn't have much time left."

Meranna led Jonah to the edge of a shipwreck. Miguel lay lifeless across the hull of the broken ship. Jonah worried that they were too late. He rested his hand against Miguel's chest hoping to feel a heartbeat. It was too difficult to tell in the water.

"He's alive. But you'd better hurry if you're going to take him with you."

"Can I have another pearl?"

Meranna reached into her hair and brought out another pearl. "Not sure how much good it will do him. He's already unconscious."

"Taking the pearl from her, Jonah replied, "Thank you."

He pulled Miguel's mouth open, placed the pearl inside, and forced it closed again. It took Jonah a several minutes to figure out the best way to grab hold of the man. The weight of the pirate prevented Jonah from making much progress toward the surface. Jonah struggled, pulling against water and gravity.

*A little help would be nice,* he called out to the ocean. She remained silent. Apparently Jonah hadn't figured out how to control her. It seems it had just been lucky with Cora. He could use a little luck now.

Meranna came up alongside him. "I'm not supposed to do this," she told him as she took hold of the pirate's other side.

Together, the two of them pulled Miguel upward. Even with Meranna's help, Jonah was finding it more and more difficult to move through the water. The ocean was refusing to help, and Jonah was uncertain how to persuade her. His muscles ached, the pearl was gone, and with exhaustion overcoming him, Jonah was no longer certain he would make it. He feared he'd die after all.

"Where am I?" Miguel's voice was weak in the water.

Jonah felt relief, immediately followed by dizziness.

"He won't last out here," he heard Meranna say as he felt his body drift downward.

*Take him.* Miguel's voice commanded, his voice powerful and unyielding. *Take him now.*

Jonah felt the ocean move around him, wrapping around him cocoonlike, stabilizing him and preventing any further downward movement. He felt caught somewhere between wakefulness and dreaming. Voices drifted in and out among the current.

Meranna's voice swirled around him. "There is only one place safe to take him."

"I know," said the pirate.

"She will never let you go."

"There is no other choice."

"Maybe I should do it."

"Only I can make this happen." Miguel's voice was full of resignation, sadness. Then it changed, the commanding tone causing a torrent of ripples through the waves. *Deliver us to the island.*

Water crashed around them as they fought unnatural currents in all directions; the ocean was clearly unwilling to let them go quietly. A power greater than the ocean herself built behind the westward current, lifting Jonah and Miguel, and pushing them forward.

# Forty-One

Jonah woke with a headache. Sand scratched against every part of his body. The sun beat down unbearably hot. He coughed and felt his throat burn as sea water ejected from his stomach and lungs.

He opened his eyes to Sachlavar standing over him. The wizard leaned heavily upon his staff, his beard brushing against Jonah's chest. "Well, well. I see you've brought me a visitor."

The way Sachlavar said this made Jonah think the wizard was not impressed. He had the sudden feeling that upsetting a wizard was a very bad idea. "Wait. I…" Jonah wasn't sure what he was going to say but figured in the end it wouldn't matter anyway. The uncertain words drifted away from him.

There was a groan beside him, and Jonah turned to see Miguel lying on the beach. Too quickly, Jonah sat up, causing his head to spin. After steadying himself, he crawled over to his father.

Miguel was ashen faced. His chest heaved upward at an irregular rhythm. He appeared unable to move. Jonah reached out and touched his arm. His father screamed as though he'd been burned.

"You cannot touch him here," Sachlavar said. "He is not meant to be here."

Jonah recalled the dream. The one where Sachlavar had showed him the *Mary Margaret*, the ghost ship. He'd told Jonah it could never find the island. That Miguel was never to come here. There were protections – powerful magic – in place to prevent him from ever returning here.

"The barrier," Jonah started. "How did he get here?" He hovered over his father.

"Love."

The word hung heavily in the air between them. The wizard stood over Jonah and Miguel, a look of conflict in his eyes.

"Will he be okay?"

"I'm afraid not, Jonah. The pirate king may never come to this island. The curse forbids it. The island cannot hold such a creature."

Emotion welled up inside of Jonah. Feelings he had not realized he held for Miguel became apparent. "I don't understand. If he can never come here, how did he get here?"

The wizard knelt next to Jonah and gently placed his hand upon Jonah's shoulder. "You, Jonah. His love for you brought him here. It was the only way to save you."

Miguel coughed and turned his head to the side. His eyes fluttered, eventually coming open and resting upon Jonah. A pained smile marked his lips. "My boy."

"Don't talk," Jonah told him, shaking his head. Tears sprang to his eyes. He'd finally found his father. Maybe he hadn't been the best dad, but Miguel loved Jonah. There was something good in him. Jonah turned to Sachlavar, "Isn't there anything you can do?"

"I'm sorry, Jonah. My magic is no match for the island."

"Jonah, my boy," Miguel said in a weak voice.

Jonah leaned closer to him, careful not to touch him and cause him more pain.

"I haven't much time left. But there are things I need to tell you."

Three tears dropped down from Jonah's eyes onto his father's beard.

"I always loved you. I never meant to hurt you or your mother. Had there been any other choice, I would have taken it." Miguel wheezed, and coughed. Blood dribbled from his mouth, down his chin. "When I'm gone…" He coughed again, more blood dribbled down.

The wizard reached out and rested his hand just above Miguel's chest. "Shh," Sachlavar told him, then turned his attention to Jonah. "When your father passes, you will receive all of his powers. This will be a heavy burden, as his powers are deadly. The curse is binding. But you have strength and must learn to channel your own power. You are not yet the pirate king. You will have a choice."

"Sachlavar will help you," Miguel choked out. "But there is something else. Something I wish I did not need to leave you." He coughed up more blood, then grabbed Jonah by the arm cringing in agony as he did so, and said more earnestly, "You must capture the *Mary Margaret.* Do not let her go unchecked. Her power is too great. Too dangerous. Promise me."

Fear permeated through Jonah as he watched Miguel fight through the pain.

"Promise me, Jonah. Promise me."

"I…I…I promise," Jonah stuttered. Tears raced down his cheeks dropping across Miguel's face and onto the sand around them. "I promise."

Miguel's hand relaxed. His eyes became clear. "I love you, Jonah. Never forget."

# Forty-Two

Jonah knew Miguel was gone the moment the light erupted from him. It broke out, like a thousand beacons that had been bound in the blanket of night. The light raced around Miguel's body, swirling together into a pillar of liquid gold directly above the pirate. It hovered for a moment, then reached out in an arch that would have been beautiful had it not slammed Jonah in the chest with the force of a thousand stones.

Sachlavar caught Jonah, preventing the young man from hitting the ground. For this he was grateful. When Jonah could stand on his own again, the wizard used his staff to summon the magical breezes of the island. They raised Miguel up and carried his body out into the deep; a proper burial for a man of the sea.

Now Jonah sat in the wizard's castle looking out over the ocean. He had finally accepted the power that was in him, though he missed his father more than ever. Miguel would not be here to teach him how to harness this power. Or to teach him how to keep the curse from destroying him as it had his father. Miguel had said that Sachlavar would do that.

He ran his fingers over the eagle's feather he held. It had surprised him to find it had remained in his pocket this whole time. Brushing his fingers across it helped him feel calm. It vibrated with warmth, which Jonah had come to recognize as the hum of magic. Sachlavar had given it to him in the underwater cave telling him it was for courage. He'd certainly needed courage the last forty-eight hours. Maybe there was something to the feather after all.

Cora poked her head into his bedroom. "You okay?"

"Yeah, I guess."

"That was a crazy thing you did there, you know," she said. "You could have gotten yourself killed."

Jonah shrugged. He didn't expect her to understand why he'd gone after Miguel, especially since he didn't fully understand it himself.

"Sachlavar said Miguel's final act had saved him."

"What?" Jonah turned away from the balcony to look at her.

"He said that by using his power to save you, your father saved himself from the curse."

Tears welled up in Jonah's eyes, so he turned away, not wanting Cora to see him cry. He didn't think she'd understand.

"I thought you might need this," she said, coming up beside him. She held out her hand. In it was the golden compass.

"Thanks. But I'm not sure it will help."

"Sachlavar says you're going after the *Mary Margaret*. This compass will help you find her."

"I don't even know which direction she went."

"This compass is connected to only two things. This island, and the *Mary Margaret*."

Jonah looked skeptically at the compass sitting innocently in her hand.

"It doesn't look like anything special, but I promise you, you'll need it," she said as she tossed it to him.

"Thank you."

"Don't thank me yet. Just don't die trying to get her back. Make sure you're ready before you go after her."

As Cora walked away, leaving him alone on the balcony, Jonah carefully turned the compass over to inspect it. In that moment, he felt the familiar warm hum of magic.

# Acknowledgements

It has been a long journey to bring Pirate Magic into the world - a real learning experience, a labor of love. I must first apologize to all those of you who have been waiting patiently, or not so patiently, for this book to make its appearance. And none so much as my youngest who has believed in me so long that his Christmas wish for the last several years was "a copy of Mommy's book." This year, he'll finally see that wish fulfilled - though he won't have to wait for Christmas.

I cannot thank my family enough for the love and support they have given me. It's not easy living with a teacher-author-mom; for if it's not one major distraction, it's another. Nevertheless, most of my children previewed this book (some multiple times) in the hopes of helping me push it along. They've provided wonderful insight which only strengthened the story that emerged in the end.

It has been a remarkable joy to work with my daughter as she developed the artwork for this book. We discussed and tested out several options for the cover art early on; and though our first designs were lost along the way, a new design emerged, and her talent really shines. I have truly loved every moment of this journey with her.

Thank you, Mom, for being a true believer in my talents from the time I was small - for cheering me on, reading and editing, and never giving up on me actually making it to publication. Your enthusiasm, honest criticisms, and undying loyalty have always helped me reach a little higher to become better at everything I set my mind to.

I would be remiss if I didn't send a shout-out to Robbin Peterson, without whom I would never have pushed myself into the world of publishing. It was her dragging me along to my first writers' conference which encouraged me to embark upon writing my first novel (after years of writing short stories). It has been a wonderful experience, and I have grown so much as a writer.

A bundle of gratitude goes to Jo Forsythe – friend, mentor, and walking buddy. Thank you for your enthusiasm in the final edits -your desire for the next part to read and your excitement for each portion of the story. Your ability to put yourself both in teacher and middle school mode provided me with the much needed confidence to bring this story out into the light.

And, of course, thank you to all those who tested out a very rough version of this story in its early stages. I hope you have found the final version to be to your liking.

Thank you, all, for reading. I hope you enjoyed part one of the journey. Watch for Pirate Magic, Book 2 coming soon.

**Tara L. Nielsen** has been writing stories nearly her entire life. Her love for storytelling and passion for putting words to paper is something she has shared with her own five children and countless students over the years. One of her greatest joys is inspiring young minds to bring imagination to life, while encouraging them to reach high to find and acheive their own potentials.

### Check Out These Other Titles by Tara L. Nielsen:

The Music Box: A Story of Hope

A Soldier Brave and Tall

### Connect with Tara L. Nielsen, Author:

On facebook at:  https://www.facebook.com/AuthorTaraLNielsen

On her blog Catching Dreams at: https://taralnielsen.wordpress.com

www.ingramcontent.com/pod-product-compliance
Lightning Source LLC
Chambersburg PA
CBHW021645110726
47902CB00007B/1834